I0738432

By Lea Carter

ISBN 978-0-9989678-6-8

Copyright © 2018

Cover illustration and design
by Daniel Manfredini

<u>Wedgewood</u> is a work of fiction.  Any
resemblance to actual persons, living or
dead, is entirely coincidental.



Learn more about the author at
leacarterwrites.wixsite.com/wholesomefantasy

# Chapter 1

Cassidy hissed in pain and snatched a tissue off her desk. Deftly, she wrapped it around her papercut before she got blood on Bert's medical file.

"Will you need stitches for that?" Agnes asked teasingly from where she sat mending a tear in the sleeve of her nightgown.

"Probably not." Cassidy smiled at her old friend. "Just needs some pressure to stop the bleeding."

"You'd better let me take a look," Agnes insisted, weaving her needle partway into the fabric and setting the garment aside. A quick flit of her wings brought her to Cassidy's side, where she gently appropriated the damaged hand. Peeking under the tissue, she nodded. "Oh, that's not too bad."

"See?" Cassidy didn't really mind Agnes' fussing. Her assisting nurses, Agnes and Daphne, were the only other Water Fairies in the whole city of Weetu, the Wood Fairy capitol. It hadn't seemed important while they packed to leave their home in Noddfa, but now she could honestly say that the prospect of spending the entire winter 'safely' inside this maple tree without them was dreadful.

"Still, you might want to wrap it while you're changing for this evening," Agnes suggested, setting the hand on the desk. "And you should probably do that soon."

"Change?" Her finger forgotten, Cassidy looked down at her outfit. While the matching gray waistcoat and skirt weren't glamorous or anything, at least they toned down her shrieking yellow long-sleeved shirt a little bit. She ought to be wearing a minimum of three vibrant colors at all times according to Wood Fairy winter custom, but that gave her a headache. "I was planning to wear this outfit."

"To a dress rehearsal? Are you sure?" Agnes frowned. "You don't want to stand out." They'd gone to great lengths to avoid that, even coloring their pink hair and wing points in an effort to blend in. Daphne, the youngest member of the Water Fairy medical party, saw the whole thing as an adventure. Thankfully by now no one in Weetu was as tan as they would have liked, so Cassidy and her nurses, fair-skinned from lifetimes beyond the reach of the sun, were able to blend in much better than they had at first.

Of course, it really wasn't much of a sacrifice compared to what would happen should the treaty between their underwater tribe and the surface tribes be broken. If the secret of her tribe's existence became common knowledge, everyone on the surface would be fatally affected. Not for the first time, Cassidy questioned her choice to come to Weetu and operate on Prince

Isaac, who'd been partially paralyzed in a battle with some pirates.

"I don't think that's what *dress rehearsal* means," she mused aloud, remembering that Agnes was waiting for her to respond. "Just in case, though, I'll wear my toffee-colored gown with the crimson sash," she compromised.

"You wore that four days ago at the banquet." Agnes calmly resumed her mending.

"My other gowns are out being laundered." Cassidy frowned, annoyed. Her borrowed wardrobe only had so many choices and she'd been avoiding some of them for good reason.

"Not all of them." Agnes continued innocently sewing up the tear with precision stitches.

Cassidy folded her arms across her chest. "I am not wearing that dress." She tossed her hair, irritated further when her *brown*curls bounced around her face. "I refuse to go around Weetu looking like a coral reef."

Agnes bit her lips to keep from laughing. "Don't be ridiculous," Agnes scoffed when she'd gotten hold of herself. "Anyway," she nodded at the water clock resting on the shelf behind Cassidy. "You'll barely have time to change as it is."

Cassidy twisted in her chair to look at the primitive time-keeping device. Less ornate than most, it consisted simply of two reservoirs and a float. One reservoir emptied into the other at a carefully calibrated rate, causing the float in the second reservoir to rise. She had to squint a little to make out the times marked on the float.

"Oh no!" Springing to her feet, Cassidy flew into her bedroom, closing the door behind her. Laughing at her situation, she unfastened her skirt and let it drop to the floor while she unbuttoned her waistcoat on her way to the closet. One outfit lay strategically strewn about the room by the time she'd finished changing into the other, which was how it was going to have to stay until she got back.

"Don't forget your case!" Agnes flagged her down as she zipped towards the outer door of their quarters.

"I'm not expecting a medical emergency…" Cassidy started to protest, then shook her head. By definition, one never expected an *emergency*. Returning to her room, she took the slim leather pouch from her top drawer and tucked it into her waistband under her left arm. "Don't wait supper for me. I promised to eat with Isaac after the rehearsal."

"Again?" Agnes frowned as the outer door closed behind Cassidy. They'd talked a little about the futility of the romance begging to happen between Cassidy and the prince. Cassidy could no more stay on the surface than Isaac could join her beneath it. But they were both young and Cassidy in particular was inexperienced in such matters. A brilliant scientist and dedicated doctor, she'd followed in her widowed father's footsteps, to and from the laboratory, until his path had nearly become her own.  Shaking her head doubtfully, Agnes finished the last couple of stitches and tied off her thread.

Cassidy, meanwhile, was winging her way towards the main theater.  Two amateur productions were taking place in the other performance halls, which were in nearly constant use by Weetu's captive population, but tonight's dress rehearsal was open to invited guests only.  She smiled and did her best to ignore the looks she was attracting in the awful gown.  Fortunately for her, she happened to know the playwright personally.

"There you are!"  Prince Isaac stopped pacing in front of the theater entrance and stared, transfixed.  Her cherry-pink gown accentuated the lovely color in her cheeks.  She shook her head to clear the curls out of her face and he noted the graceful curve of her neck, as white as a swan feather.  He couldn't imagine a life beyond the reach of the sun, yet as he looked at her, he found himself tempted.  "I," he swallowed, "was starting to think you weren't going to make it."  Thank goodness she was wearing her glasses or he might never have recovered.  Her spectacles served only one purpose—that of hiding her mesmerizing hazel-green eyes, the likes of which could not be found among any of the four surface tribes.

"I almost didn't," she admitted with a laugh. "If Agnes hadn't reminded me to change, I would probably still be at my desk, studying Bert's file." Silently, she marveled at how easily he'd been moving only moments before. Thanks to sophisticated Water Fairy medical equipment, and the astonishing healing powers of the local potions, Isaac had recovered in record time. His severed right forewing was another matter entirely.

He laughed with her, then cleared his throat. "Where would you like to sit?" Leading her inside, he surveyed the rows of empty seats as if it was a packed opening night.

"Over there, perhaps?" Cassidy played along, indicating the row nearest their friend and burgeoning playwright, Bert. She'd grown accustomed to Isaac's dry humor by now, but she still felt sorry for Bert, who was signaling frantically at them. Like Isaac, he'd been wounded during the battle against the pirates that recently plagued Fairydom's four surface tribes. The amputation of Bert's leg, however, was something she could not repair.

"Hmm. Do you really think that would be wise?" Isaac frowned mischievously. His heart twisted painfully when he saw Cassidy smile at Bert—or any other man, for that matter—even though he knew she was just being friendly. Winter was half over and she would be returning to the Water Fairy Tribe in the spring. Which was why he was spending every available moment with her. "He looks quite the type to talk through the entire play," he joked. Two short months ago, when Isaac first met Cassidy, he, like Bert, was dependent upon a wheeled chair.

"No more dawdling," Cassidy admonished him, brushing a brown curl back out of her face. "You know how much this dress rehearsal means to him." She still wasn't quite sure what a 'dress rehearsal' was, just that Bert was fidgety with nerves when he asked them to attend.

Neatly cornered by her compassionate logic, Isaac dropped all pretenses. "Shall we?" He gestured towards Bert.

Bert almost relaxed his ramrod straight posture when he saw that they were finally coming over, but four hundred years of military service made that his natural bearing.

"You cut it awfully close," Bert informed them sternly as they slipped past him to their seats. "Everyone else is already here." By 'everyone else,' he meant Isaac's parents, King Walter and Queen Fiona of the Wood Fairy Tribe. They'd arrived early and their presence was doing nothing to settle Bert's nerves.

"You must forgive me." Cassidy made a point of taking the blame—and the seat nearest Bert, in the hopes of keeping them from spending the entire play swapping friendly insults. Wood Fairy etiquette, such as it was, was very different from the more formal atmosphere that prevailed in the Water Fairy tribe, but she flattered herself that she was getting the hang of it. "I have an important surgery tomorrow and I quite lost track of time when I sat down to review the files after lunch."

Bert smiled sheepishly at her. The reconstructive surgery she spoke of was for his lower left wing, which was shredded by the vile brass needles worn by a pirate who attacked him from behind.

"I can forgive that," Bert agreed. He nodded to the pair of young troupe fairies blowing out the candles that lined the walls of the theater seating area. "I just hope they can." He grinned. "They might even be as nervous as I am!"

The troupers backstage would have laughed if they'd heard him say that. Performing was the lifeblood of their group, one of the primary reasons the king's steward engaged them for a winter of distractions and amusements in the city of Weetu. Sure, things went a little sideways with the discovery that the troupe master, Phil Girard, and his flunky, Dizzy, were involved in a series of jewelry and antiquity thefts. Harry, their new leader, figured the troupe was better off without them. Sure, he had to pull double duty now, playing the tragically sensitive Prince Cambrian of the Sky Fairies as well as keeping track of the props, but things could be worse. And often had been.

Harry, who was busy applying the final touches

touches of makeup to his costume, sensed the eager mood of what he now thought of as his troupe and smiled. This new play, *WinterDelayed*, was not a comedy like their last play, *What's for Supper?*, but he felt it had a lot of potential. The mystery of this winter's late arrival was still a topic of discussion in the restaurants around Weetu, so the audience was guaranteed to be engaged. For a basically true story, it had it all, too. Danger, adventure, romance, combat, and a victorious ending. He shivered. It had taken some serious guts for the Sky Fairies to challenge not only enemy windships but a monster snow cloud, too!

Rising, Harry tugged at the front of his doublet until it was smooth. "Can I have your attention, everyone?" He extended his lightly-tinted wings enough to lift himself to where he could be easily seen. "We all know who's out there, so I'll keep it simple. Remember your lines. Hang onto your wigs." Like most of the rest of them, Harry wore a blue wig that covered his painfully close-cut hair. "And remember that we are not just acting out scenes from an untried playwright. We are spinning dreams of grandeur. We are sharing hopes of feeling the sun's rays again." Making fists of his hands, he held them up, one above another, miming his next words, "We will *wring* tears of envy from the Wranglers that they were not present at this glorious battle with Dame Nature." His voice swelled with excitement.

"Curtain?" called a roustabout anxiously. The theater manager looked like she was about to come raise it herself!

"Curtain!" Harry agreed, back to his normal voice. Looking at the eager group about him, he instructed, "Places everyone!"

Bert almost sighed with relief when the curtain finally began to rise. This was his first dress rehearsal. Ever. He leaned forward to hear the opening line without realizing it.

"Father!" Harry-Prince Cambrian flew in through a 'window' and landed center stage. "The scouts are back. They report that there is not so much as a snowflake between here and the high peaks!"

Partway through the rehearsal, the cast 'took to the skies' aboard a thin windship shell that was supposed to represent the *Wind Sorter* (the now-fabled cloud chaser) A handful of stagehands were assigned to help create 'the illusion of savage winds raging about the windship' by shaking the sails vigorously. It was going well until one of them misjudged the distance between the end of a spar and an actor's head, knocking the poor fellow to his knees.

Bert dropped his face in his hands and muttered something unintelligible.

Cassidy would have rushed up to aid the injured actor if she had not seen someone slip out from the behind the backdrop to do just that.

Isaac was suffering, too, but for different

reasons. This entire play was based on the letter of introduction Prince Cambrian sent with Doctor Cassidy. A few paragraphs, really, those deemed suitable for public knowledge. After praising Water Fairy medicine highly, Cambrian's mood had turned grave as he reflected on the dangerous mission other Sky Fairies were undertaking.

Isaac couldn't help spending most of the play gloomily pondering the fate of Fairydom—would there still be a Sky Fairy Tribe in the spring? And if there was, would all of the surface tribes live to see summer? He straightened in his chair in time to hear 'Prince Cambrian' deliver some very dramatic dialogue to the cheering crowd of extras gathered about the windship shell. Judging by the backdrop, which strongly resembled the docks at Regalis, they were returning triumphant and he'd missed most of what had to be a highly imaginative third act.

"Nay, save your praise." Harry flung up his hands and the cast obediently quieted so 'Prince Cambrian' could deliver his lines. "We had old Dame Nature on our side. How then could we fail to restore the balance of the seasons?" Majestically throwing back the protective hood of his weathersuit—almost completely dislodging his blue wig—he led the others from the windship shell to center stage, where they were greeted by a few more dutifully cheering extras from the wings.

Isaac began clapping politely as soon as he saw the curtain begin coming down. He did not have to look behind him to know that his parents were applauding as well. The play would serve its purpose, educating and entertaining the citizens of Weetu without revealing the hidden Water Fairy tribe.

"Well?" Bert asked Isaac eagerly. He fiddled with the brake on his wheeled chair to keep from giving way to anxious anticipation. After a rough and ready life on the wind, working his way up from able-bodied windfairy to captain, he found show business surprisingly terrifying. "Stop clapping and tell me what you really think of it!"

Isaac looked hopefully to Cassidy for an enthusiastic answer, but she was still staring at the curtain wide-eyed. This was only the second theatrical production she had ever attended above the surface of Fairydom's sea, and Isaac knew that she would have questions. They would discuss them later, away from prying ears and eyes, but with no hope of romance.

"I am no theater buff," Isaac complained to Bert. "What do you want me to say?" Waving one hand at the stage, he continued before Bert could respond. "The scenery is excellent. The casting is better than most winter dramas, which is astonishing given that this is the same set of trouper fairies that regaled us with their brilliant rendition of the comedy *What's for Supper?* less than a month ago." Isaac could not help grinning as he remembered the hilarious play; it featured everything from a disastrous mix-up in grocery deliveries to an unexpected supper guest.

"Isaac." After months of working with him in the water pump room, Bert had finally come to terms with addressing Prince Isaac by just his name. "The story. What did you think of the story?"

Isaac scratched his jaw contemplatively. "The story is fine," he proclaimed at long last. "I just do not see how you can be comfortable writing an entire play around so few concrete details!" He twisted around so he could look Bert in the face. "We cannot even be sure their plan worked."

Bert laughed aloud. "My friend, you have no understanding of storytelling. The story may be only one quarter truth and three quarters imagination. What matters is that the audience enjoys it!" He held up a finger to emphasize his next point. "And in mid-winter, the audience will enjoy almost anything." He waved away their chuckles. "You know that I am right. In two short months it will be spring and things will be different. When it is warm enough, the citizens of Weetu will pour out of this sugar maple's reopened doors and dare anybody to make them go back inside. For now, they are living from diversion to diversion. Why, I daresay that most of them have already lost a sense of which meal is which."

"Is that why you spent so much time portraying the dangers of the snowstorm?" Cassidy frowned, shivering in sympathy with the brave fairies who risked so much. Thoughts of the dangers of winter only added to her yearning to be back in her underwater city.

"Exactly!" Bert beamed at her. "Not even the Sky Fairies, with their skill for manipulating the weather, can tolerate the winter conditions that rage over the surface of Fairydom four months of the year. And building up the suspense will greatly increase the audience's delight when our heroes arrive safely at home."

Cassidy nodded and sat back. It was hard not to correct him, even though she barely knew more than he did. Her cousin, Kuntza, wrote a little of the situation above the surface in the same letter he sent asking her to leave her beloved home and spend the winter healing at Weetu. Those brave windfairies depicted in the play had not made it home; not *yet*. Each surviving storm chaser crew had scurried off to a separate village high in their mountains, where they hoped to find sanctuary for the deadly winter months. Then, if the *monster*snowstorm hadn't obliterated the Sky Fairy tribal territories as they knew them, destroying even their storied mountain fortresses, they would return home in the spring.

"Bert." Isaac folded his arms across his chest. "Why do they talk like that?"

"Like what?"

"Like…" Isaac nodded at the stage. "Like that last speech. 'We had old Dame Nature on our side.'" He cocked an eyebrow in Bert's direction. "I have never heard anybody talk like that."

"Not even in a play?" Bert grinned.

Isaac tried to keep a straight face, but in the end he yielded to the answering smile tugging at the corners of his mouth.

"It is an old artistic tradition," Bert explained, feigning loftiness. "Besides. Prince Cambrian is a poet and will not mind my taking a little artistic license with such a wonderful story."

Isaac certainly hoped someone else would have the dubious pleasure of informing Prince Cambrian that he was Fairydom's latest hero as far as Bert's play, *WinterDelayed*,wasconcerned.

"Thank you so much for inviting us." Cassidy, sensing a somber mood building in Isaac, smiled at Bert. "It really was a fascinating experience."

"You're not leaving?" Bert protested as they rose. "The evening has only just begun! I must go over costume details; remind half of the cast that they should never, ever get between the others and the audience… Not to mention what happened with that falling spar." His nose wrinkled in disgust. As if a Sky Fairy windship spar would just come loose like that!

"Bert, I promise." Isaac clapped his friend on the shoulder. "We will not mention it."

"No, not a word." Cassidy pressed a finger to her lips. "Of course, we probably will not be able to help discussing the play a little over supper." She nudged Isaac's arm with one elbow in Wood Fairy fashion and he naturally slipped that arm about her. Because they were in public, she permitted it as a friendly gesture. Since her blunt declaration that she would be returning home in the spring—whether he loved her or not—Isaac had graciously assumed the role of chum instead.

"But no details." Isaac put his free hand on his heart as if making a pledge. "They will just have to wait and watch *Winter Delayed* for themselves." He winked knowingly at Bert. The theater would be stuffed with eager fairies on opening night the way that a jar was stuffed with pickles, regardless of whether or not Isaac and Cassidy began a whisper campaign. Nevertheless, he could tell that it made Bert feel good to think of hundreds of fairies all around Weetu discussing his play.

"Alright, you two lovebirds." Bert did his best to hide his surprise at the way they hastily drew apart. He thought they were perfect for each other. "Just be sure he takes you home early." He grinned up at Cassidy from his wheeled chair.

Cassidy smiled warmly at him. "And you be sure that you arrive a little early tomorrow morning. Agnes will need some time to prepare you for the procedure."

Bert cheerfully saluted, then released his chair brake.  "Now get lost, you two.  This is my chance to talk to the king and queen!"  Expertly he gripped the right wheel and forced the left forward, spinning his wheeled chair about in a perfect half circle.

# Chapter 2

Isaac lingered to watch as Bert eagerly wheeled himself up the aisle.  When Cassidy arrived at Weetu almost two months ago, Isaac had been confined to a very similar wheeled chair, paralyzed from the waist down.

"What are you thinking?"  Cassidy would have been happy to find out she was wrong about Isaac's somber mood, and his teasing way with Bert a moment before seemed to indicate just that.  Except that now Isaac was back to that faint, almost invisible frown that drew his eyebrows together.

"Just remembering how much I used to envy the fairies like Bert, who only lost a leg and a wing in the pirate offensive."  Isaac bowed his head and put one hand lightly on Cassidy's lower back, ostensibly to steer her along towards the restaurant.  But really because it was the closest she had let him come since her ultimatum in his father's office.

Cassidy allowed him to guide her through the imaginary crowds of theater goers while she considered his words.  She'd learned a lot from the injured Wranglers and windfairies she was treating, enough to know that Wood Fairies were taught from childhood that a debilitating injury was essentially a matter of time.  Even the apprentice Wranglers she knew already had some idea of what they were going to do after they were permanently disabled.  It was part of their culture.  Yet they fought fiercely to regain whatever flexibility, mobility, and endurance they could, because physical independence was also an integral part of their culture.

"Where shall we eat tonight?" Isaac asked to break the silence.

Cassidy looked around at Weetu's bustling citizenry and tucked her hand through Isaac's arm.  That got his hand off her back, where it had been causing her to experience mildly erratic heartbeats.

As the silence stretched out between them, Isaac tried to ignore the suspicion that he knew exactly where she wanted to eat.  He enjoyed eating at the Trattoria, but surely she would choose somewhere else after four nights in a row?

"Could we go to the Eagle and Serpent?"  She appreciated Isaac's gallant willingness to eat at the Trattoria with her, but it didn't take a genius to notice the way his eyes strayed in the direction of the Eagle every time they walked past the turnoff.  The casual eating place was a favorite hangout of the Wranglers and it wasn't too difficult to abide as long as she sat between Isaac and Sugar, their massive mutual friend.

"I think that could be arranged," Isaac grinned.  He was so delighted that he could have kissed her.  But then, he was always ready and willing to kiss her.  The few kisses he had stolen before she constructed a wall of logic between them haunted him. Unfortunately, she had not given him the slightest bit of romantic encouragement in the last two months.

Cassidy did her best to grin back. As much as she adored Isaac's Wrangler buddy Sugar, a man of astonishing height and breadth, the other patrons tended to presume that because she was one Wrangler's friend, she was everybody's friend. And their definition of 'friendly' as often as not, involved some form of physical contact, be it an arm flung about her shoulders or a 'friendly' jab in the arm. Now, she had never been one to stand upon ceremony, no bowing or curtsying to her just because she was a Lady of the Botere clan. Nevertheless, she was learning that she could breathe much better when there was no one within a hand's breadth of her. In point of fact, being touched without warning or permission left her tense and off-balance.

"Isaac!"

"Look who's here!" The ever-present loafers welcomed them as they approached.

"Hya, Doc." She nearly cringed out of her own skin when an older, retired Wrangler tugged at one of her curls. "How you been?"

"Fine," she answered stiffly. She couldn't seem to catch her breath until Isaac had cheerfully greeted them all and tugged her clear of them, apparently blissfully ignorant of her predicament.

"Sugar!" Isaac waved cheerily as soon as he spotted his friend, sitting as usual at a table just outside the restaurant. "Have you room for two more?"

"Isaac!" Sugar waved back. "C'mon over," he boomed. "Always room for you and Doc Cassidy!"

Cassidy beamed at Sugar as she slid onto a stool beside him. One of the many things about the Wood Fairy culture that she struggled with was their habit of shortening names or assigning nicknames. Of course, Sugar's nickname made sense to anyone who had ever seen him consume an entire pie in a single sitting. And since he began calling her 'Doc' or 'Doc Cassidy,' the attempts of the others to shorten her name to 'Cassie' had thankfully died out.

Isaac, still standing, grinned at Sugar, whose long arms were making short work of stacking the mugs and plates left behind by his previous tablemates. Sugar even managed to make stacking the mismatched mugs look easy by always putting a big one at the bottom.

"So," Isaac rested his boot on the stool he planned to occupy. "What have they got that is good tonight?"

"That depends." Sugar slid the dirty dishes towards Isaac.

"On what?" Cassidy asked innocently.

"On how hungry you are!" Isaac and Sugar laughed in unison.

"Oh." Cassidy managed a laugh. Yet another difference between winter in Weetu and winter back home. The sea continued to provide even when there were icy patches near the shoreline. Granted, some foods were more difficult to harvest this time of year... Cassidy tugged her thoughts back to the present. She was going to have to be careful, or she would become as homesick as Agnes.

"Now, no fretting." Sugar smiled easily at her. "We are not at the short end of supplies yet." One of only three boys in a family of twenty-two children, Sugar had naturally picked up a thing or two about womenfolk. Like how to tell when their smile was only skin-deep. As Cassidy's always seemed to be when she was at the Eagle.

"Is stew alright?" Isaac asked Cassidy, his smile faltering. He loved a good squirrel stew, but he loved it best of all when the winter winds shrieked so loudly through the branches that they could hear the old sugar maple singing a mighty challenge to all elemental comers. He hardly knew what Cassidy liked. She rarely spoke of herself or of her life at home, which left him doing most of the talking.

"Of course." Cassidy clasped her hands in her lap rather than put them on the soiled tablecloth.

"Best take them with you." Sugar nodded at the stack of dishes. "Chirk might give you a labor discount."  Chirk owned and ran the Eagle and the Serpent, and was as cheery as his nickname implied.

Cassidy's smile widened at that.  During the winter season, Weetu was primarily an exchange city.  Service for service, including dishwashing in exchange for food, etc.  When Rosie first explained it to her, Cassidy thought it sounded odd.  Now, though, after seeing it in action, it made a lot of sense.  They could either spend the winter passing money back and forth, from patron to proprietor, then from proprietor to employee, or they could work together and save the hassle of money for the spring, when there were fresh goods and supplies to be bought from outsiders.

Isaac rolled his eyes, but took the dishes anyway.  As a Wrangler, he could claim a free, basic meal at any of several restaurants in Weetu.  Nevertheless, it made more sense to keep Chirk happy than not.  Burnt stew was the inevitable consequence of an unhappy chef.

Sugar picked at a snag in the rough tablecloth until Isaac was out of earshot, then cleared his throat.

"Doc?  How come you're eating here tonight?"

Cassidy, not wanting to admit that she was there solely for Isaac's sake, just smiled.

"You two do most of your courtin' at the Trattoria, seems like."

Cassidy blushed and earnestly set both hands on top of the table. "We are not courting, Sugar," she corrected. "We are just friends." When Sugar just looked at her without blinking, she hastily added, "I suppose I can see where you might get the wrong idea, of course. We do spend quite a bit of time together…"

Sugar put one huge hand over both of hers. "Friends?" Sugar could track a spider up one tree and down another, much to the astonishment of many of his fellow Wranglers. To him, reading a woman's body language was almost as easy, though it helped if he got to know them a bit first. "Do you always make yourself miserable for friends?" He glanced into the crowded eating room, past the tables to the multi-purpose fire, and finally over at the enormous sink where Isaac was depositing the dirty dishes. "I ain't sure I oughta be saying this to you," Sugar admitted. "But I never was one to stand by when trouble was brewin'." He waited until she looked up at him. Again, he looked straight back at her. "You think you are doing right by him, agreein' to come and spend time with his Wrangler friends." Sugar frowned, hating to have to say it so plain. But he'd never seen deception, however well-intentioned, benefit a relationship. "When I reckon you know, deep down, all you are really doin' is foolin' yourself. And tryin' to fool him, who you claim you ain't involved with."

Cassidy dropped her eyes.  "How did *you* know?"  Apparently her best efforts at hiding her distaste hadn't fooled Sugar.

"Easy enough to see."  Sugar kept his voice conversationally low, not wanting to attract attention by whispering.  "For anybody who is lookin'."

"Then why…"  Cassidy bit her lip before she could finish asking why Isaac had not noticed how uncomfortable she was here.

"Because he ain't lookin'."  Sugar cocked his head to one side.  His usually close-cropped hair flopped a little with the motion; he was waiting for spring to get it cut again, one of many peculiar Wrangler rituals.  "He only sees what he wants to see.  Otherwise he would have noticed how you tighten up every time you come in here."  He smiled when she lifted puzzled eyes.  "You tuck your wings tighter, you hold your shoulders straighter.  You even clasp your fists tighter, 'cause you want to avoid touching anything or anyone at the Eagle."

Cassidy could feel an embarrassed heat rising in her cheeks.  Sugar was right.  She was so worried about being embraced without permission or warning; about getting buttonholed by someone who wanted to proudly recount nightmarish stories of their Wrangler exploits; or just flat driven mad by the persistent chaos that reigned there, that she was ready to leave before she entered.

"Seems to me…" Sugar took a deep breath. This was dangerous ground he was treading on. "That you want to be more than friends with him."

"Impossible." Cassidy retorted sharply.

Sugar's eyebrows shot up. Her choice of words told him a lot. Well, that and the way Isaac looked at her whenever he thought nobody was looking at him.

"Folks where you are from," he frowned inquisitively, "they ever want what they can't have?"

Cassidy rose abruptly. "I should go." A frightening variety of emotions were twisting and turning in her gut, threatening to overwhelm her right then and there.

Just then something landed with a thump inches from where her hands had been resting. Inhaling sharply, she reminded herself that the jointed wooden object, painted to resemble one of the more dangerous surface snakes, was just a toy. A child's toy, belonging to one of the oldest, most insufferable children she had ever met.

Skite shrank back from the jibe he had been about to toss after the snake when her cold gaze settled on him.

Cassidy choked back the acerbic remark she felt like making in reference to delayed maturity levels and just flew away, her wings beating rapidly.

"Some folks just have no sense of humor."

Skite turned to agree with the fairy beside him only to find that it was a very angry-looking Prince Isaac.

"And you are one of them."  If Isaac's hands had been free, he might have taken the action that Skite's weak chin seemed to be begging for. Since they were not he settled for, "Do that again, and I will personally see to it that you are banned from the Eagle for the rest of the winter."  He stood stiffly, watching her fly away, while Skite slunk into a corner.

Sugar, who heard Isaac, sighed softly. Cassidy had feelings for Isaac, even if she did not know how to fit in with his Wrangler friends. And Isaac had feelings for her, so much so that Sugar figured something was holding him back or they would have announced a double-wedding instead of just Princess Gallica and Sir Stuart's.

"Alright."  Isaac banged two plates of stew and biscuits onto the table where Sugar sat. "Why did she leave?  And how come you didn't stop her?"

Sugar casually swept one of the plates over to his side of the table.  "You might want to sit down a'fore I answer that," he suggested mildly.

Isaac slowly took Sugar's advice, lowering himself onto the stool Cassidy had just vacated.

"Doc's a fine woman."  Sugar started by stating the obvious so that he could be sure Isaac knew that he knew. "Smart. Pretty. Strong. Got a temper, I reckon, but seems to have a good handle on it." He stopped there rather than mentioning that if she had lost her temper at Skite just now, he had been planning on holding her back. There was something of steel in that woman. Unfortunately, she didn't know what the rest of them did about Skite—that he was worth a dozen Wranglers in a pinch—and giving him a lecture would've made her look downright mean and waspish to the others.

"Sugar," Isaac growled warningly.

Sugar calmly forked some stew into his mouth, chewed, and swallowed. "Refined, too." Consuming an entire biscuit in a bite, Sugar washed it down with half a mug of cheap peach nectar. "Yep. Real refined. Dresses up the place, just havin' her around."

Isaac felt anger beginning to stir, but could not put his finger on what was causing it. Sugar had not said a single thing wrong.

"She ain't dainty, exactly." Sugar drained the rest of the mug and reached for the pitcher to refill it. "Just well-mannered. Quiet." A shouting match started inside. The subject seemed to be whether winter would last two months and a week more or just seven weeks more. "Yep." He pointedly took a sip of his nectar, set the mug down, and took up his fork again. "Real refreshing, having someone like her around here."

Isaac stared around the Eagle with new eyes, his heart sinking further and further until it had dropped past his stomach and into his toes. Workwear was the Eagle's dress code, patches and all. Since everyone was more or less off-duty, there was not a shined boot in sight. And quite a few of those boots were propped up on convenient stools. Some were even on tables. The *thunk* of knives embedding themselves solidly in the practice target on the far side of the room invaded his thoughts and his shoulders sagged. The *slurping* sounds of others consuming their stew was the last straw.

"This is all she has seen of the Wranglers," Isaac muttered. "This and our scarred, wounded bodies." He looked helplessly at Sugar. "She has no idea of what it is to see them as more than loafers and idlers, forever lounging about the Eagle."

"You mean she ain't even seen the apprentices?" Sugar smiled. Things were beginning to look up.

Isaac started to shrug, then stopped. The apprentices! Of course. Nothing stopped their training, not even winter.

"I think she could stand to see more of them." Isaac had come to his feet without realizing it. Now he stopped to rest his hands on the table, to be grateful he could do little things like stand up on his own again. "She certainly could. Excuse me, I just thought of something I need to arrange."

Sugar would have returned Isaac's farewell

nod, but Isaac left too quickly.  Shrugging, Sugar plopped Isaac's still-full plate on top of the one he had just emptied.  No sense letting good food go to waste.  His appetite might have been ruined by having to open the eyes of two of his dearest friends a little wider, except that he was hoping Isaac's plan would work. Whatever it was.

Cassidy, her mind still whirling, found her way to the deepest, dustiest part of the medical maze.  She had no idea what the rooms where she took refuge were originally intended for, but they would suit her purposes just fine.  One hand on her heaving stomach and the other pressed against her mouth, she slid to the floor.  She made the mistake of reaching up to rub her eyes and the barrier burst.  Hiding her face against her knees, she began to sob.  Hot, angry tears soaked the fabric of her skirt as she struggled to untangle the emotions that had driven her to find solitude.

How could she have been so stupid?  So naïve as to think that she was being *generous* in agreeing to spend time with Isaac's friends? Family, more like.  Was she really absurd enough to believe that she could fall in love with Isaac while turning up her nose at a vital part of who he was?  Isaac's clothes might be a little dressier, better cared for, but underneath their tan skins, they were exactly the same.  Rough and ready, more interested in getting food in their bellies than how politely it got there.  Well...Isaac's table manners were quite good, actually.

Not that her own behavior was anything to boast of.  Sugar was right.  The other patrons loved Isaac dearly, so what was it that kept them away from his table at the Eagle?  His charming dinner companion, of course.

Her tears spent, she wiped her eyes with the back of her hand and tried to calm her breathing. The first few times they ate there, she had hardly been able to breathe for the crush of admirers, slapping her on the back, tousling her curls, and so forth.  They were apparently all friends with the Wranglers she had operated on and wanted to let her know how much they appreciated it.  She laughed bitterly as she remembered how 'courteous' she had been, taking care to not spend too much time with any one of them, nor too little.  Focusing on Isaac and Sugar because they were more than casual acquaintances.  Trying to laugh when she seemed expected to…and expressing her disapproval of their lifestyle in a hundred little ways that, like a hundred little papercuts, eventually reached a cumulative level of discomfort the others no longer chose to overlook.  What an idiot she was.  This Wrangler culture was not remotely like what she was accustomed to.  Life at home was calm and ordered, revolving around science and education. In attempting to preserve her sense of decorum, which was firmly based in the customs of her own tribe, she had managed to snub most of the Wranglers.

Sniffling, she wiped her nose on her handkerchief. Wrangler: her new word for 'riddle.' Wranglers could be as refined as Isaac and as sensitive as Sugar. Others were just plain aggravating—like Skite, who cheerfully entertained himself at any expense except his own. What was it that drew such different fairies to the same group? Such a bizarre assortment, crossing both etiquette and economic boundaries, was previously unknown to her.

She leaned back against the wall, exhaling upwards so that her hair was lifted off her damp forehead. The wall was no doubt as dusty as the floor, but she was beyond caring about such a trivial matter as her appearance. The truth behind the depth of the pain she felt was slowly forcing its way to the forefront. She had made social faux paus before and no doubt would again. Also, as awful as it might sound, she would still be perfectly happy if she never ate at the Eagle again; the food there was only passable, after all. Just so long as she continued eating with—and walking and talking and being with— Isaac.

The truth cleared its throat, metaphorically speaking. It was getting impatient with her. Sighing, she faced it—how could her feelings for Isaac be so one-sided? As in, providing he saw *her side* of things, they got along just fine. What kind of woman was she, anyway? She was acting as weepy and as gloomy as any fictional romantic heroine Daphne had ever told her about. But where was her overwhelming dedication to the comfort and happiness of the man she loved? Her dramatic but willing self-sacrifices?

Worst of all, where was her integrity? How could she claim—even to herself—to be in love with him at all after telling him flatly that they could never be together? She had meant it, too; unless or until she could choose which secrets she was keeping from him, a romantic relationship felt dishonest. However, her good sense seemed to dissolve like silver in sulfuric acid whenever Isaac got within an arm's length of her. She found a dry spot on her handkerchief and wiped her nose with it.

*What would Father think if he knew? Or... Mother?* For the first time in a long, long time, she wished she could talk with her mother.

Sighing wearily, she closed her eyes. Pity love was not something she could take a sample of and study under a microscope. Then she might be able to find a cure for it.

# Chapter 3

The next morning, Bert watched Cassidy closely as she and Agnes held a final consultation before they worked on his wing. She'd already injected a 'numbing agent,' as they called it, and he was starting to lose sensation in his back. Bert watched everything they did with a lively curiousity. He was a naturally observant fellow, which was part of why he hoped he'd be a good playwright. While he knew he had a lot to learn about recreating what he saw and heard and felt in such a way that it could be performed on the stage, he couldn't seem to help hoping that someday he'd be widely-known and successful. And before that, he might just solve the mystery of Isaac and Cassidy's behavior.

Cassidy looked up just then and caught him looking at her. She'd already injected a 'numbing agent' and she could tell from the way his wings were starting to dangle free that it was working. Smiling, she patted Agnes on the shoulder. It was time to get started. She had slept like a rock after last night's cry. Agnes was already asleep by the time Cassidy slipped quietly in. And, thanks to Daphne's absorption in the latest work of fiction she had borrowed from the library, Cassidy managed to flit into her own room without being seen. The dress she was wearing at the time, poor thing, was still wadded up on the floor waiting to be cleaned.  If that was possible.

"Nervous?" Cassidy asked Bert while she soaped her hands and wrists in the sink.  The rooms where they were working now were much larger than the five room medical suite they were originally assigned.  Oh, they still slept there, but this business of being able to move freely about, visiting patients and documenting their progress, it was a luxury she had taken for granted before coming here to Weetu.

"Some," he admitted, glancing at Rosie.  He knew she wouldn't be actively participating in today's procedure, but it was a relief to look up and see her familiar face.  "I never figured that fixing my wing would involve cutting it again."

Cassidy nodded her understanding.  A clean, fluffy towel absorbed the moisture from her hands while she prepared to explain the procedure just once more.  It would work whether he understood it or not, of course.  She simply considered it good manners to…  Shoving thoughts of etiquette aside, she got down to business.

"Your wings, all fairy wings, are as fragile as they are strong."  She smiled and slipped on her surgical gloves.  "And just like a cut in your skin can be healed, wings can be, too, with the proper material.  We will use these," she nodded toward the tray of paper-thin green sheets that Daphne was bringing over, "as organic bandages to fool your wings into believing that there is just a small, ordinary cut to be healed. The sheets mimic healthy tissue around such a cut, and at the same time provide a path for the extensive healing to move across the gap."

Daphne exhaled in relief as she safely deposited her tray with two dried starfish sheets on the counter beside the operating table. Her first job that morning had been to trim the sheets to Cassidy's specifications, so there would be enough to cover the area they were working on without wasting any of the starfish sheets.

Agnes had the more difficult task of preparing the rehydrating solution. The formula was precise and much too important for Daphne, the junior nurse, to try yet.

"Agnes will be here in a moment to finish preparing those to be attached to your wings." Cassidy avoided looking at the tray that Daphne brought next and the razor-sharp scalpels it contained. She was trying to calm Bert, not make him more apprehensive. "Today we will start repairing these areas," she indicated two large gaps in the picture of his hindwing that Agnes had drawn and posted on the wall, "because they will need the most time to heal. I will remove a tiny amount of scar tissue from the edges, then use a weak adhesive to hold the sheet in place." The damage to Bert's hindwing was so severe that the field medic had resorted to cauterizing Bert's compromised veins and cutting away the parts of the membrane that were beyond his help.  There was still enough of the original damage from the pirate's brass needles to make Cassidy spitting mad every time she stopped to think about the vile weapon.

"Which will let my wing heal back up just like nothing ever happened, right?"

"Yes, but…"

"But it takes time."  Bert grinned.  "As long as I can still write while they heal, I can be patient."

"Ready, Doctor," Agnes announced, noting that Bert's interruption prevented Cassidy from pointing out that the sheets would need to be tended and kept damp.  Only after the wing membrane and veins were healed underneath them would the sheets be allowed to dry up and fall off.

"Go ahead," Cassidy instructed her.

Bert watched, fascinated, as a green sludge poured out of the flask Agnes was holding and onto the paper-thin sheets in the tray.

"Are you sure you do not want to be put to sleep?"  Cassidy offered.  "This could be quite painful."

"I believe you."  Bert looked up from where the sheets were gradually absorbing the liquid from the sludge and puffing up like sponges.  "But I might use this in a play someday, so…" He shrugged.

"Then you had better tell me," Cassidy took up one of the scalpels and pressed the dull end of the handle into Bert's back between his fore and hindwings, "if you can feel this?"

Bert frowned in concentration, then shook his head. "Feel what?"

Cassidy made sure she let him see her elbow move as she drew her hand back and reversed the scalpel. This time it was the sharp end of the blade that she lightly touched against his skin.

"Doc, are you being serious?" Bert shook his head again. "I'm not feeling anything."

"I assure you," Cassidy traded the scalpel for the wingboard, a lightweight balsawood frame they would affix the hindwing to while it healed. Ready, she beckoned to Agnes. The numbing salve had clearly taken effect. "I am quite serious."

Agnes slipped her gloves on and came over to help. Gingerly taking hold of Bert's hindwing by the peripheral membrane, she eased it away from his body.

Cassidy realized that she was holding her breath while she waited for the hindwing to be stretched out flat enough for the wingboard she was holding. It was no surprise to her when she looked over her shoulder at Rosie, who had been invited to observe, and found that Rosie was holding her breath, too.

"Ready." Agnes' centuries of experience stood her in good stead as she held the hindwing in place without straining the scar tissue.

Cassidy was already fitting the wingboard around the wing and Daphne was at her elbow with a bowl of weak adhesive. Working together, the three of them got Bert's wing safely attached to the wingboard in short order. They then attached the bottom of the wingboard to a wooden support on the table to prevent things from moving during the surgery. Agnes double-checked that the support was close enough to Bert that they would not stress his hindwing's basal region, either.

"Alright." Cassidy nodded when that was done. It was almost her turn. And if her hand slipped, she could do more damage than good. Taking up the scalpel she had used to test Bert just a minute or so before, Cassidy took a deep, cleansing breath.

Daphne was busily spreading some of the thick, green solution just inside the edges that Cassidy was about to trim back. This was the final phase of preventing infection while promoting healing. Likewise Agnes was standing by, her fingers already poised over the sheet shaped for the first area.

When Daphne stepped clear, Cassidy stepped in. It looked rather like a dance to Rosie, who understood the technique in theory and was glad of a chance to see it performed. Rosie winced as the scalpel cut into the delicate membrane, cutting away the damaged, scarred tissue. The sludge followed the scalpel down into the cut like a pet would follow its owner. Cassidy stepped back to allow Agnes in. Agnes plucked the first sheet free of the sludge and pressed it firmly in place. They repeated the process once more, and this time Rosie noticed that Cassidy cut away just the part of the scar tissue that Agnes was prepared to cover. That left several finger widths of scar tissue still in the hindwing, but apparently that was it. Cassidy was taking her gloves off and Daphne and Agnes were scraping the remaining sludge from the preparation tray back into the flask it had come from. It could be stored a few days and used in the next surgery.

"Rosie?" Cassidy turned to face her hostess-guest. "This would be a good time for questions," she smiled.

Rosie exhaled slowly. They had discussed the materials Cassidy would be using over breakfast that morning, so Rosie knew that her tribe would never be able to replicate the procedure without first opening trade channels with the Water Fairy Tribe. The sheets were apparently harvested from a strange sea animal called a 'starfish,' which had the amazing ability to regenerate its limbs when they were lost. That was also one of the keys to the fabulous Water Fairy decoction that was enabling some of Weetu's patients to overcome their spinal injuries. Rosie couldn't help wondering what other medical marvels were hidden from them in the sea.

Behind Cassidy, Agnes was reminding Bert that, once the edges dried, sealing the sheet in place on his wing, he was free to leave. Providing, of course, that he remembered to keep the sheet damp.

"You say you will repair the cauterized sections of the media and posterior cubitus veins at a later date?" Rosie confirmed.

"Yes, that is right," Cassidy agreed. "At the moment, there is nowhere for the blood to go, no vein for it to flow through. But the wing membrane will grow back and when it has done so sufficiently to support the vein's regrowth, we will cut away the cauterized sections and insert an organic tube to carry the blood out from the basal region to the trailing edges of his hindwing." She was privately glad that the affected veins were the media and the posterior cubitus, smaller veins that posed less risk to the overall health of the hindwing and usually rebranched on their own.

"And the sheet will work with the tube to regrow the surgically removed tissue, including the vein?"

"Exactly."

"What about the wingfolds?"

"They are a little trickier," Cassidy agreed. "The wing membrane will grow back across the gaps and there will be some natural tendency of the new membrane to fold where the old one would have. However, to make sure Bert regains the full, tuck-able motion of a healthy hindwing, we will teach him some exercises after the wingboard is removed."

"And when will that be?" Bert inquired with obvious interest.

"Ordinarily, I would estimate months or even a year for the wing membrane and vein to fully regrow and harden." Cassidy grinned at him. "But thanks to the healing potion Rosie will be giving you, that might happen a lot sooner."

She only wished she could take the measurements and document Bert's progress personally. The implications were tremendous, particularly for the Water Fairies who suffered lightning injuries during the course of their duties. Or even those who got hurt while harvesting the sea. It was long past time for the Water Fairy Tribe to rejoin the rest of Fairydom; they stood to lose too much if they continued in their isolationist ways. If only there was something she could do about that right now, instead of having to wait for the spring thaw!

"This is truly amazing." Rosie had leaned close to Bert's hindwing and was studying it carefully.

Cassidy roused herself enough to give Bert a friendly warning. "It will be terribly itchy after the numbness wears off."

"Wonderful." Bert was trying to look over his shoulder or under his arm to see the results when Daphne handed him a small mirror. "Thank you." He chuckled when he got his first good look at it.  "I doubt this will ever catch on as a fashion statement."

Caught truly by surprise, all four of the women began laughing.

"Here."  Daphne appeared beside him again, holding a sling-like strap.  "Let me put this over your shoulder to keep the wingboard in place."

"It will still move," Bert protested as she hooked the strap to the wingboard by means of small holes in its upper corners.

"Not very much."  Daphne smiled and held up the second piece of the harness, which was essentially a belt.  "Because the basal section of your hindwing is unharmed, a little swaying and stretching will be good for it, help to loosen up the muscles."  She ran the belt through the loops on the strap and brought the belt ends together to fasten it in place.

"Wait!" Bert exclaimed.  "If you buckle it back there, I…"

"You will not be able to adjust the position of the wingboard," Cassidy finished for him.  "And that is a good thing.  The belt and shoulder straps are just too ordinary.  An hour or two and you would be trying to adjust it without meaning to."  She shook her head.  "Daphne adjusted the length of the straps and belt from a medical perspective, with the intent of keeping your hindwing in a stable position while it heals."

Daphne was now dutifully pressing lightly on the starfish sheet with a clean cloth, checking for areas that would try to drip.

Bert took a deep breath, found that he could manage it with the belt on, and nodded. "I am convinced." Through the mirror he watched as Daphne released the screws that were holding the wingboard in place on the table. It was a relief to have its top edge out of the indent it was making in his back and side. He straightened up slowly and noted that the wingboard felt about the same weight as a messenger pouch. "Is it alright if I go to the recovery room for a while?"

"Of course." Cassidy smiled. A handful of her Wrangler and windfairy spinal patients were in there, harassing the Wood Fairy nurses with questions about when they would be well enough to leave and so forth. A few of them would need the braced walkway she requested for Isaac immediately after his surgery, but most were making impossibly rapid recoveries. "I am sure the others will be happy to see you. Just remember to check on the sheet at least once an hour. It must remain damp."

"Hmmph." Agnes didn't even bother to look up from the equipment she was cleaning so she could re-sterilize it. "He will remember. Or I will personally remind him again."

Bert's eyebrows went up. There was no question in his mind that Agnes would indeed hunt him down and drag him back to the medical maze should she feel it was required.

"Cheer up, Bert." Isaac grinned at them all from where he stood, leaning against the door jam. "You can always ask for an apprentice that needs some diplomatic hours." He'd timed his arrival just right. Cassidy was still there, but the procedure was already complete.

"Diplomatic hours?"

Isaac trained his smile on Daphne, who had asked him to explain, just like he hoped.

"Oh, yes. Wrangler apprentices must learn a lot of things, including diplomacy."

"In this case," Bert's powerful arms flexed as he eased himself off the table and onto his remaining leg, then down onto the edge of his modified wheeled chair, "the diplomacy lesson would take the form of remembering your mission while either bored stiff or thoroughly distracted by the events going on about you." He smiled thankfully at Rosie, who had moved quickly forward to hold his wingboard while he eased back in the chair seat until his shoulders were resting against the leather strap that was standing in for the entire chair back. Once settled, he released his chair brake and tested to make sure his wingboard was out of harm's way while going forwards or backwards.

"So, the apprentice's mission would be to check your wingboard once an hour?" Daphne surmised.

"Precisely." Bert nodded.

"It might even count as service hours," Isaac

mused, rubbing his jaw.

During his hours of therapy after Cassidy's arrival, she expressed her admiration for the way the apprentices were built into the program. The older apprentices were assigned specific Wranglers to serve, including driving their wheeled chairs wherever in Weetu they wanted to go. The most responsible members of the next oldest class spent most of their service hours—amounting to a month per year—inside the pump rooms, helping the patients work their muscles while drawing water or fresh air into Weetu.

"It could, I suppose." Bert rolled his shoulders forward and back experimentally.

"You could request Jared from the water pump room," Rosie suggested with a smile. "He is a good lad."

Isaac had to agree with that assessment. Jared was the apprentice who worked with him through his therapy.

"Take this with you." Rosie handed Bert a water bag with a red leaf stamped on its side, marking it as holding a medicinal potion. "Sip it as the numbing wears off. It will accelerate your healing and dull the pain." She had crimped a wing once and knew firsthand just how exquisite wing pain could be.

"Thank you." Bert clipped it to his real belt so it would stay on his lap while he worked the wheels of his chair. Pausing beside Isaac, Bert offered him his hand. "Thanks for stopping by to check on me."

Isaac's logic kicked him in his guilt, but he smiled anyway. Bert's welfare was not his primary reason for coming by, it was true; however, if not for Bert's operation, Isaac would have had to go somewhere else to locate Cassidy this morning.

"How could I resist?" Isaac grinned. "I wanted to see what I was getting into!" He was scheduled for his first wing operation the next morning.

# Chapter 4

After Isaac had cheered Bert on his way, he found himself standing awkwardly to one side while Cassidy and her nurses set the room to rights.  Twice he tried to interrupt so that he could invite Cassidy to join him in his morning duties, but both times Rosie chose to ask a question at just the wrong moment.  He was beginning to think she was doing it on purpose.

"So there are ample opportunities to harvest what we need without harming the starfish animals," Cassidy finished answering Rosie's latest question.

"Fascinating."  Rosie tried to think of another question to ask Cassidy.  It had been a while since such an opportunity to tease Prince Isaac had presented itself.

"Cassidy."  Isaac spoke abruptly. "May I have a word with you?"

Daphne, Cassidy's younger assistant, immediately left what she was doing to take over what Cassidy was doing.

Cassidy was slow to yield the task, mundane as it was, because avoiding Isaac still seemed like the best way to keep Water Fairy secrets. Reluctantly, she turned to face him.

"I thought you might come with me on my rounds this morning."  Isaac's smile slowly faded as he waited for her to respond. "You mentioned wanting to investigate the way we do things on the surface," he added when it seemed like she was going to just stand there.

Cassidy considered, unaware of the slight frown that puckered her brow.

"Thank you," she said at last. "I really should remain here. There are things to do before…"

"We can do them." Daphne leapt in before the conversational door could be shut and locked.

Cassidy shot a look of thinly veiled desperation at Agnes, who was replacing the sketch of Bert's hindwing with the sketch of Isaac's left forewing. It was literally the last thing that had to be done before tomorrow's operation. Even Isaac's starfish sheets were already cut, since Daphne did them at the same time as Bert's. The two friends stared at each other for a few seconds, then Cassidy squared her shoulders.

"Thank you, Your Highness." Cassidy allowed Daphne to help her remove the surgical smock she was wearing. She held out her hand, palm down, at approximately chest height.

Isaac slid his forearm under her hand without giving it a thought. And then it was too late. Instead of going arm in arm, or even hand in hand, they were setting off like two strangers at a Silver Fairy ball.

Cassidy was glad of the silence between them at first. But as they entered more populated areas of Weetu, she grew concerned. He barely reacted when he was hailed, returning only the faintest of smiles or short nods to the well-wishers they encountered.

"Is something wrong, Your Highness?" she asked after they turned off from the main tunnel.

"Hmm?" While Isaac's heart was firmly set on winning the Lady Cassidy, his mind was busy with thoughts of what he needed to accomplish that morning. "Oh, forgive me." He glanced around them. "I seem to have been walking unawares. It is a good thing this is one place in Weetu I can find half-asleep!" Indicating a door on their left, he led her over to it. "Thank you so much for agreeing to come with me this morning. I could hardly say I had shown you Weetu without visiting the Wrangler apprentices."

Cassidy braced herself as he opened the door for her. What had she gotten herself into? Or rather, what had *he*gotten her into? She found herself in a wide hallway that stretched out beyond what she could see with just the light of the cold fire.

Isaac pretended not to notice the way she was glaring at him and opted to continue with the formal manner she had chosen. It occurred to him as he allowed her to precede him through the heavy door that she always fell back on formalities; whether she was tired or uncomfortable, or whatever. Interesting. He wondered which she was now…and why with him?

"I always start with the youngest apprentices." Taking his place beside her again, he pressed a finger against his lips for silence. Easing the door to the first room open, he peeked in.

Cassidy watched in wonder as his face lit up. Then he opened the door fractionally wider and let her see, too. Her heart dropped when she saw that the room was a nursery! Were these the *apprentices* he was going to show her?

"Attention!" Maisy, the apprentice in charge whispered when she saw Isaac in the doorway. Everyone who was not feeding someone else, or changing a diaper, looked up and nodded at the prince.

"At ease," Isaac countermanded, also in a whisper, as he let himself and Cassidy into the room. "How are the triplets?" he asked Maisy.

"Less trouble than most of the rest of them," Maisy smiled, stepping back so that Isaac could see them better.

Cassidy's heart melted when she looked in an oversized crib and saw three tiny babies wrapped in each other's arms. The way that Isaac deftly reached into the crib to rearrange one of those arms, which was dangerously close to another triplet's nose, without disturbing them, told her a great deal about him. Like what kind of a father he would be.

"And how are all of you?" Isaac asked once he was content that each of the triplets was breathing. "Getting all of the supplies that you need?"

"Yes, thank you." Maisy smiled.

As was his practice, Isaac took a moment to go around the room, checking each of the cribs, speaking to each of the apprentices on the morning shift.

Cassidy tried to keep her doctor's mask on while she followed along. The professional veneer allowed her to keep an emotional distance until they reached the last crib. A little butterball gurgled at her and waved its arms as if expecting to be picked up.

Isaac chuckled softly. "Go ahead," he encouraged her. "Otherwise he will start to fuss."

Cassidy's hands somehow got past the milling arms and legs to the baby's torso. Sliding one hand under the baby's back and the other behind the baby's head, she eased him towards her.

Isaac placed his hand lightly on the back of her waist as she bent further and further into the crib, just in case she started to fall in—or at least, that's what he told himself. And so it was that Cassidy found herself straightening into his arms, her own arms full of warm, precious baby. She almost started to cry, the ache in her chest was so tremendous. Never in her five hundred years had she missed having a family as badly as she did now.

"This is little Teddy." Isaac smoothed the tyke's fluffy hair, even though he knew it was hopeless. Sure enough, Teddy's hair sprang back up as soon as Isaac lifted his hand. "He came to us from a village far to the east when his mother passed away."

Cassidy lifted tear-filled eyes to look at him in surprise. "He is an orphan?"

"Not exactly." Isaac hesitated. "His father is a Wrangler, and cannot take care of him right now. So he has a home with us for a while."

Cassidy looked back around the room, seeing the cribs with new eyes. "All of them?" She could hardly believe it.

"It is the rightful legacy of every Wrangler who defends our tribe and others, that their children will be taken care of," Isaac asserted proudly.

Teddy's caretaker offered Cassidy a baby bottle, but she handed him over instead. She was already in too deep with the charming infant.

"Better not tell Daphne about this." Cassidy tried to laugh when they were on the other side of the door. "She will move in there, bag and baggage."

Isaac smiled at the feeble joke and gave her a moment to catch her breath. He was always sorry to see a new occupant in the nursery, since that meant another Wrangler or family member had died. However, after a few hundred years he usually managed to focus more on the good the nursery represented.

"Do they all grow up to be Wranglers?"

Isaac frowned, bothered that she was keeping her face turned away from him. "No, not all.

Just those who choose to do so."

Cassidy shut her eyes tightly, confused to her core.  How could she be ready to cry again so soon after last night?  Besides the obvious.  Wrangler babies growing up to be Wranglers, to fight and die and leave behind more Wrangler babies who…  For how could they help but grow up to be what they were so clearly being raised to become?

"Well, thank you for the tour."

"Wait a second."  Isaac caught her gently by the shoulder as she started to walk away.  "That was just the first stop."  He dropped his hand from her shoulder to her wrist.

Cassidy jerked her hand free.  "Very well."

Thoroughly confused now, Isaac skipped some of his regular stops and guided her down a branch tunnel.  Morning classes were well underway by now, so he stopped to show her one of them.

"You must see the details," the teacher was saying.  "Observe this bird.  The way her head is cocked to one side.  The way her tail feathers are spread, as if she is getting ready to take off."  The tip of a long stick traced the items to which the teacher was referring on an enormous drawing.  "Observe and draw the details."  Noticing his two guests, the teacher nodded briefly at them, then took a question.

"Should we even notice the bark?" asked the young fairy.  "Because my friend says oak trees are best, but I think maple trees are best, so I always use maple bark on my drawings. We live in a maple tree, you know."

"Yes, I know." The teacher shook his head kindly at the student. "It is very important to draw the kind of bark that is in the picture. Even if you like maple the best, Wranglers should be able to draw all kinds of bark." When the same hand shot into the air, he answered the anticipated question by saying, "Wranglers who can draw what they see get important assignments." As he had hoped, the hand was lowered.

Cassidy's frown was deeper than before when Isaac smiled down at her, so he took her back out into the hallway.

"What is wrong?" he asked.

"How can you teach those children as if everything revolves around being a Wrangler?"

Isaac stared blankly at her. "I do not think I understand the question."

"You heard him," she flared. "'Wranglers who can draw what they see get important assignments'," she quoted the teacher. "So these children are taken in as infants and trained to live, eat, and breathe the idea of growing up to be Wranglers."

Isaac caught her by the shoulders and this time he held on. "Stop right there." He scowled down at her. "That class has exactly one Wrangler orphan in it. The other seven students are here because they wanted it so badly they have left their families for the winter and are staying here at Weetu."

Cassidy stared up at him, shocked.

He released her, took a few steps away. "I wanted you to see the Wrangler program, to understand how hard we all worked to reach active Wrangler status. To understand that it is bigger than the clientele at the Eagle." He stopped when she winced visibly, some of his anger at her censure draining away. Running his fingers through his hair, he sighed. "Wranglers learn a little bit of everything. They tend babies. They cook, sew, and sing. Musically-inclined Wranglers are worth twice their pension during a long, dull posting." Desperate to get his point across, he walked over to her again. "They learn history, politics, basic medicine, art!" He swung his hand towards the room they just left. "We teach them how to debate and when to debate." A smile teased at his lips. "Just before tackling a bird's nest is the wrong time to debate an order, for example."

Cassidy, shaken to her core by how badly she had misjudged things, tried to smile back at him. "What is a bird, exactly?" she finally asked.

Isaac felt like a fool. Another piece of the puzzle had just smacked him in the face. Facts did that, sometimes. What would a Water Fairy know of the dangers on the surface? Of the practical reasons for the Wrangler Corps' existence?

"I was going to save this for last," he took her gently by the wrist, "but I think you should see it now." Tucking her hand in the crook of his elbow, he began walking slowly toward the athletic area.

The tunnel before them widened, giving way to a decent-sized chamber. Inside the chamber, a group of wide-eyed apprentices was counting off for a game of Wasps and Fairies. A mock-up of a wasp nest hung from the ceiling and would act as home-base for those playing wasps.

"The younger apprentices work on their flexibility, reflexes, and reactions through games like this one," Isaac paused so they could watch. "These games are designed to prepare them for the more difficult field exercises."

"What are they supposed to be?" she asked, indicating the half of the group being outfitted with conical devices. When the device belts were strapped about their waists, the cones hung down behind them.

"They are going to pretend to be wasps," Isaac explained. "Wasps are much smaller than birds, but larger than fairies. The wasp larvae eat spiders, which is good. Unfortunately, the adults attack fairies that are in what the wasps consider to be their territory."

"I see." Cassidy nodded. "We have sea animals who defend their territory also."

Isaac was glad to hear that!

"This wasp nest is actually quite a bit smaller

than the real thing," he continued. "Its main purpose is to teach them the layout of a wasp nest and how to maneuver inside one."

"So in this game, both sides are learning?" Cassidy deduced.

"Exactly." Isaac was relieved that she seemed to be beginning to understand. "Those playing fairies will try to get inside the nest, drop fake smoke bombs, and get out without being captured."

"Smoke bombs?"

Isaac nodded. "It is the safest way to drive wasps from one nest to another one in a more suitable area." He caught her eye, then resumed walking. "By the time they are ready to move on, they will have also learned the best places to drill in the walls of the nest for maximum smoke bomb effectiveness."

"Can either side win?" Cassidy asked as they were about to exit the chamber.

Isaac stopped again and looked her in the eyes. "Absolutely. That is another vital lesson."

Cassidy followed obediently when he set off again. Her mind remained on the activity in the chamber they just visited until she noticed his steps slowing.

"The older apprentices are sparring in there," Isaac informed her, coming to a stop before a hole in the wall wide enough for three fully-grown men to come barreling through unimpeded.

Cassidy cringed at the sound of several somethings smacking solidly against each other. Like most adult Water Fairies, she was an expert with a suge, or flexible sword that was as long as she was tall, but she rarely sparred with anyone.

"By the end of the winter, they will either be active Wranglers or not." Isaac felt his wings start to twitch in memory of his own final year and forced them to be still. "The apprentices who make it this far have been taught and tested and tried to their limits."

"But…" Cassidy looked up at him, consciously deciding to ask instead of assume this time. "Why?"

"Because they need to know what their limits are," Isaac explained helpfully. "Being a Wrangler is a dangerous job, one of the most dangerous on Fairydom's surface. We arm them not only with weapons and tools to get the job done, but with the facts. Cold, hunger, fatigue, fear, these are just some of the enemies that we can neither hide nor flee from. At the end of their training, an apprentice must know themselves well enough to know they can do the job."

Cassidy took a deep breath. "This is all much more sophisticated than I thought," she admitted.

Isaac stifled the platitude that sprang to his lips. He would hardly be acknowledging her implied apology if he made light of the misunderstanding. Instead, he squeezed her arm softly.

"Shall we go in?" he invited. Sensing her reluctance, he moved his hand from her arm to the small of her back, hoping to reassure her as they walked through the entrance.

Cassidy was once more astonished at what she saw. A handful of young fairies were sparring one on one with each other. However, the greatest source of the noises she had been hearing was coming from the other side of the chamber.

"That," Isaac leaned one arm against the railing that ran around the room, separating the walkway from the sparring areas, "is our dummy hummingbird."

Speechless, Cassidy stared back and forth between Isaac and the puppet that filled most of the room. The puppet's two feet were carved out of the chamber floor, while its tail 'feathers' brushed against the far wall; leaving Cassidy to wonder if it was really possible for a surface animal to grow to such a size.

"But it's enormous!" she squeaked.

"Actually, they're quite small. For birds, I mean." He decided not to tell her that there was a squirrel sharing Weetu's tree with them. After all, there was no way for the squirrel to fit through the tunnel they used to reach its nest.

They watched together as a squad of apprentices attacked the dummy bird, bursting out from behind some fake foliage. Two of them maneuvered a small cannon into position, then dry-fired it. While the whole squad followed up with a mass assault, their instructor checked the cannon's position.

"If this was a real hummingbird," Isaac explained, "that cannon would have launched several hundred twigs of netting to ensnare the wings."

"Get back 'ere!" Bellowed the instructor, halting them mid-attack. "This cannon is off-center. Any netting fired from this would have gone wide, lettin' the bird escape. You two!" He pointed at the two in charge of the cannon. "You just put your squad on the hummingbird's mornin' menu! Twenty run and tumble laps; maybe that will teach you to aim straight!"

Isaac grinned, remembering his own apprentice squad. One of the first lessons they learned was that they functioned as a unit. His legs ached at the thought of the leagues they'd run together.

"Not you lot!" The instructor stopped the rest of the squad from running with the two being punished. "I got two more months to make Wranglers out of you lot, so the rest of you are gonna stay 'ere and go through it again."

Isaac frowned. "Excuse me, Cass."

She opened her mouth to protest that terrible nickname, but she was too late. He had already stepped over the railing and was sliding down the sloping wall to its base.

# Chapter 5

"One moment." Isaac called ahead to the instructor, a burly fellow he had never liked very much.

"Weelll now, if it ain't His Highness." McGrath, the instructor, rested two hammy fists on his waist. "I hope everybody brought their clean hankies today."

"No need to surrender, McGrath," Isaac quipped. "I have come to have a word with you in peace." A few titters from the confused apprentice group reminded him that this was not the time or the place for friendly jabs; especially given that there was not a friend about with which to exchange them. "I was just showing Doctor Cassidy around the Wrangler training program," he nodded at where Cassidy was waiting for him on the walkway above, "when I saw your unusual training tactic."

"Unusual?" McGrath slipped his thumbs inside the pockets of his britches. "How do you mean?"

"Splitting up the punishment." Isaac knew from past experience that McGrath ignored subtlety and routinely misunderstood wit. "Is that a new training policy?" If it had been, Isaac would have been the one telling McGrath about it, not the other way around. And they both knew it.

"Yeah," McGrath sneered. "I come up with it. Works real well, too."

Isaac counted to twelve before he dared speak and then it was to command the squad. "Take your laps." What he planned to say next would better be spoken in private.

"Hold it." McGrath glared at him. "How dare you?"

Isaac focused on McGrath despite being aware that others were turning to look at them as McGrath's voice got louder.

"You come in 'ere, all hoity-toity and tell me how to train a squad? You got no right!"

"I have every right." Isaac kept his voice at a conversational level through an enormous amount of willpower. "I outrank you."

"You outrank me?" McGrath spluttered. "Come off it. No other Wrangler would have the gall to tell a trainer how to do his job."

"That is true." Isaac forced himself to admit it, much as he hated to give McGrath so much as a hand's breadth of credibility. Trainers were selected with the utmost care, though some allowances might be made for those forced to retire early due to traumatic injuries, such as McGrath's double-wing amputation. Clearly that had been a mistake. "However, they surely would feel free to remind each other that this is not the Wrangler way. A squad must think and act as a unit, whether in mock combat or punishment laps."

"Is that a fact?" McGrath had finally noticed that all activity in the room had slowed or stopped completely. "Of course, Your Highness." He touched an imaginary cap with two crooked fingers in a gesture of servility. "Right away, Your Highness." His eyes and tone mocked Isaac.

Cassidy watched in mounting alarm as apprentices exchanged knowing glances. This, she felt sure, would not be anything like the friendly brawls she had witnessed at the Eagle. When those were over, the combatants dusted each other off, patched each other up, and went back to discussing politics or playing Stratagem or whatever it was they were doing originally.

Isaac was counting silently again. It had been foolish of him to rush into the situation. Correcting McGrath could have waited, come through the regular channels. Waited until a chamber full of apprentices was safely out of earshot and McGrath's pride was only minimally involved. Worst of all was the composition of the group presently—and actively—eavesdropping on them. Nearly two-thirds of them were the children of Wood Fairy nobles. If he relied solely on his rank, how many of them would still see it as a function of his position as prince?

"I can see only one way to settle this." Isaac unhappily began unbuttoning his jacket. This was going to hurt. "A Wrangler challenge." An excited whisper flew around the room.

"You? Against me?" McGrath folded his arms across his chest. McGrath was already in the standard issue Wrangler workwear uniform. "Are you serious?"

Isaac tamped down on his anger yet again. Calling up a smile from his repertoire of social skills, he just nodded.

"Then I will choose us some weapons." McGrath's grin was pure vitriolic glee. "You there." He pointed at one of his apprentices. "Clear a ring."

Cassidy decided enough was enough and flew down to stand beside Isaac.

"Are you doing this to impress me?" she asked in a low tone as she took his jacket from him.

Isaac surprised himself by laughing. "You might give me a little credit," he teased her. "You keep your secrets well, but I do know how much you dislike violence."

"Then why?" Cassidy, seeing that he was going to leave his cravat on, stretched out her wings and lifted herself to hover where she could more easily untie it. "You will be better off without this for the next few minutes, I imagine."

Isaac sighed. "I am not sure I have enough time to explain why right now." Glancing over her shoulder, he saw that McGrath was testing weapons for balance. It had to be for show, because McGrath surely knew every weapon in the room by heart. "I am ashamed to tell you that we have had several charges of arrogance filed against some of the apprentices in this chamber.   And they all used the same justification: their parents are Wood Fairy nobles, so why shouldn't they treat the other apprentices like servants?"

Cassidy slowly settled to the ground in front of him, his cravat in her hands.  "You are doing this to make a point?  One that you could just as easily make in some other way?"

Isaac took her by the elbow and led her to the edge of the informal ring the apprentices had cleared.

"I am trying to lead by example.  As the crown prince, I would be within my rights to order McGrath to do anything I can make seem reasonable.  In this chamber, though, I am a Wrangler first and a prince second.  That is what I am trying to teach them."

"But…"

"Cass."   Isaac dropped his hand from her elbow to her hand, brought it to his lips and kissed it.  "Small problems have a way of getting bigger, like, well, like the holes in one's boots.  I have to try."

"Whenever Your Highness is ready," McGrath's voice sneered from behind him.

Isaac winked at Cassidy, then turned to face his opponent.  No sooner had he done so than a quarterstaff was launched at him like a spear. Side-stepping easily, Isaac caught it onehanded.

Years of practice took over as he ran through a short training pattern, testing the quarterstaff for balance and reach. This was a training weapon for older apprentices or active Wranglers and lacked the padding that graced those used by the younger classes. As he finished, Isaac was pleased to look up and find McGrath watching him through narrowed eyes.

"A Wrangler challenge." Isaac's voice rang through the still chamber. "As an active Wrangler of the order of the eagle and holder of three green maple leaves, I challenge McGrath, Wrangler trainer of the order of the fox and holder of two green maple leaves and one scarlet plume." McGrath had received his scarlet plume for wounds received while rescuing two members of his squad during a squirrel attack; it was little enough to do for someone who would have to retire from the Wranglers because he had literally lost his wings. "The matter between us shall be considered settled after this, regardless of who wins."

Cassidy blinked in surprise at Isaac's last words. Arguments could last for generations in her tribe, particularly if they were about matters of science. It was unlikely that they would ever adopt the Wrangler way of handling disputes, yet Cassidy was beginning to see it for what it was, instead of what she had originally thought.

McGrath, taken off-guard by the way his rank and commendations rolled off Isaac's tongue without outside prompting, was a shade less eager to fight. "Agreed." McGrath stepped closer to Isaac.

Isaac watched stoically as McGrath feinted a strike at his shoulders. The next blow was not a feint, however, and Isaac was hard pressed to avoid the sweep at his legs. When McGrath reversed the motion, bringing the tip of his staff up hard and fast, Isaac had to jerk back to keep his staff from being ripped from his hands.

Finding himself falling backwards, Isaac twisted at the waist, planted one end of his staff on the floor, and swung his feet up in time to catch McGrath in the stomach mid-rush. Completing his flip, Isaac went on the offensive.

His thrust was blocked. He dodged McGrath's overhand cut at his head only to get a stinging cut on his wings that dropped him to his knees. Assuming that McGrath would attack from behind as well as before, Isaac rolled onto his right hip in time to watch the business end of a quarterstaff slice through the air where his head had been. Still rolling, Isaac brought both hips around, got a knee under him and lunged to his feet. McGrath had overextended himself in the expectation of a decisive finish to their bout, but Isaac waited for him to recover.

"What are you waitin' for?" McGrath spat at him.

"You." Isaac grinned back.

With a wild yell, McGrath launched himself at Isaac.

A few of the blows raining down on Isaac got past his defenses as he blocked, parried, and dodged, leaving him wishing that he had another pair of hands holding another quarterstaff. As he had hoped, however, it was short-lived. McGrath took another chance and Isaac saw his. Knocking McGrath's staff aside, Isaac struck him once on the left shoulder. After that, it was mostly a matter of keeping McGrath off his rhythm.

"When was the last time you fought an active Wrangler?" Isaac asked conversationally as he side-stepped, then struck back, his staff connecting solidly with McGrath's meaty right forearm. Wood rang against wood as Isaac hit McGrath's staff dead center, not because he thought he could make McGrath drop it, but rather because he expected McGrath to hang onto it. Sure enough, McGrath's grip had tightened after the first blow and the second rattled his hands badly.

"Remember, you chose the weapon." Feinting a step to his left, Isaac circled right. Swinging in under McGrath's guard, he rapped him sharply on the ribs. He nearly got the end of McGrath's staff in his face afterwards, and did get a crack on his left shoulder that almost made him howl. Pain was a known enemy, however, and he coldly shoved it aside. Reflexively, Isaac brought his left hand forward and down, taking advantage of the split second that McGrath was out of position.

McGrath dropped his staff and cradled his left arm against his chest.

"You broke my collarbone!"

"Do you yield?" Isaac swept McGrath's quarterstaff out of reach. He was taking no chances.

McGrath was on the verge of snarling something nasty when he saw that Isaac was poised to continue. Abruptly, he began to laugh.

"D'ya see that?" He looked around the group for his squad. Finding them, he jerked his chin in Isaac's direction. "That is how you fight properly. Always on guard. Always ready to attack. Until I yield, the bout is not over." Flexing his left land, then his bicep, McGrath decided his collarbone might not be broken after all. Tucking that hand in his pocket, he held out his right hand to Isaac. "I yield. You fought well."

Isaac took McGrath's hand, impressed despite himself. *This*was leading by example. And it would probably save a few lives in the field.

"I will think twice before I challenge a trainer again," Isaac grinned. He meant it as a promise to himself, too. An ounce of diplomacy could have saved the gallon of 'doctor's water,' a bitter herbal concoction, that Rosie was going to dose him with when she got ahold of him. Oh well. It served him right.

"Here." Cassidy gave Isaac back his jacket and cravat. "Let me see your shoulder," she instructed McGrath.

"Wait." McGrath looked at their audience. "You lot, get back to your wasp training. My squad, get your medic kits. You just might learn somethin'."

Cassidy waited impatiently until McGrath's apprentices had reassembled around them.

"Collarbones are located here." She indicated the general area, then began examining McGrath's. "If they are broken…"

From where Isaac stood, buttoning his jacket back up, Cassidy had never looked lovelier than she did now, surrounded by apprentices, teaching them. He draped the cravat about his neck and folded his arms across his chest. What was different here? Why was she so at home in the training area and so uncomfortable at the Eagle? Just then, the apprentices obediently snapped open their medical kits for her to examine them; McGrath's collarbone was officially *not*broken.

Isaac saw the connection as Cassidy alternately praised and scolded the apprentices for the state of their kits. At the Eagle, she was just another hungry fairy who could easily choose to eat somewhere else, somewhere that had higher standards for the etiquette of its patrons. Here and now, she was actively contributing to the education of these apprentices and doing it in a way that called on her strengths. She was needed.

"In a case like this," Cassidy put her hand on McGrath's arm, "which potion powder would you use?" When all of them reached for a particular bag in their kit, she nodded. "Excellent. Now I need someone to tell me what the proper ratio of powder to water would be for a bad bruise like McGrath has." From the corner of her eye, she watched McGrath's face for confirmation that the volunteer was giving her the right information. She hadn't yet begun memorizing how to use surface treatments because she wasn't sure for how much longer she'd have access to them. "Very good. Please prepare, using only the equipment in your medical kits, a pain potion for McGrath. The rest of you watch closely. This should help simulate the pressure of a real emergency situation."

McGrath was chuckling as he offered Cassidy a half-bow. "Thank you for your time, Doctor Cassidy."

"My pleasure." Cassidy gave him a half-curtsy back and moved to join Isaac up on the walkway. They were well out of earshot of the others, so she felt safe in asking a few questions. "You say hummingbirds are small?"

Surprised, Isaac followed her gaze to the dummy bird. "Yes, the smallest of all the birds."

Cassidy nodded, then took hold of his loose cravat ends. Deftly, she wound them around each other, fluffing and tucking as needed. When it was ready, she reached up to retrieve his cravat pin from her hair.

"Careful." Isaac caught her hand. "It is tangled." Gently, he worked the pin free, all the while stifling the urge to let her hair all the way down. "Here."

"Thank you." Cassidy's hands trembled slightly as she pinned his cravat. If she could react to him like this in a chamber filled with noisy apprentices, she was going to have to redouble her efforts to never be truly alone with Isaac. Deciding to straighten his collar anyway proved to be a mistake.

Isaac took her gently by the shoulders, turned so that his body blocked them from most of the spectators, and stole a kiss. When she kissed him back, her arms going 'round his neck, he forgot his plan to be the perfect tour guide that morning. Pressing her to him, he lifted her off her feet and took three long steps around the edge of the doorway. There was always a chance that someone might wander past, but at the moment he did not care.

"Isaac." Cassidy looked up into his dark, chocolate brown eyes and it was as if she could see centuries stretching out before them. The warmth of his hand on her waist, the tickle of his other hand slipping behind her neck, it was all part of the picture. Loving Isaac and being loved in return. Worrying about him, as she had just now during the bout. Nearly bursting with pride in him, as she had just now after the bout. Losing her temper with him, for the first few decades anyway. Eventually blossoming into parenthood with him at her side…

Softly, softly Isaac covered her lips with his. He treasured every heartbeat of holding her close—hers as well as his. What more could he ask for, but to wed the woman he loved?

"Isaac." Breathless, Cassidy hid her face against his chest. "No more. Please."

Disappointed, Isaac pressed his cheek to her hair. "I cannot bear to hear you say it again," he murmured. "No talk of leaving."

Cassidy's tears fell on his jacket as she nodded. She did not have the strength anyway. Come spring, she would have to return to her tribe. Right now, she was going to close her eyes and stay right where she was until…

"Isaac!" She tried to straighten away and found herself nose to nose with a wide-eyed Isaac. At that distance, she could not breathe without inhaling his scent. "I promised Gallica I would join her for the fitting this morning."

"Then I should probably keep Stuart company." Isaac's sigh gently stirred an errant curl, but he obediently stepped back. His eyes never left hers as he tucked her hand possessively under his arm. His best friend, Stuart, would marry his sister, Princess Gallica, within the month. It was an unusually short engagement, acceptable mostly because of their lengthy friendship.

Silently, they moved away from the training area. The classrooms and the nursery fell behind them, until they were once again amidst the crowded main tunnel chamber.

"I should go that way." Cassidy indicated an upper tunnel.

"I will probably find Stuart checking on the blacksmiths." Isaac reluctantly released her hand. "By now they should be halfway through our winter order."

"What did you order?"

Isaac, who had been about to turn away, stayed where he was. "The usual." His gaze dropped to her lips. "Replacement cannon for our foreign postings. Enough round shot, grape shot, and hollow shot to see them through the spring."

"Is spring one of the more dangerous seasons on the surf…?" Cassidy caught herself mid-word and flushed violently. *This* was why she had to be careful! Because she indulged herself in detaining Isaac, she had nearly given herself—and her tribe!—away. No surface fairy would call it 'the surface.' Nor would they ask if spring was dangerous! They would already know.

Chapter 6

Distressed, Cassidy flew away without another word.  It was an effort for her to reach the upper tunnel with her slightly stunted Water Fairy wings, though not so much as when she first arrived at Weetu.

"Cassidy!"  Gallica clasped her hands in relief and flew quickly to her friend.  "I was just coming to look for you!"

"Gallica, please forgive me."  Cassidy allowed herself to focus on Gallica's distress.  "I had no sooner finished Bert's surgery than something came up."

"Knowing how absorbed you can get in your work, I am surprised you remembered this at all!"  Gallica laughed and slipped her arm chummily through Cassidy's, leading her off towards the fitter's.

Cassidy laughed weakly, grateful that the color in her cheeks would most likely be attributed to her flight up from the lower level.

"Anyway."  Gallica squeezed her arm.  "I need you to help me convince my mother that I should wear a white bark cloth gown to the wedding."

Cassidy almost sighed.  When Isaac invited her to attend the wedding as his companion, she never dreamed it would include arbitrating the battle of wills between Queen Fiona and her daughter.   Worst of all, Cassidy agreed with Fiona!  The spider-silk cloth was *so* soft and *so* filmy that she could hardly resist stroking it.

"Gallica."  Queen Fiona was waiting for them in the doorway of the tailor's shop, arms folded across her chest.  "Really.  Cassidy is our guest, not a professional campaigner."  That was as close to a rebuke as Fiona would come in public, but she held Gallica's gaze for a moment to be sure she was understood.  Fiona, too, was tempted to treat Cassidy like a member of the family, especially given the way Isaac was behaving; unfortunately, Cassidy remained firm on the point of returning to her tribe in the spring.

"Yes, Mother."  Gallica was only mildly subdued.

"Gallica!  Finally."  Gallica's maid of honor and matron of honor simultaneously appeared on either side of Fiona.

"Get in here, will you?" Eliza, the matron of honor, laughed.  "I only have an hour before I'm due for my shift at the hospital!"

"Are you ever going to stop trying to order everyone around?" Tina, the maid of honor, winked in everyone's direction.  "You can take the officer's leaves off the Wrangler, but you can never take the officer out of the nurse!"  Gallica just laughed and dashed in with them.

"One moment, my dear," Fiona touched Cassidy lightly on the arm as she was about to enter the shop. "Forgive me," she reached up to smooth Cassidy's hair, tucking in a loose strand here and there. "You must have had quite a morning." Finished, she was lowering her arm when Cassidy caught hold of it. Fiona was startled to see the sheen of tears in Cassidy's eyes when she looked at her. "My dear. What is it?"

Cassidy took a deep breath, shook her head slightly, and released Fiona's arm. Much to her surprise, Fiona slipped that same arm about her shoulders.

"While you three argue with Master Clyde," Fiona announced, leading Cassidy into the shop, "Cassidy and I are going to put our heads together on the perfect outfit for the bride's brother's companion." She smiled when the three friends burst into giggles at her intentionally silly phrasing. "Come with me," she murmured to Cassidy.

Sweeping Cassidy along with her, Fiona made one small tactical error in her plan to get Cassidy alone for a talk. She chose the one and only fitting room with a half-finished spider-silk wedding gown inside.

Cassidy stopped abruptly when she saw it. Taking another deep breath, she stepped away from Fiona and towards the gown.

Fiona watched closely as Cassidy reached out to stroke the gown. The expression on Cassidy's face was a mixture of wistfulness and resignation, if Fiona was reading her correctly.

"Cassidy."  Fiona decided it was time to take a chance.  "I realize you are in a difficult position. Not only are you far from home," she chose her words carefully lest anyone should be close enough to overhear through the heavy drapes that separated them from the others, "but you have taken so much responsibility upon yourself. I cannot help but think that, if I were in your place, I would very much like to have someone I could talk to."

Cassidy, who had naturally looked over at Fiona, now looked back at the dress.

"Of course, you have your nurses," Fiona allowed gently, not wanting to pressure her.

Cassidy laughed sadly.  "My nurses," she repeated softly.  "Agnes was my mentor when I was in nursing school."  Noticing two simple, wooden stools sitting against the wall, Cassidy slid them out and motioned for Fiona to join her. After they were both seated, Cassidy discovered she had lost her place in her thoughts.  She instinctively understood that Fiona's offer was sincere, yet was having trouble finding a starting point for explaining the mess she had gotten herself into.

"I rather thought Agnes was more than a professional acquaintance."  Fiona, sensing Cassidy's inner struggle, leaned her shoulder against the wall.  An open, calm posture might help Cassidy to relax as well.

"Yes, much more."  Cassidy gave Fiona a

grateful smile. "She used to help me study for examinations and gave me a great deal of practical advice on how to handle different kinds of patients. When I went on to become a surgeon, I naturally asked her to work with me."

"An honor for you both." Fiona nodded her understanding.

"Yes. She is a wonderful friend." Cassidy smiled again. Rubbing her damp palms on her knees, she tried not to sigh. She had already tried talking with Agnes about the situation with Isaac; somehow they always ended up agreeing that it was important not to reveal tribal secrets. "Very wise. Very practical."

"I am so glad that you have her to counsel with," Fiona said gently, her quick ears having caught the flat note in Cassidy's voice when she said 'practical.' Was Cassidy looking for some *im*practical advice? To whom could she turn in this city of strangers? "I do hope your visit here is not all work, though. Surely you and Daphne have found some time for recreation?" Again she watched Cassidy carefully, remembering that Rosie had called the younger nurse 'a bit daydreamy, but perfectly capable.'

"Daphne." Cassidy's soft laugh was a little lighter this time. "She spends every spare moment reading."

"Ah yes." Fiona smiled. "I found her in the library the other day. A very sweet, young lady."

Cassidy almost sighed at Fiona's subtle emphasis on 'young.'

"My visit to Weetu has had some unexpected consequences." Somehow, Cassidy managed to look Fiona directly in the eyes. It was so much like looking into her own, dear mother's eyes that it took Cassidy a moment to reorient herself before continuing. Her mother died when she was very young, the result of an unfortunate laboratory accident. "Your Majesty, surely you understand. Whatever my personal feelings, I must put my," she glanced at the drapes, wondering vaguely that they had not been disturbed as yet, "responsibilities first."

"What exactly are your personal feelings?" Fiona asked bluntly, a little disappointed that Cassidy had chosen to hide behind titles.

"About…about what?" Cassidy blushed and dropped her eyes.

"Cassidy." Fiona put her hand lightly on Cassidy's. "Isaac, my *only* son, is in love with you. Whether or not you share his feelings, I only want to help."

Tears crowded Cassidy's throat as she responded, "I do share his feelings. And therefore, no one can help me."

Master Clyde busied himself with straightening the drapes he had just passed through.

"Ah, a thousand pardons." After a few millennia of working with female customers, he had learned the delicate art of when to notice tears and when not to. "The other ladies are making their final selections, and I am at last," he bowed, first to the queen, then to her guest, "at your service." He was also hoping they would not be so difficult as the bride and her ladies, who had all insisted on bark cloth gowns. While bark cloth was an immensely versatile cloth, particularly in Weetu where the Wrangler culture dominated even the fashion scene, he personally thought it a trifle too common for a bridal gown.

"Marvelous." Fiona beamed at him. "And what have you to offer us?"

Clyde clapped his hands, rubbed his palms together, and opened a wall panel.

"We begin with cloth swatches."

Fiona waved her hand dismissively. "Doctor Cassidy will be accompanying Prince Isaac. Her gown must be suitable to the occasion."

"Of course, of course." Clyde bobbed a few half-bows, clearly distressed. "And as the bride has chosen a lovely white bark cloth, may I suggest…"

"You may not." Fiona gave a tiny inward sigh of resignation. While not truly surprised by Gallica's decision, Fiona was torn between memories of her own, satin wedding gown and the bald fact that this was Gallica's decision to make. "Doctor Cassidy favors the spider-silk. And she is accompanying my son, not competing with my daughter."

"Of course." He bobbed again. Holding the swatches to his chest he said, "It would be my pleasure to make the lovely Doctor Cassidy a gown from any cloth she chooses."

"Excellent."

"Unfortunately," Clyde's voice rose slightly, "I have only just been informed that we have run out of that cloth. It will be at least a week before more can be brought from storage and…"

"You will use that dress." Fiona nodded at the dress they were sharing the fitting room with. "The material is mine. Please remodel it for the doctor." Rising perfunctorily, she added, "While you begin, I will check on the others."

Cassidy watched in shock as Fiona swept out of the room. Catching Clyde looking thoughtfully between her and the dress, she asked, "Is that really her dress?"

"Oh yes." Clyde nodded. "She commissioned it for the princess the same day that the engagement was announced."

Cassidy closed her eyes, pained on Fiona's behalf.

"I have never been to a royal wedding. Will it be proper for me to wear a white gown when I am not the bride?"

"Traditionally it is only the bride who wears white at the ceremony," Clyde agreed, faintly curious as to what backwoods village such a skilled surgeon could possibly have come from. "But never fear. The cloth will take any color."

Unlimbering his measuring tape he asked, "Will you stand, please?"

When he had the figures he needed, he peered at his notepad, then at her face. "Do you always wear those glasses?"

"I…" At a loss for a truthful answer, Cassidy settled for a nod.

"Hmm." Flipping to a new page on his notepad, he glanced between his customer and the half-made gown. "Have you any Wrangler insignia that you would like featured on the gown?"

Cassidy laughed. Then, sobering quickly under his surprised gaze, she shook her head.

"I always wanted to be a doctor."

"Hmm." He waved at the stool. "Sit, sit. This may take a moment." Weddings were one Wood Fairy social event where tradition called for simplicity in attire, even in mid-winter, when everyone wore loud colors and various accessories to combat the dull brown tunnel walls they saw all day and all night. It was a refreshing change after two months! "Tell me, do you come from a large family?"

Cassidy cocked an eyebrow at him, but he never looked up from where he was sketching something on his notepad.

"I am an only child."

"Hmm. Just you and your parents, then?" He tried to keep his surprise at her answer to himself.

Cassidy assessed the question, wondering what it had to do with dress design. That riddle remained unsolved when she responded.

"My mother died when I was quite young. I lived with my father and his mother after that."

"Hmm." Flipping to another page, Clyde tried again. There was something unusual about Cassidy, something he could not quite put his finger on. Something besides her obvious dislike for talking about herself. "When did you first know you wanted to become a doctor?"

Cassidy's eyes closed, the memory of her mother's untimely death as fresh as the day it occurred.

"I would rather not talk about it."

Clyde grumbled softly to himself. This was going terribly. If he could just find something she was passionate about, some window into her personality to help him envision her gown. Sadly, she seemed as antiseptic as her chosen profession.

"Perhaps," Fiona suggested from the doorway, "you would tell us about your father."

Cassidy hesitated yet again. Her father was a master of the sciences and a senior member of the ruling council of the Water Fairy Tribe, a position he had more or less inherited from his mother, Damaris Botere. None of which she could tell the tailor. Cassidy was earning a deep hatred for secrets. They were like a wedge, coming between her and those she wished to befriend.

"Is he as tall as you are?" Fiona prompted.

"Oh." Cassidy nodded. "Yes, just as tall as I am. But his hair is," she swallowed 'a darker pink' in favor of, "wavy, not curly."

Fiona, understanding both sides of the situation before her, was racking her brain as well.

Cassidy, tired of being on the receiving end of the questions, asked, "May I see your notepad, please?" When he reluctantly handed it over, she paged through the crossed-out sketches. "Your pencil, please?"

Cassidy felt a bit reckless as she swiftly sketched the basic lines of one of the more popular Water Fairy dress styles. At last she had thought of something about her tribe that she could share with abandon—providing she claimed ownership of it. As she adjusted the style here and there so that it was more in harmony with current Wood Fairy styles, she smiled. There was nothing quite like it above or beneath the surface so far as she knew.

Fiona watched, amazed at how swiftly and surely Cassidy moved the pencil around the page. This was an unexpected development.

"Here." Cassidy returned it to Clyde. "Can you remodel this dress to look like that?"

Clyde stared at the sketch, his eyebrows raising gradually.

"I will be glad to try," he agreed at last. There was a new respect, and perhaps just a little awe, in his manner as he bowed his way out of the room, intent on finding his head apprentice.

Cassidy shrugged slightly at Fiona's questioning expression.

"My aunt is an artist."

"I see." Fiona cocked her head to one side. "Would you join me for lunch?"

Cassidy rose. "Thank you, no." Her stomach was in knots of various shapes and sizes after the morning's events. "I am not hungry."

Fiona took her by the arm. "Then fly with me."

They waved at the others, who were busily engaged in teasing each other in feminine Wrangler fashion, then slipped out the exit together.

"Thank goodness we have another two weeks before the ceremony," Fiona laughed for effect as they passed a group of other ladies who were out touring the shops. She appreciated it when Cassidy joined in with a chuckle. Behaving as though everything was fine was not something that came easily to Fiona during her early years as Wood Fairy Queen. And while Cassidy answered to either Lady or Doctor Cassidy Clark, Fiona had come to the conclusion that Cassidy's role in the Water Fairy Tribe was considerably more than just toting an ancestor's title around.

Fiona continued to smile and wave to her subjects as she led Cassidy through a back way to her private drawing room. It was quite similar to the larger, official sitting room that she shared with her husband, but its function was distinct and different.

"Please."  Fiona indicated one of the three overstuffed chairs that surrounded a knee-high table.  "Would you care for a beverage?"

"No, thank you."  Cassidy shook her head as she lowered herself into the chair.

Fiona dismissed her maid with a smile, then seated herself near Cassidy.  Here they could sit undisturbed for quite some time, in silence or in earnest conversation.  Long enough, Fiona hoped, for Cassidy to explain what she meant when she said earlier that because she loved Isaac back, no one could help her.

"You have a lovely room," Cassidy ventured. It was the same room where she was introduced to Isaac.  Even at their first meeting, she felt an attraction to him that was unlike anything she had ever before experienced.  Which made perfect sense, considering that she'd devoted so much of her time and energy to her studies.

"Thank you."  Fiona smiled.  "This is the first room that I ever decorated."  Leaning back in her chair, Fiona allowed herself to reminisce.  "After Walter and I were married, we were given these rooms to live in.  His mother suggested that I would want to redecorate them, sort of put my own touch on them.  Then Walter brought it up." She chuckled.  "I finally had to admit that I was afraid to because I had no idea how to decorate a room."

Cassidy laughed, too. "What made you change your mind?"

"Walter did. He brought me in here, sat me down on a horrid old chair with a weak leg and a stiff back, and told me that I could rearrange the room as many times as I liked. After all, the royal household had enough furnishings in storage to decorate a dozen rooms. So, instead of worrying about somehow getting it wrong, he urged me to take my time and get it just right." Fiona leaned over as if to confide something. "The hardest part after that was getting to the point that I knew what I wanted."

Cassidy smiled weakly. "Your Majesty…"

"Call me Fiona. Please."

Cassidy swallowed. "If you are asking me if I know what I want, Fiona, I do. I want two things: to follow my heart, which is turning ever more insistently towards Isaac; and to protect my tribe, which I can do best by keeping to myself and returning home in the spring." Summoning her courage, she looked at Fiona steadily. "I cannot have both."

Fiona considered carefully before asking, "Is there no way that you could come back after making your report?"

"And do what?" Cassidy kept her tone neutral. "Every time that I reach for my glasses, I am reminded that I am living a lie." She reached up with some irritation to lift said glasses back into a comfortable position on her nose. "Every time I have to stop and reevaluate what I was about to say, even to Isaac, I am further convinced that I could never be happily married to a man from whom I had to keep secrets."

Fiona nodded slowly. "I am more grateful for your honorable nature than you may ever know." She refrained from broaching the subject of the Water Fairy Tribe rejoining the rest of Fairydom because she already knew that Cassidy was visiting without the knowledge or approval of her tribal council. Thus, it would only distress them both to discuss a change they could not personally effect.

They lapsed into silence then, both of them needing time to think. Cassidy heard it first—a faint *drip,drop*. Thinking that she was imagining things, she flicked a glance at Fiona. They continued, not speaking, for several more seconds before Fiona closed her eyes in exasperation.

"It happens every winter. There is a sink behind that partition," Fiona gestured in the general direction, "and the mechanism leaks every winter."

Cassidy raised her hand slightly from where it was resting on the smooth chair arm.

"Please do not apologize. I think it has given me an idea."

# Chapter 7

Sir Stuart wiped an arm's length of sweat from his forehead as he watched Isaac take his turn. The blacksmith's storeroom had been a riot of carefully labeled barrels, boxes, crates, and kegs when they arrived two hours ago. Since he and Isaac had to move everything at least once anyway to complete the inventory, they had agreed to organize it as well. After all, why should this winter be any different?

Stuart fanned his face with the inventory sheets. The manual labor was bad enough; it was the heat roiling off the forge in the next chamber that was going to be the death of them both.

"Thirty." Isaac grunted the final count as he heaved one last keg of nails into place atop a tidy stack. He leaned on the stack a moment, relaxing his back muscles and gritting his teeth against a twinge. He flattered himself that he'd hidden his weakness from Stuart, who'd allowed him to do his fair share of the work.

"You know," he said to Stuart, wiping his own forehead, "I think Sven does this on purpose." He felt no more sense of pride as he surveyed the tidy rows and stacks than he imagined an ant did after hauling mine carts up a long shaft in the Sky Fairy mountains. It was just something that had to be done. Again.

"Of course he does." Stuart nodded Isaac

towards the nearly-empty skin of doctor's water. "He makes the nails and round shot and grape shot and bar shot and everything else and just tosses the containers anywhere he pleases in this old storeroom."

"Leaving us," Isaac stopped guzzling water long enough to add, "to put everything in proper order during the inventory."

"Next year," Stuart made a final mark on the top inventory sheet, "I am assigning this job to every Wrangler who claims to be bored."

"Uh-uh." Isaac stretched his arms upwards, then bent to touch his toes. His back popped gratefully. "Remember? I tried that once."

"Oh yeah." Stuart followed Isaac out into the smithy. "How could I have forgotten the six months of revenge we endured after it was over?"

"We?" Isaac was incredulous. "Who was it that got spider leg hair in his stew unless he was the one cooking supper?"

"We both did," Stuart laughed. "But I was the one who always got the helmet full of mud."

"Well, that was your own fault," Isaac informed him.

"What?!"

"You should *never* put on an upside-down helmet without checking inside it first."

"Oi! Either of you lads seen the prince?" Sven growled good-naturedly at the sweat-soaked duo emerging from his storeroom. "This page says his mum is lookin' for him." The long rod of pure silver that he took down from the wall looked like a walking cane in his massive hands.

Isaac chuckled along with the others as he made his way over to the sink. After splashing some water on his face and hair, he felt a little more like himself. His white shirt and dress slacks were past help, unfortunately.

"You have a message for me?" Isaac asked the page, reaching for the cleaner-looking of two towels. It was stiff as a board from drying in the blast of heat from the furnace, so he patted his face dry instead of scrubbing it.

"The queen bids you to come to her private drawing room right away," the lass announced.

"That sounds important," Stuart announced when he came up from his own rinsing.

"Do tell." Isaac draped the damp end of the used towel over Stuart's dripping wet head. "Here." He handed the completed inventory to the lass. "Deliver this to the Minister of Finance, please, and inform the Minister of Intertribal Trade that you have done so."

"At once." The lass took off as fast as her young legs could carry her.

"That was an awfully big assignment for someone whose wings have not even grown to size yet," Stuart observed as he hung the now thoroughly-dirty towel back where Isaac found it.

"Nonsense." Isaac slung his jacket over his shoulder. "She just has to ask an ambitious older page where to find the Minister of Intertribal

Trade and half of the job will be done for her." He waved at Sven. "See you in two months!"

"Try to stow things in order between now and then, would you, please?" Stuart could not resist adding.

"Where do you think you are going?" Isaac asked, finding Stuart at his elbow.

"To eat lunch with my fiancée," Stuart informed him haughtily.

"What, smelling the way you do?" Isaac made a face at Stuart to cover the pang that struck him in his emotional breadbasket. He already cared for Stuart like a brother, but it sometimes stretched Isaac's good nature to the limit to be around so much happiness when he was so unhappily in love.

"I smell better than you do," Stuart asserted with a grin.

"You both smell equally bad," a voice informed them from behind.

"Yes, Your Majesty." Isaac grinned at his father.

"I take it the inventory went well?" King Walter grinned back, moving to fly along with them. Just ahead of them, actually, but he hoped they wouldn't take offense.

"As well as usual," Isaac shrugged.

"Sven is a few weeks ahead of himself this year," Stuart reported.

"Which means the mess was worse than usual, I suppose."

"Much worse!"  Isaac and Stuart agreed at the same time.

They all threw back their heads and laughed at that.  Good king that he was, Walter was pleased to note that most of his subjects who were nearby began to smile as well, even though there was no possible way for them to know what the joke was.

"What have you got there, Dad?"  Isaac asked, pointing at the scrolls under his father's arm.

"Your mother sent a page to fetch me—and the blueprints of the water pump system."

Isaac blinked, temporarily speechless.

"Intriguing, is it not?"  King Walter remarked. "I cannot wait to find out what she wants with them."

Isaac managed a nod.

"I would love to go along and see for myself," Stuart was only half-joking, "but I promised to have lunch with Gallica."  Recognizing the beginning signs of a friendly warning forming on King Walter's face, he quickly added, "After I get myself cleaned up, of course."

"Smart man," Walter chuckled as Stuart disappeared down a connecting tunnel.

"Good thing Mom loves me anyway," Isaac muttered as they hurried along.

Walter glanced at his son, remembering their recent conversations about love and courtship, then focused on the tunnel ahead of them.  To date, he had left the matter to Isaac and Cassidy's good sense. Why, even a father could only intrude so far in someone's life before they were warned off, and Walter was saving that for something critical. However, if things kept on as they had been, Walter just might have to take his chances.

"After you." Walter half-bowed to Isaac as they approached the door of Fiona's drawing room.

"Oh, no." Isaac was beginning to doubt the wisdom of not stopping to, um, freshen up first. "After you."

"If you insist." Walter was barely through the door when he stopped so abruptly that he blocked Isaac's entrance with his back.

"Dad, what…?" Isaac's voice trailed off as he found himself looking over his father's shoulder and into Cassidy's wide eyes. "Oh."

"Fly for it," Walter whispered. "I will cover your escape." But the door was already closing behind them.

"Too late." Isaac groaned.

"Stop right there, young man." Fiona flew over to a hidden cupboard and whipped out an old tablecloth that she kept around especially for situations like this. "Cassidy, catch the end, will you?"

"I am not that dirty!" Isaac protested in growing embarrassment as his mother guided Cassidy through the simple process of draping the tablecloth over his favorite chair so that he would be able to sit in it without damaging the upholstery.

"You never know," Fiona informed him pragmatically. "And let me tell you this much: it is nearly impossible to get blacksmith soot out of this upholstery." She chuckled. "In fact, if your valet, Noland, gets all of those soot stains out of your clothes, he can sell his secret and retire a rich fairy!"

"This is very sensible," Cassidy hurried to say as she smoothed her side of the tablecloth. She wilted a little when Isaac frowned at her. She had only been trying to help.

"Very." Walter kissed his wife lightly on the cheek. "Now, if we are done playing dress-up with the furniture," he raised the scrolls he was holding, "I was given to understand that these are important?"

"Extremely." Fiona took him over to her desk so he could set them down, an action that just happened to leave them both with their backs to Isaac and Cassidy.

"Sorry," Isaac mouthed at Cassidy. On the inside, he was fighting his frown to a standstill; a sheepish smile took its place on his face.

Hiding her dismay at the state of Isaac's white shirt, Cassidy fluttered over to him and smoothed his wayward hair.

"Are you alright?" she murmured, her concern over his skinned knuckles and a half a dozen bruises forming on his bare forearms far exceeding standard medical procedure.

"Never better." Isaac glanced down at the hand she had unconsciously taken hold of and raised hers to his lips. She paled a little, but stayed where she was.

"Ah, here we are." Fiona's voice sang out in triumph. "The original plans for the well pump."

"Actually, I only brought those along because I was not sure why you wanted the rest of these." Walter handed that scroll to Isaac, who had appeared at his elbow. "If you need the actual working plans for what we are using now," he unrolled a different scroll with a flourish, "this is the best place to start."

"Excellent." Cassidy leaned over the scroll, all business. Her command of the common surface tongue did not include plumbing terms—besides which, the bulk of the writing on the scroll was in what she supposed was the Wood Fairy language—but she understood the sketches pretty well. "Here." She put her finger on a blue line towards the bottom of the sketch. "This is water?"

"Yes." Walter nodded. "The pipe," he tapped on two black, parallel lines that ran perpendicular to the water, "runs down through the tree and into the water."

"The water is pumped up through the pipes and into the reservoir," Isaac pointed at a circle situated at the top of the pipe. He had no idea why Cassidy was interested in this.  "From there…"  He stopped when Cassidy waved the information away.

"If someone wanted to get down to the water line," Cassidy looked up from the sketch. "How would they go about it?"

Isaac and Walter exchanged glances.

"There is a service shaft," Walter admitted eventually.

"It is a very *long* service shaft," Isaac added quickly.

"Long enough to reach down to the water line?" Cassidy probed hopefully.

"Yes."  Walter nodded.  "Not easily, but…yes."

Cassidy thoughtfully pinched her lower lip between two fingers.

Isaac, alarmed at the idea that had just exploded into his mind, opened his mouth to deny it.  Cassidy might be homesick, but he flatly refused to let her try to swim there!

"Why do you ask?"  Walter had gone from curious to concerned.  As much as he would have liked to welcome Cassidy into his family, her line of questioning could be taken as hostile.  Unlikely though it was that the Water Fairy Tribe would stoop to an invasion when they could simply wipe out the surface tribes by denying them clean water, he dared not close his mind to a potential threat.

Cassidy emerged from her thoughts to study King Walter's face.  His stony expression reminded her of a night not too long ago in his offices. To keep his trust, she had destroyed a useless relic of an ill-advised Water Fairy lightning experiment. And she understood why he still had to be suspicious. It was one of the many curses of leadership, a master that never took a day off or let down its guard.

"I have some small hope of contacting my tribal leaders," Cassidy answered succinctly.

"Through our water pumps." Walter finally managed to say.

"Through your water system, yes." Cassidy corrected with a smile. "If we could stop the pumps temporarily, and if I can reach your water source through the service shaft," she leaned back over the scroll to point at the approximate spot, "then I believe I can get a message to my tribe."

Walter frowned. "Is this message so urgent?"

Cassidy wished her hands were hidden under the table instead of resting on top of it; she could have twisted her fingers nervously then. The information she had gathered about the situation on the surface was important to their long-term health.

"It is important," she answered at last. Especially to her, since she was planning to request permission to begin establishing official diplomatic relations with the Wood Fairy royal family.

"How would you send this message?" Isaac only just managed not to ask if she was planning to swim the message over herself.

Cassidy bit her lip—this was where things got tricky.

"I have a machine," she chose her words with care, trying to reveal as little of Water Fairy secrets as possible. "And they have a machine. Once my machine is in the water, it should be able to, sort of, talk to their machine." It was the best explanation she could give, though it had to be puzzling to a culture in which machines were hand-operated.

"I…" Walter looked at Fiona, then at Isaac. They looked as confused as he felt. In Weetu, machines made manual labor easier, but that was about it. "Will your machine damage the pumps or the pipes?"

"No, not at all." Cassidy shook her head vehemently. The machine would send the message out through sound waves in the water, much in the same way that the animals of her underwater world communicated, and the pipes would never know the difference.

"And can you guarantee that no harm will come to the populace of Weetu as a result of this experiment?" Walter was inclined to allow Cassidy to try it, but he had to know the answer to that first.

"I cannot command my tribal leaders," Cassidy answered honestly. "I can only offer to let you read the message before I send it." She was reluctant to offer that because there was always the chance that the Water Fairy council would reject the idea of rejoining the rest of Fairydom. However, it seemed she had no choice.

"How long would it take you to send this message?" Fiona's voice broke the silence.

"That is difficult to predict," Cassidy admitted. "The…machines are always monitored. Yet, they are not expecting a message from me, so I would have to wait for them to respond to be sure it was received."

"And their reply?" Isaac raised his eyebrows. "I assume you'll want to know what they think of your unexpected message."

Cassidy certainly did!

"I suppose you could make that part of your message to them," Isaac suggested. "I mean, you could include a time when you will return to listen for their response."

Cassidy nodded thoughtfully. She couldn't predict how long it would take the council to gather and discuss her message. "I could ask them to let us know when to expect an official reply. That would be simplest, I am sure."

Walter, Fiona, and Isaac looked at each other.

"The reservoir holds enough water for a full day," Isaac began.

"For an average day," Walter corrected mildly. Sighing, he made a decision. "I will consider it. We haven't had a water shortage in Weetu in decades." He frowned, musing over what he'd just said.

"Thank you, Your Majesty." Cassidy immediately resumed mentally composing the message.

"In the meantime," Walter felt quite brilliant, "I will hint to my staff that we need to reevaluate our emergency procedures. That will give them time to inadvertently spread the idea amongst the civilians of Weetu, who will in turn draw much more water than they actually need and enthusiastically support a very realistic emergency drill featuring the scenario of frozen or broken water pipes." His eyes twinkling, Walter kissed Fiona on the cheek and left to get the ball rolling.

"And I will return these scrolls to the archives." Isaac used his jacket as a makeshift tote, placing the rolled up scrolls inside it, then tying the arms of the jacket firmly around them.

"Forgive me." Cassidy curtsied to Fiona. "I should begin composing the message."

"There, you see, Mother?" Isaac grinned. "I told you there was no need for that," he nodded at the unmarred sheet covering his favorite chair.

Fiona just laughed and began gathering it so she could refold it.

"No, I can do it," Fiona reassured Cassidy when the lass started forward as if to help. "Hurry along and get that message ready."

Isaac caught Cassidy lightly by the elbow and guided her to the door, which he opened for her. They could not discuss this matter in public, but at least he could walk with her for a while.

"Speaking as your doctor," Cassidy began, "may I ask what happened to you?  You look even worse than you did after your bout with McGrath."  She clicked her tongue softly against the roof of her mouth.  "If you are not careful, you will be too badly banged up to have your wing surgery in the morning."  Now that she had completed all of the spinal surgeries that had even the faintest glimmer of success, it was time to focus on the numerous torn and broken wings.

"What, these little bruises?" Isaac clarified, lifting one arm for inspection.  After seeing Bert attached to a wingboard, Isaac was even more relieved that Cassidy allowed him to put off his own surgery until after the formal dinner that evening.  "They're only skin deep and will probably be gone by morning."  He shrugged and took her by the elbow again.  "Anyway, bruises are a natural consequence of inventorying Sven's storeroom."

"Sven?" Cassidy gaped at him.  "Sugar's father is the blacksmith you were going to see?"  In her excitement, she had forgotten about the inventory.

"Sven is the best blacksmith in Weetu.  His apprentices do most of the ordinary work, like our winter order of nails, buckles, and whatnots, but he does the fancier orders himself—anything with moveable parts, even metal limbs.  If you can dream it up, he can make it."  Noticing the thoughtful frown on Cassidy's face, Isaac asked, "Why, do you need a blacksmith?"

Cassidy frowned thoughtfully. "As a matter of fact, I do. In order for this…project to succeed," she smiled at a passing couple, "I will require several lengths of silver wire." The ultrasonic communications device she was going to use to contact her tribe was meant to be held in one hand and operated with the other, which would be impossible in the proposed situation. Even if the pipes were large enough to allow her to descend as far as the pump mechanism, getting the device itself in open water would be ideal. The less interference there was when they sent the message, the better the chances were that the message would reach as far as one of the dozens of receiving stations strategically positioned on the sea's floor. Hence, the silver wire, by which she hoped to lower the device past the pumps.

"Oh." Isaac was faintly disappointed on Sven's behalf, having expected her to ask for something a little more unusual. "That will be no challenge at all for Sven."

Chapter 8

When they reached a connecting tunnel, Cassidy bid Isaac goodbye and flew as quickly as she could to the rooms Rosie had assigned her and her nurses.

"Agnes?" she called out. "Daphne?"

"I am in here," Agnes called back from another room. "Daphne is probably at the library."

Cassidy was laughing as she followed the sound of Agnes' voice, but when she saw what Agnes was doing, she stopped short.

"Where did you find that?" Cassidy asked, meaning the stained dress that Agnes was washing in the sink. She had left it on the floor of her bedroom, where the bed would shield it from sight.

"Right where you left it, I imagine." Agnes spoke in Margua, their tribal language. Her soft tone took any sting out of her practical answer. "I let it soak for a while," she swished it around in the oversized sink, "and I think I was able to get it cleaned up alright." Removing the plug that held the soapy water in the sink, Agnes lifted the garment to wring it out.

"Let me," Cassidy offered, also in Margua, as she reached to unfasten her cuffs. She rolled up her sleeves as Agnes stepped aside. "You did not have to do this."

"That is true," Agnes conceded, taking a seat. "I could have just added it to the laundry."

Cassidy ducked her head, wondering why she had not done that herself. Nobody would have known how or why the dress got so dusty and dirty. It was likely that no one would have even asked. But no; she'd felt like she had to try to hide it. Moving over to the sink, which was empty now except for the dress and the little rivulets of water coming from it, she picked up the dress and began twisting the rest of the water out of it with a vengeance.

"If I had known you were planning on wringing its neck," Agnes observed dryly, "I would not have troubled myself with it."

Cassidy relaxed her straining shoulders and laughed. It really was good to have Agnes to talk to. Resuming her work with considerably less force, she finally got enough water out to satisfy her. Turning the faucet on, she rinsed the fresh layer of soap scum off the sides of the sink and replaced the plug.

"I suppose you knew all along that I cried last night."

"Yes."

"I suppose that is why you offered me some of your medicinal infusion this morning at breakfast." She tried to laugh, but choked on it. Unrolling the dress, she shook it out a bit, then released it to slowly descend to the bottom of the rapidly filling sink.

"Yes." Agnes usually sipped her infusion at night, when she was sore after a long day's work, and rather thought Cassidy should have made the connection sooner.

Cassidy turned the faucet off. Reaching into the lukewarm water, she began sloshing the dress about, taking care not to splash herself or the counters.

"If you want to talk about it," Agnes ventured, "we have a few minutes."

"What else is there to say?" Cassidy asked, pushing and pulling the dress from one side of the sink to the other so the clean water could reach all of the material.

Agnes disciplined a sigh. "You must feel very strongly about him if he is worth a post-weeping headache."

"It was much more than that." Cassidy raised the top half of the dress out of the water, returned it, then repeated the procedure with the bottom half. "Disappointment, frustration... I never knew love could be something terrible."

Agnes smiled warmly at Cassidy's back. After her millennia of married life, Agnes understood how very naïve Cassidy was.

"Love is many things, including terrible." Rising, Agnes retrieved a large, thick towel and carried it over to Cassidy for her to wrap the dress up in once she was ready. While Agnes was standing at Cassidy's elbow, she spoke her final words on the subject; unless, of course, Cassidy brought it back up at some point. "There is a very wise, very old Wood Fairy saying," Agnes told her. "Love, like a tree, must learn which winds to bend with and which to stand tall against." She touched Cassidy reassuringly on the arm, then returned to her seat at the table.

Cassidy closed her eyes, weary of the whole matter. Casting her mind back over the time she had spent with Isaac, she was intrigued to realize how powerful an effect her decision not to allow him to court her had on their relationship. Instead of flirting, they engaged in sincere conversation. One-sided, but that couldn't be helped given her situation. Over the course of the last two months she had seen him in action, both physically and intellectually. She knew he was possessed of a temper as well as a keen sense of humor, and respected him for the self-restraint she had seen him exhibit. She blushed as she also thought about how immensely she enjoyed it when his restraint slipped and he kissed her.

"He wants me to stay."

"Oh, my." Agnes frowned. This was more serious than she thought. "Stay on the surface?"

Cassidy turned towards Agnes quickly, before she could get started comparing Weetu with the underwater paradise they called home.

"Why not?" Forgetting her hands were wet, Cassidy gripped the back of the nearest chair in her excitement. "I could spend a lifetime healing and teaching at Weetu. And learning. Their potions have absolutely fantastic medicinal properties, which I could probably improve, given enough time and the right resources..." Her voice trailed off as her thoughts focused on those last three words. *The right resources.* If she stayed, she would not have the resources to which she was accustomed. And what would she do when she ran out of things like starfish sheets?

Slowly, Cassidy drew the chair out from the table and seated herself.

"It is a lot to think about," Agnes offered kindly. She could tell from the sad look in Cassidy's eyes that the young woman was already beginning to grasp what she would have to sacrifice should she choose to remain. Agnes simply wanted Cassidy to be happy, which was why she dared start the conversation. An informed decision could be lived with, at least.

The door to the hallway opened and closed, warning them that someone else, probably Daphne, had arrived. Agnes, willing to leave Cassidy to her thoughts, stood and fluttered over to the sink. Giving the dress a final swish, she removed the plug one last time.

"Daphne." Cassidy looked up when the younger nurse entered the room. "Please put your things away and come join us."

Daphne, disturbed by Cassidy's somber expression—not to mention the fact that she was speaking in Margua!—made haste to obey. And so it happened that she spent a few minutes on the edge of her seat at the table before Agnes finished hanging the dress over the sink to dry. Once they were all seated, Cassidy took a deep breath.

"I think we may be able to send a message home." She let the others absorb that for a moment.

"You are not seriously thinking of using my traveling transmitter-receiver?" Agnes sputtered.

"I certainly am," Cassidy rejoined calmly. "It's a good thing that you brought it along."

"I did not *bring* it," Agnes protested. "I simply failed to remove it from the luggage it came with!" She wished that she had not told Cassidy about finding it amidst her things; better yet, she wished she had left it home. Whatever plan Cassidy had in mind for using an underwater communications device from *inside a tree* had to be dangerous!

"Will it work?" Daphne asked eagerly. The Wood Fairy library had whetted her sense of adventure, making her more susceptible than usual to believing in what was logically impossible.

"It will be complicated. It might even fail. However," Cassidy straightened a little, "I have discussed it with King Walter, and he has agreed to help us."

"How?" Agnes asked skeptically.

"By granting us access to the water pipes. They descend from the reservoir above us through the tree to the water beneath us." Cassidy absent-mindedly began drawing the pertinent parts of the plumbing diagram from the scrolls on the table, her damp fingers leaving traces as they moved across the polished surface. "We can go most of the way down through a service shaft. After that, we lower the transmitter piece by a silver wire and use a lightning reservoir to send a coded message."

Agnes shook her head, still not believing what she was hearing.

"There will be interference from the pipes," she objected. "Also from the roots, rocks, and whatever else is down there!"

"I am aware of all that," Cassidy replied. "I would at least like to try."

"Are you asking us or telling us?" Agnes asked, her eyes narrowing slightly. Having wielded authority herself, Agnes was acutely aware of the distinct difference between the two approaches.

"Mostly telling," Cassidy admitted with a faint smile. "We were sent here to heal and to test the truth of the stories carried to us by pirates. I will report on that as succinctly as possible. And then I will petition for authority to establish official diplomatic relations with the surface tribes."

Agnes' mouth sagged open in shock. Daphne simply stopped breathing.

"I will have to compose the petition very carefully. I am relying on you both to assist me with it." Finished, Cassidy leaned back in her chair and waited uneasily for an explosion.

"Tell me you are not suggesting this," Agnes inhaled slowly, "drastic measure of resuming diplomatic relations with the surface just so that you can stay here."

Cassidy and Agnes both ignored the way Daphne's eyebrows crept higher on her forehead.

"I give you my word." Cassidy looked Agnes squarely in the eyes. "I believe that we, as a tribe, stand to gain far more than we could ever lose by taking this step."

Daphne waited hopefully, but that was all either of them had to say on the matter.

"And now," Cassidy looked at the water clock, which was calmly splashing the seconds off as if it had not possibly witnessed history in the making. "We should all begin getting ready for supper."

"Is the banquet tonight?" Daphne gasped and looked down at the plain dress she was wearing. Without bothering to wait for an answer, she leapt to her feet and flew into the room she shared with Agnes. "I have nothing to wear!" she wailed.

Agnes and Cassidy shared a small smile at Daphne's exaggeration.

"I am sure that we would be welcome even if we went in our surgical gowns," Agnes offered from her seat at the table.

Cassidy looked around as a knock sounded at the outer door.

"I will get it," she volunteered, waving Agnes back into her chair. "It might be about the message." Much to her surprise, it was Gallica at the door.

"Hi!" Gallica was grinning from ear to ear. "Mind if I come in?"

Puzzled, Cassidy opened the door even wider.

"Thanks!" Turning her back to Cassidy, Gallica caught hold of something and pulled it inside the antechamber.

"What in Fairydom is all of this?" Cassidy asked, staring in astonishment at the clothes' rack Gallica was apparently travelling with. A few dozen formal outfits, of varying styles and sizes, rocked slightly from the momentum.

"Ladies. Your wardrobe for the evening." Gallica announced grandly.

Daphne entered the room just then and let out a squeal of delight.

"For us?" she asked.

"Yes!" Gallica confirmed brightly. She scuffed the toe of her boot on the smooth floor of the antechamber and looked sideways at Cassidy. "I meant to make this offer to you a few days ago, but I have been so busy lately that I completely forgot. Sorry about that."

Cassidy smiled and nodded, accepting the apology. She also nodded at Daphne, who was eyeing the rack impatiently. Daphne was considerably shorter than Cassidy and a bit narrower about the waist than Agnes, so they couldn't wear the same outfits anyway.

"I think," Gallica plucked an outfit from the rack and offered it to Cassidy, "that you should wear this one."

Cassidy touched the filmy, shimmery silver-green dress softly. Holding the dress up to her shoulders, Cassidy pressed her free hand to her abdomen, keeping the dress from falling lower while she leaned forward to check its length. The sleeves tickled her arms as she straightened.

"It is lovely," she smiled at Gallica. "Thank you."

"What is it made of?" Agnes asked, coming over to admire it.

"It is made from the fibers of the lamb's ear plant," Gallica told them. "They have the softest leaves and the fibers hold their natural color well."

"Agnes, you would look wonderful in this," Daphne bubbled from where she stood by the clothes' rack.

Agnes was pleasantly surprised as she considered the simply cut gown Daphne had found. It appealed to her especially because it was feminine, but not flirty. As a happily married woman, she was not interested in dressing to catch someone's eye.

"What a delicate shade of lavender," she sighed, taking it from Daphne's outstretched hand.    A brief examination proved that it should fit her comfortably.    A wave of homesickness washed over her as she wished her husband, Duncan, was there to see her wear it. To talk with. To just *be* with. Agnes cleared her throat and forced her attention to the clothes' rack.    "But what will you wear?" she asked Daphne.

"Well," Daphne hesitated.    "I thought I might wear this one."  She ran her hand down the impudently yellow skirt of a dress that looked about her size.

Cassidy looked discreetly in Gallica's direction.   Bold colors were the norm during winter in Weetu, but she certainly did not want Daphne accidentally attracting the wrong attention.

"Oh yes," Gallica nodded vigorously.    "I thought you might pick that one!"

Satisfied, Cassidy cleared her throat.

"We had better try these on," she suggested.

"They should fit pretty well," Gallica assured them confidently.   "We got your measurements from your laundry."

Cassidy laughed first and the others joined in.

When Gallica managed to stop laughing, she reached for the door knob.   "I better go finish getting ready. You know where to meet us?"

Cassidy nodded.    "Your mother said we should be at her private drawing room at half past seven."

"Perfect," Gallica nodded. Waving goodbye, she let herself out. It was late for her personal eating schedule, and probably for Cassidy and her nurses, as well. Conversely, it would be early for many of the other guests who kept different schedules in the never-ending day-night of winter in Weetu.

"That was very thoughtful of them," Agnes murmured, subconsciously attributing some of the credit to Queen Fiona.

"Very," Cassidy agreed. Now that Gallica was gone, Cassidy had a chance to evaluate the abrupt appearance of the clothing from a cultural standpoint. Tonight was obviously going to be more elegant than she originally anticipated. In fact, that was probably the very reason Gallica and Stuart had taken such care while they ate together the last week or so, going over formal Wood Fairy table etiquette, utensils, and so forth.

Finding that Agnes and Daphne had drifted off to their rooms to get ready, Cassidy hurried to do the same. By the time she had showered, pinned her hair back a bit so she would be able to eat hair-free food, and added a little face powder to take the shine off her pale skin, her stomach felt like a swarm of lightning eels had taken up residence. She was not sure if it was her talk with Agnes or the kisses Isaac had stolen earlier that were making her so nervous. Or perhaps it was the way she had kissed him back.

Acting on an impulse, she went to her top drawer and took out a long, slender box. Reseating herself at her dressing table, she opened the box to reveal a choker made of perfectly matched pearls, resting on a red satin inlay. Taking hold of the clasp pieces on either end of the string, she lifted the choker to her throat and considered. The usually lustrous pearls were dim and dry from spending too much time away from their moist, underwater home. Fastening the choker in place, Cassidy paused, one hand on her throat, to study her brown-haired reflection. It was like seeing a stranger wearing her mother's choker.

"Cassidy?" Agnes' voice carried through the closed door to Cassidy's bedroom. "We are going to be late."

Cassidy was trembling slightly when she reached for the doorknob and turned it. The shocked expressions on Agnes' and Daphne's faces as she stepped into view were bad enough. The curtsies that followed only made her feel more isolated. Was the comfort of wearing her mother's jewelry really worth the side effects of drawing attention to the fact of her rank?

"Lady Cassidy," Agnes murmured respectfully as she rose. "We await your pleasure."

"Thank you for calling me," Cassidy responded as graciously as she could. "I should hate to keep our hosts waiting." Gathering her skirts, she led the way through the outer door.

Stretching their wings, they glided silently through the halls, something Cassidy admitted she would miss being able to do when she returned home. Guards straightened as they passed by, while a few of the less-inhibited civilians gawked openly. The clock was just striking half past when they rounded the corner and saw the royal party waiting for them by Queen Fiona's private drawing room.

Cassidy folded her wings, allowing herself to settle softly to the floor close to the royal party. Her choker, woken from its slumber by the warmth of her skin, had begun to give off a soft, white glow.

Agnes and Daphne flanked her, curtsying deeply. For her part, Cassidy merely inclined her head to King Walter and Queen Fiona.

# Chapter 9

The next morning, Isaac strode into the surgery with a smile on his face and his mother on his arm. Last night had been more or less a success. More in the eyes of the regular guests, the ambassadors and nobles, he thought, and less in Cassidy's opinion. He felt his smile dim a little when she entered the room, her head bowed over what he supposed was his medical file.

"Take a seat on the table, please," she instructed without looking up.

Isaac's level of concern continued to rise as she turned the procedure itself over to Agnes and Daphne in favor of answering his mother's questions. They did an excellent job, of course. The only pain he felt was due to the fact that Cassidy continued to avoid eye contact with him.

"The process of harvesting and preparing the sheets is quite complicated," she told the queen, who'd asked. "However, due to their versatile nature and the overwhelming results, we've found it worth our while."

"Yes, of course," Fiona agreed, wishing silently that there was some way to get steady access to them for her tribe. She and Walter had discussed at length the long-term effects of allowing Cassidy to practice her medicine. It was such a risk. They could've glossed over Isaac's healing, shuffling Rosie to the forefront in any recounting, which would've made things much simpler. However, they'd chosen not to in order to allow Cassidy to treat as many as she had the resources for, primarily because they both felt compelled to offer the best they had so long as it was available.

Now, while Fiona would never regret the benefit received by those treated, she could also see much more clearly the harm done. Morale alone would sustain a crushing blow after Cassidy left. The next round of injuries—spring, summer, fall—would leave the wounded wistfully dreaming of treatment they could never receive. Not to mention the thousands of fairies from other tribes who needed this medicine. Fiona glanced at Cassidy, wishing there was some way to change the future.

"There," Daphne announced, meticulously salvaging the cuttings. "Now we just need to attach your harness and you'll be done."

Isaac couldn't help noticing that Cassidy took a half-step back, as if to put more distance between them. He'd supposed she'd be heading the procedure this time, or at least be as involved as she'd been last time. As he lifted his arms to allow Agnes to buckle him into the harness, he watched Cassidy, wishing he understood what was bothering her.

He thought back to the night before, wondering if something had happened during the banquet to upset her. She'd looked lovely in her lambs ear gown, as he'd expected. Her exotic jewelry had prompted a few compliments and a lot of whispers. Still, she'd seemed alright during the first few courses. She'd kept an eye on Daphne, but then, so had he. He'd been the one to suggest seating her next to the young lieutenant, and naturally felt some responsibility for seeing that she was being well taken care of.

The spiced cheese course had taken Cassidy by surprise. The dessert course—exquisite chocolate miniatures of the tree that was their home—delighted her, and the delicious strawberry sipping nectar seemed to relax her as they mingled with the other guests before saying goodnight. Yes, that was it. At some point between leaving the table and bidding him goodnight, she had seen or heard something that upset her. That was still upsetting her.

"We should like to send it as soon as possible," he heard Cassidy say, her voice drawing him back to the present.

"I understand," nodded Fiona, trying to ignore the anxious uptick in her heart rate as she accepted the sealed paper Cassidy held out. "I will see to it that Walter examines this at the earliest opportunity."

"You've very kind."

Fiona patted her hand and flew over to kiss Isaac on the cheek. "I must say," she favored everyone in the room with a swift smile, "this process is most astonishing."

Isaac grinned as well, nodded when she told him she had to give his father Cassidy's message. It was only as she left that he realized Daphne and Agnes were also missing, no doubt gone off to tend to the starfish sheet remnants. He cleared his throat to get Cassidy's attention.

"I thought we might continue our tour of Weetu today," he suggested even though she didn't look up from what she was doing.

"Sorry." She shook her head. "I need to stay available in case the king finds time to review the message with me." She shot him a tight smile. "Must be time for me to finally sit down and review the research that Agnes and Daphne have been doing."

An unpleasant prickle across the back of Isaac's neck warned him that something more was going on. It had served him well as an active duty Wrangler; even saved his life a time or two. In this case, however, he was at a loss as to what it might mean. Sliding off the table and onto his feet, he crossed the room to Cassidy in two long strides, ignoring the wingboard.

"Cassidy?" He waited, her soft perfume a pleasant contrast to the smell of antiseptics and the drying slime, but she refused to look at him. Gently, he slipped two fingers under her chin and forced her head up. "What's wrong?" The longer it took for her to answer, the farther his heart sank.

"It's complicated."  She'd resumed keeping her distance for a reason.  His scent, his touch, the fading hope in his eyes—they all distracted her from the facts.

Frustrated, he took a step towards her, and when she matched it with a step away from him, he proceeded to close the gap until he had her backed against the wall.  "I've wrangled wild ants," he informed her, lowering his head so he could look straight into her eyes.  "They couldn't get away from me, either."  He sighed at the obvious distress in her eyes and took a half step back to relieve some of the tension between them.  "Cassidy.  Darling.  Just tell me what's wrong."

She pulled away before he could touch her. She knew the gesture was meant to comfort her, but the last thing she needed was to become more muddled.  During the banquet some of the guests she'd met quietly lamented the loss of a merchant windship over the sea that fall.  They'd had relatives onboard, whom they naturally believed were dead.

She'd never been in favor of detaining the *advena,*the strangers from other tribes who stumbled into Water Fairy territory, yet she'd understood the need to keep their existence a secret.  Last night, face to face with the grief her tribe's paranoia had directly caused, she'd almost become violently ill on the spot.  Even now, staring into Isaac's worried brown eyes, most of the arguments she'd used to convince herself in the past seemed invalid. That wouldn't change the past or even the present; and at the last census, there had been over seven thousand *advena* on record. If a new treaty was negotiated, it would inevitably involve repatriating the *advena* and their descendants. It would involve telling Isaac the one secret he might never be able to forgive.

"We're what's wrong," she said, upset with herself at the way her voice quavered. "Even if," she began shaking her head, "if I could stay, you wouldn't want me to."

*He'll hate me*, her fears whimpered.

"What?" Isaac swept her into his arms, held her close. "I want you," he stated firmly, pressing his cheek to hers. "I want to watch you experience the surface, to see your face the first time you see a sunrise." He gently smoothed her hair. "I want you to smile when you see me. Or think of me. I want you to miss me the way that I miss you when we're not together. I want you to listen when I speak because you think I say things worth hearing. I want you to be mine and me yours. I want to ride with you in ferry chairs after we grow too old to fly, and to see our great great granddaughters smile like you do."

It wasn't until he felt a hot tear running down both their cheeks that he admitted to himself she was somehow keeping her distance, despite being wrapped in his arms.

Cassidy raised the hands that had been hanging at her sides and forced them between their bodies. Gathering her strength, she pushed away from him. From the future he had just offered her.

"I'm not sorry I came to Weetu." The thought of leaving tore through her like a dull knife, but she couldn't think of a way to add that without it sounding like encouragement. Gathering her skirts, she whisked away from him, the vision of the hurt look on his face chasing her through the halls back to her quarters.

Racing to her sink, she turned on the cold water, splashed her face with it until her head ached. It did nothing to dull the exquisite pain in her chest from breaking her own heart. Even the lump in her throat stayed firmly in place in spite of her best efforts to wash it down with the sweet, flavored beverage she found on the counter.

At last, at a loss for what to do, she seated herself at the desk where Agnes and Daphne had stacked the papers with their research findings. For several seconds, she just stared at the papers. She didn't mind the work. Some of her happiest hours were spent poring over research papers and peering through her microscope. It just seemed…futile this time. The odds were high that they'd never be able to use this information. Spring would come, the surface world would thaw, and they would slip back to their undersea home, never to return.

Her inner scientist reached for the top paper anyway. *It's never futile to learn.* Almost before she knew it, she was deep in the familiar rhythm of taking notes, absorbing information, and organizing the papers. Hours must've slipped by, judging by the cramp in her writing hand, before anyone disturbed her.

"A moment," she called in answer to the knock on the outer door, pausing to pop her protesting back before she finished rising from the desk. The ache in her neck was more familiar than comfortable, yet she felt she had no reason to complain. Any time thoughts of Isaac—and the *advena*—were kept at bay was time she was grateful for.

To her surprise, she found Gallica waiting for her on the other side of the door.

"My father would like to see you." Gallica announced. She waited hopefully while Cassidy hastily swiped at the ink on her fingers, but Cassidy's response was not informative in the least.

"Yes, of course." Once she felt presentable, Cassidy began hurrying to the king's office. Her anxiety levels continued rising during the flight, but her chest constricted further at the awful thought that her encounter with Isaac earlier just might impact the king's decision about whether or not to let them signal their tribe.

She gripped her hands behind her back while she waited for the servants to announce, then admit her.

"Sit down, Lady Cassidy." King Walter gestured at the chairs before his desk. He kept his hands on the arms of his own chair to hide his white knuckles. The magnitude of what her communiqué contained had almost prompted him to share it with his advisors before making a decision. His dread of losing access to Water Fairy medicine had grown almost into fear by now. Every time he heard someone talking about the astonishing new treatments, the hopeful future, he'd had to clench his stomach against its violent heaving.

"I take it you've read our proposed message." She indicated the sheet of paper on his otherwise empty desk.

"Four times." Watching her closely, he saw her pale from white to almost translucent. "You want to open diplomatic relations between your tribe and the rest of Fairydom."

"I do." Cassidy forced herself not to shrink under his stare. And not to answer the question he hadn't actually asked. She'd matched wits with the best of her tribe, successfully for the most part, so she knew that volunteering information could have disastrous results.

"You realize that this is not a decision the Wood Fairy Tribe can make for all of Fairydom," he pointed out delicately. He hated that he had to bring that up.

Another non-question. This point had

occurred to Cassidy as well, while discussing the wording of the message with Agnes and Daphne. If they'd arrived during the spring or summer or even fall, there would've been a good chance of getting specially assigned representatives of each tribe to Weetu, making the renegotiation of the treaty a challenging but doable task. As it was? She nodded slowly, hoping she was right in thinking that he had already thought of a way around the apparent obstacle. She resisted the urge to fidget while waiting for him to continue.

Walter found himself relaxing a little, impressed with her fortitude. Even full-fledged ambassadors had been known to crack under the strain of silence. He relaxed his grip on his chair arms, flexing his fingers a little, relieved to have that over with. His tribe stood to gain so much that he'd been sorely tempted to ignore that fact for fear of discouraging her.

"What exactly do you hope to accomplish by sending this message to your tribe?" This, he needed to know for himself. Whenever he thought he was getting a better deal than any sane fairy could expect to, it made him uneasy.

Ah. A question. They were making progress.

"I intend to report my findings and advise them that I believe the time for remaining apart has ended."

Walter tapped his fingers lightly on the padded arm of his chair, acutely aware that she had answered his question as stated. Without padding or bragging or making promises she couldn't keep.  He leaned forward, abandoning the idea that there was something to be gained by appearing aloof.

"I've seen enough in your short time here to agree that the surface tribes would benefit enormously from having the Water Fairy Tribe among us again.  Your medical resources alone…"  He cleared his throat of the emotion that choked him when he thought of the rapid recoveries his son and others had made since Cassidy's arrival.

Responding to his forthrightness, Cassidy ventured to assure him, "We would benefit as well.  My nurses and I have barely begun our research into your local medicinal resources.  The possibilities are staggering, particularly when combined with our advanced surgical techniques and unique decoction ingredients."

Walter took a moment to ponder her words. "Then you truly believe there is a chance the five tribes will be reunited?"

Cassidy felt an involuntary shiver down her spine at his words.  "If I did not," she answered breathlessly, "I would not suggest it."

King Walter's responding nod launched a sequence of events that set Weetu on its ear. While the rumors that there would be a water-shortage test had spread as planned, everyone Cassidy spoke with seemed stunned it was actually happening.  Their dismay heightened at the additional announcement that the pumps were already turned off, preventing them from drawing extra water to supplement their needs. A few still tried, only to be cautioned by the authorities that the entire city was relying on the reservoir. In a matter of hours, Cassidy, Agnes, and Daphne found themselves in the damp innards of the pumps.

"Here." Isaac held out his hand for the small satchel Cassidy was carrying. "If that's the machine, we're ready to place it in the water." He hated the fact that his wingboards would prevent him from doing the dangerous job himself, but at least they'd managed to persuade Cassidy that it was something best left to the maintenance crew.

Walking carefully to avoid slipping on the slick floor, Cassidy brought the satchel over and took her first look down the service shaft. The narrow shaft dropped away from the edge, going down and down and…

"Hey." Isaac caught her by the shoulder as she swayed forward. "Are you alright?"

With difficulty, she looked away from the shaft. "I feel sick," she murmured just loud enough for him to hear.

Alarmed, he pulled her away from the opening and closer to him. "Don't tell me you can't handle heights!"

"I…don't know." She rested her head against his shoulder, hoping the room would stop spinning. "I've never…" She swallowed and shook her head. "We don't have anything like that in Noddfa."

Isaac hastily looked around to make sure Adrian wasn't close enough to have heard her mention her hometown. Simultaneously he realized just how badly she must've been affected to make a mistake like that.

"Well, don't worry," he advised, slipping his arm about her waist to give her something to anchor her thoughts to. The memory of her bewildering comment from earlier helped him maintain a casual tone as he reassured her, "It happens." There was even a treatment for her dizziness, this just wasn't the time. "Here." Taking the satchel, he held it out to Adrian, the maintenance crew chief. "All the way down, Chief," he instructed. "Then you come straight back up." They'd agreed that a minimum of witnesses was best, even though Adrian had gravely sworn to keep confidential anything he saw or heard while volunteering to assist them.

"When you get to the water level," Cassidy didn't even open her eyes, "open the satchel and take out the machine. Bring the satchel back, but gently lower the machine into the water. Be careful of the silver wire." She finally looked at him. "Stay clear of the wire *and*the water. That's very important." The lightning reservoir wasn't even connected, but she gave the warning anyway.

Isaac nodded sternly at Adrian to reinforce her words.  He had no idea why it made a difference, but he could tell by her tone of voice that it was critical.  He forgot all about Adrian, however, when he felt Cassidy start to pull away from him.

"Not so fast," he admonished, tightening his grip.  "Are you sure you feel better?"

"Yes, I'm quite sure."  Cassidy had hard work not to smile at his obvious attempt to rationalize continuing to hold her.  Flattering as it was, she knew not to linger.  Gingerly, she made her way over to where Agnes was waiting by the portable lightning reservoir.  They would eventually connect it to the transducer that Adrian was carrying via the makeshift silver tether.

"I hope this works," Agnes confided as they watched the silver wire unspooling itself and disappearing into the shaft.

"As do I," Cassidy agreed, taking a seat beside her.  The unit itself wasn't overly complicated, so the small adjustments they'd made to fit the circumstances shouldn't affect its functionality.  Yet that was only one of a dozen things that certainly could go wrong.  They waited in a mutually uncomfortable silence until the spool of wire abruptly creaked to a halt.

"He's there," Isaac announced, his voice seeming to echo in the previously silent room.

Cassidy looked away from where he was leaning into the shaft, watching Adrian's progress.

"Ready!" Daphne announced from where she stood by the spool. At Cassidy's approving nod, she immediately began rotating the spool by hand.

They planned to leave the transducer down there for the full day, with one of the three of them monitoring the key at all times for a response. If there wasn't a response in that time frame, things got considerably more complicated. Retrieving the transducer before reactivating the pumps was a necessity. Even if the Wood Fairy equipment didn't damage it outright, the noise interference from the pumps would make it impossible to use the system for communication. Still, even the slightest chance of receiving the response she was so desperate for made it seem foolhardy to quit before they absolutely had to.

"Forty!" Daphne called out. They'd done some calculations the night before, based on the stated depth of the shaft and the approximate length of cable each turn would release. She continued unspooling the wire, lowering the transducer still further. "Fifty!"

"Hold." Cassidy turned to Isaac. "How much longer do you expect Adrian to be?"

Isaac let out the breath he'd been holding. "It's a very long climb," he reminded her. "We can use the safety line to pull him up, if that will help."

She shook her head. "We'll wait." They still had to run an echolocation test to make sure the transducer was actually beneath the bottom of the shaft, but it was much too dangerous to do it before Adrian was clear of the unshielded silver wire.

# Chapter 10

Cassidy and Daphne moved up to stand beside Agnes while she connected the lightning reservoir to the key, blocking what she was doing from the view of Isaac and Adrian. Typically, a Water Fairy carried a standard-sized key with them wherever they went so they could communicate at any of the publicly available stations. Since this machine was designed to be used while travelling, however, it came with its own—much smaller than average--key, which Agnes now deftly flipped into position.

"Ready."

"Run the echolocation test."

Agnes twisted the wire key on its pivot and touched the free end to the correct contact. A burst of static came back that made everyone in the room jump.

"Keep trying," Cassidy instructed in a low voice. Grimly, she hurried over to where Isaac and Adrian were standing with concerned expressions on their faces. "I need to ask you to leave the room, please."

"Thanks for your help, Adrian." Isaac held out his hand to the man, who shook it. "Please go tell Sir Stuart that you were successful." Turning back to Cassidy, Isaac smiled a little stiffly. "I'd prefer to remain." Actually, he'd rather leave, put some distance between them.

He'd even tried without success to persuade Stuart to take his place as the official attendant. Not because he shared Cassidy's assertion about the inevitable end to their relationship; because the hurt of her saying it was still so fresh. And now that he was here, duty required that he remain.

She took a deep breath. "Of course." She told herself that it was because he was the prince and had every right to be there. She also told herself that he wouldn't even understand what they were doing so they couldn't technically be betraying any Water Fairy secrets…

"Clear!"

Cassidy swung towards Agnes' voice. "Transmit a lead." If their signals reached one of the border stations, the lead would let the technician know they were waiting for a response before sending a complete message.

Isaac watched, perplexed, as Agnes began tapping one end of a thin piece of metal against a slightly elevated square patch of metal. He couldn't catch a rhythm, so he deduced that it must be some sort of code, like the ones he'd learned in the Wranglers. Except that he had to be able to see or hear another Wrangler for those codes to work. He briefly considered pacing back and forth alongside Cassidy, only to reluctantly dismiss the idea in favor of stowing Adrian's safety harness. It was better that he keep his distance, anyway. Inwardly he smirked at himself.

Now was a fine time to be figuring that out! Shaking his head, he got to work.

He'd just finished recoiling the safety line and was hanging it up when the tapping sounds stopped. Judging by their sober expressions, though, it wasn't time to leave. Noticing they weren't even talking amongst themselves, he found himself a corner to hunker down in and continued to observe them in silence. They were all staring expectantly at the machine in front of Agnes. It wasn't doing anything as far as he could tell.

"Again," Cassidy ordered.

Agnes ran a finger under her limp collar, lifting it off her neck as she transmitted the lead a second time.

Isaac's attention was jerked from their faces to the equipment when, suddenly, the key began moving on its own!

"Contact!" Agnes nearly yelled even though they could all see and hear it as well as she.

"Send my identification signal." As a high-ranking member of the Botere clan, sending Cassidy's identification signal was the same as labelling the message 'confidential' and would automatically result in a sworn key operator being sent for. It was absolutely vital that the contents of this communication be given only to the ruling council.

"We got through?" Daphne squeaked in disbelief.

"The border stations are always staffed," Cassidy reminded her, disguising her own elation behind a calm tone of voice. While they waited for confirmation that a sworn operator was present, she absent-mindedly ran a hand over her curls, enjoying the sensation. Her hair felt almost normal in here, where the air was heavy with water from the service shaft. She held her breath when the key began moving.

"Alright," she exhaled, recognizing the incoming signal. "Transmit our message."

Agnes proceeded to do just that, making it through the entire process without a single mistake. They all listened closely as the operator responded: *Message received. Await response forty-eight hours.* And that was that. In a matter of minutes, the stress of the last few days was over.

Cassidy brushed a hand across her eyes, the relief almost too much for her.

"Hey." Isaac spoke from his corner. He could've sworn he saw Cassidy sway, ever so slightly. "Is everything alright?"

Cassidy blinked at him. She'd forgotten he was there. Naturally, he would have understood very little from their terse remarks and absolutely none of the code.

"We got through. We'll know more when they respond in forty-eight hours."

"Wonderful!" Isaac smiled and looked curiously at the equipment. The less time it spent traversing the corridors the better, in his opinion.

"Is it alright to leave this equipment here or do we need to take it back to your quarters 'til then?"

"The room is kept locked?  Always?"

"Always," he assured her.  "The less traffic in and out of here, the cleaner it remains for the pumps."

Cassidy smiled faintly, understanding better why everyone had been required to leave their shoes at the door and don boots from inside the room.  The floors were damp and a bit slick, but also the boots would be much cleaner than their ordinary footwear, which trekked all over Weetu.  A far cry from her personal laboratory, where she also donned a fresh, clean overgown upon entering, yet the same basic principle.

"Then most of it can remain," she decided.  Catching Agnes' eye, Cassidy looked pointedly at the lightning reservoir, then engaged Isaac in what she hoped would be a diverting conversation.  "I suppose you have a lot of questions."

"Let's save that conversation so my parents can hear it, shall we?"

Cassidy stared at him, surprised and hurt by the coolness of his tone.

"If we're all ready?"  He deliberately refrained from looking over his shoulder at Agnes and Daphne.

Cassidy ignored the obligatory arm he offered, instead sweeping out of the room with Agnes and Daphne at her wingtips.  They all watched closely while he locked the door behind them, made sure he pocketed the key, then they resumed moving briskly along the hallway. At the first available branch, Agnes and Daphne turned off. Cassidy went with Isaac while the others whisked the lightning reservoir back to their quarters for safe-keeping. Not wishing to look at him, Cassidy flew on ahead, probably the rudest thing she'd done during her stay there. By Water Fairy standards, anyway.

While she waited for him in the foyer outside the king's office, she paced, a terrible question going round and round in her mind. *What have I done?* She re-examined her motives for suggesting that her tribe renew diplomatic relations with the surface tribes, forcing herself to take her feelings for Isaac into account. There were a number of other reasons, of course, a select few of which she'd included in the message as persuasively as the limited communication would allow. Still…she couldn't help confessing—at least, to herself—that despite all of her protests, she'd allowed her personal feelings for Isaac to affect her reasoning. She was still wrestling with the realization when Isaac finally walked in, scowling.

"Wait." She eyed his wingboard. "Has that been bumping into the back of your head when you walk?"

"Of course it has," he retorted crossly.

"Then it needs to be adjusted." She met his eyes calmly, secure in her role as his doctor. "Hold still."

Isaac grimaced but didn't move away when she approached. He closed his eyes to steel himself against the scent of her perfume, the feel of her shoulder brushing his chest as she adjusted his harness.

"Did I hurt you?" she asked, noticing his closed eyes as she straightened away.

"No." Pivoting on his heel, he strode to the doors of his father's office and shoved them open.

Cassidy slipped in behind him to find that the queen, Princess Gallica, and Sir Stuart were already waiting with the king. Six chairs, counting the king's, were arranged in the shape of a circle. Quietly, she stationed herself by the nearest empty one, seating herself only after King Walter nodded permission.

"Welcome, Lady Cassidy." Walter decided to err on the side of formality, at least this once. "We have been anxiously awaiting an update on your progress." He left the door as wide open for her as he could because they'd agreed to keep the possibility of a new treaty between the two of them until it was more than an idea.

"It went well. Better," she admitted, "than I ever could have hoped." Hiding her hands in the folds of her skirt, she continued, "We are to return in forty-eight hours to get their reply."

"That's it?" Gallica slouched down in her chair. "I was expecting something more…" She hesitated, searching for the right word, then shrugged helplessly. "*More.*"

"Diplomacy takes time," Walter reminded his daughter gently.

Cassidy nodded her agreement. "First they must call an assembly of the ruling council, which will then have to consider the limited information we were able to provide."

"I see." Walter cocked his head to one side. "I certainly hope that it will allay their fears."

"As do I."

"A ruling council?" Stuart leaned forward in his chair. "I suppose once they've discussed it, they'll report to the king?"

"Which will take even longer," Gallica muttered.

"There is no one ruling family in my tribe." Cassidy corrected the misconception mildly. "A dozen families first settled our territories, and their descendants now lead our tribe." She watched them exchange surprised looks.

"So, you have a dozen kings?" Stuart was confused.

Cassidy almost laughed at that. "No, not exactly. The ruling council is our tribal governing body. They make some decisions by unanimous consent, others by a majority, and so on."

"I would think that would make the laws of descent terribly confusing," Stuart observed, his eyebrows knit together in bewilderment.

Cassidy shook her head. "When a council member passes away, the direct descendants who are old enough to hold the office are gathered and examined by the remaining members of the ruling council. Only those who demonstrate exceptional knowledge of our laws and customs are even considered."

"I take it the examination is not the sole determinant?" Isaac guessed.

"Very few make it past that first step," she agreed. "And in the event of multiple qualified candidates, the other descendants choose between them by secret ballot."

"Wait." Gallica frowned. "I don't understand. The final decision is sometimes left in the hands of those who were deemed unqualified for the position themselves?"

"I see a certain logic to it," Walter conceded. "One does not have to be an expert lawyer to know a good heart, after all."

"Precisely." Cassidy smiled at him. "Any clerk can read a law book. A councilor must have the best interests of the tribe at heart."

"Councilor?" echoed Stuart. "What a refreshingly direct title!"

Gallica frowned thoughtfully. "But what about your title? *Lady* Cassidy."

Cassidy felt her cheeks turning pink. "That is just an academic title," she returned dismissively.

"Academic?" Gallica persisted. "Like a

teacher?"

Cassidy smiled at that. "Goodness, no. Teachers educate our youth. Doctors study and practice specific disciplines. Those who complete the available curriculum for three or more subjects are referred to as Scholars."

"And Ladies?" Isaac prompted from where he sat, relaxed in his chair.

Cassidy concentrated on smoothing the skirt of her dress. "Barons and Ladies have made some substantial contribution to the sciences."

Walter and Fiona exchanged looks. Cassidy's apparent embarrassment told them a great deal about the Water Fairy Tribe and how much they valued learning.

"I seem to remember you telling me you were also a…" Walter's brow furrowed as he hunted back through their conversations for the correct term. "A zalden?"

Cassidy's lips twitched, but this time she managed not to smile. "A zaldun. Yes."

"A warrior."

"Yes," she reiterated. "Warrior. Protector. Guardian." It was an unwritten law that every Water Fairy living in the border realms should master at least one weapon, though she squirmed a little just thinking about how that tradition began. Most of those living in the border realms hadn't trusted the surface tribes to keep the treaty, so they practiced and trained daily in case of an attack. She blamed similar suspicions for the way the *advena* originated.

"I suppose," Isaac leaned forward, resting his upper body on his elbows and linking his fingers together, "you studied all of the available curriculum?"

"I did." Cassidy refused to feel insulted by his upraised eyebrows. A little hurt, perhaps. Which was entirely different from insulted. Much worse, if she was being honest.

"The pumps will be restarted in an hour or so," Walter cleared his throat. "And in forty-eight hours we can turn them off temporarily, just long enough to receive the response. But for now, we wait."

Fiona took his cue and came lithely to her feet. "I detest waiting," she laughed. "It makes me rather fidgety."

"I suggest we take a turn at the woodshed." Gallica rose and linked her arm through her mother's. The woodshed was where the city's supply of fuel for the winter was kept, mostly in enormous logs that had been drying since last spring and just needed cut down to the size of the various stoves and ovens. "I find that cutting and stacking wood is a marvelous way to expend my nervous energy."

"Perfect." Fiona smiled at her daughter. Maintaining the city's morale throughout the winter was of primary importance. Seeing a few members of the royal family doing their bit in a difficult job should help with that enormously.

Stuart caught Cassidy's eye. "Would you care to join us?"

She laughed, relieved that Isaac wasn't showing any interest in coming along. "I think I would."

Isaac had two good reasons for not slumping down into his chair and sulking. The first was that he was too old for such childish behavior; the second was that he was afraid the wingboards would come loose again. That was part of why he'd leaned forward to ask Cassidy that question, but then his emotions had twisted inside him and the words came out as disbelief.

Once they were alone, Walter got to his feet and commenced putting the furniture back in its usual pattern. He'd already decided to keep the extra chairs, for now.

"Say it." Isaac prompted.

"You were rude to her."

"I know." Scowling, Isaac leapt to his feet and swung his chair into line with the others.

"I was under the impression that you felt rather differently towards her."

"I do. That is, I did. I mean..." Isaac paused, took a deep breath. "Weren't you ever rude to Mom?" He cringed the second he realized what he'd said.

Walter hesitated, unsure as to whether or not that was a question he should answer.

"Never intentionally."

Isaac ran his fingers through his hair, feeling

twice the guilt now. "I thought I was making progress. I was convinced that she'd changed her mind and was going to stay."

"Hmm." Walter squinted at his son. He'd never tolerated sulky behavior from Isaac before and they were both too old to start now. "So, you only love her when you think she's going to do what you want."

"What?" Isaac was incredulous. "No, that's not what I said at all." He held up his hands, palms forward, for emphasis. Even as he stood there, his words rang in his ears... *I do. That is, I did.*

"Sounded like it to me." Walter leaned on the back of the chair he'd just repositioned and studied his son closely. Satisfied that he'd gotten through to Isaac, he probed gently, "Something has happened to make you think she won't stay?"

"Yes." Isaac sighed and settled the final chair into the new arrangement. "She told me she's leaving. No." He held up his hand, index finger extended. "She told me I wouldn't want her to stay."

Walter considered for a moment. "And it never occurred to you that she might know what she's talking about." Isaac opened his mouth to speak, then sank into the nearest chair, his mouth still hanging open. "Just because she's colored her hair brown and speaks our language, that doesn't mean she's one of us, Son." Walter seated himself opposite Isaac. "We have absolutely no idea what her life was like before she came here. Oh, I know. You two have spent a lot of time together," he continued before Isaac could interrupt.

Isaac absent-mindedly flexed his shoulders to move his wingboard into a slightly less uncomfortable position and waited for his father to continue. He'd been so…presumptuous. Foolish. Conceited. A lengthy list of uncomplimentary adjectives tumbled through his mind.

"I believe she truly enjoys your company. I also believe she has developed feelings for you that, given time, might mature into something more than a dalliance. However." Walter paused for emphasis. "There is a great deal more at stake here than two young hearts. We're teetering on the edge of history, Isaac. Whether or not the Water Fairies choose to renegotiate the treaty, you and yours will be impacted."

"Everything could change." Isaac gripped the arms of his chair. "Everything from existing import and export agreements to tourism and travel. Even menus at restaurants."

"Education," added Walter soberly. "Should we send teachers or Tribal Historians to help fill in this great gap in their timeline?"

"Should we receive their teachers?" Isaac countered.

"Will they even be willing to send them?" Walter shook his head, the idea of sharing his burden with eleven others suddenly sounding very appealing.  The Water Fairies might be onto something with that ruling council idea.  Of course, votes of six to six would be tricky.  "Or will they prefer to keep their secrets?"

"And what secrets do they have that are so terrible I wouldn't want to spend the rest of my life with the woman I love?"  Without realizing what he was doing, Isaac pressed his palms against the sides of his head, as if by so doing he could somehow ease the process of mind-stretching he was currently undergoing.

"The little bit that we've learned during these last few weeks has barely scratched the surface of their world.  And it may be that we'll never really need to know more, because," Walter conceded, "they could decide they like things just fine the way they are."

# Chapter 11

Cassidy blinked a little, trying to convince herself to finish waking up. A full-body stretch felt fantastic, but left her wanting to snuggle back under the covers. She'd never had that problem at home in Noddfa. The rhythm of the waves—the sea's heartbeat—lulled her to sleep each night and lured her awake each day. As soon as she opened her eyes at home, a magnificent, sprawling vista filled her view. Schools of fish swimming past her bedroom filled the deep blue water with flashes of color and swirls of movement. The seaweed beds were usually alive with underwater harvesters by the time she woke up, and she would fly up to wave at the workers from the ceiling of her glass bubble before closing her privacy drapes and changing into her day clothes.

She always ate breakfast with her father—sometimes in silence, occasionally in animated discussion of a new discovery or frustration; but always with the comforting knowledge that they had each other and their work. She could really have used his advice right now.

Sighing, she shoved back the covers and sat up. The emptiness inside her after thinking of her father was more than breakfast could fill, she knew. Nevertheless, today was far too important for her to spend the morning lying abed. Today they would receive the council's reply. Slipping out through the gap in the bed curtains, she rinsed her face with cold water from the sink, refilled the water clock, and picked out a dress for the day.

The pale green glow of the foxfire lighting was gentle on her newly opened eyes. She marveled at how natural it seemed to tie back the bed curtains before smoothing the bedding, and had to fight back a perverse wave of nostalgia for the place she was visiting. The place she wouldn't even be able to leave for another two months, at the minimum!

She was still shaking her head at herself when she exited the bedroom and entered the common area. And stopped in her tracks. It was gone! She touched the top of the table to be sure she wasn't imagining things, but the pad of paper with the two potential responses to what they thought the council might say was definitely not there. They'd all sat up late last night, laughing at themselves for trying to outguess the council yet needing something to do with the anxious energy pervading the room.

She straightened from checking the chair seats and under the table and winced, putting one hand to her back for support against the twinge. She might resort to the woodshed again in the future, particularly once they had the council's response in hand, but right now she was still too sore from her last visit. She smiled grimly at her declaration of being a warrior and slid into the nearest chair, suddenly not caring that an extremely confidential document had vanished. It would most likely turn up before they returned to the pump service shaft, unlike her supple flexibility—the neglect of which had caught up with her.

"Still hurting?" Agnes spoke in Margua, their native tongue, her voice kind and sympathetic, as one who'd reached the age where being sore somewhere or another was normal. "Let me warm up last night's steep."

Cassidy started to decline, then surrendered the point. Agnes was right and would win the argument if one got started. Besides, the steep would soothe her sore muscles and reduce the inflammation, making it easier to resume her daily workout.

"Thank you." Cassidy responded in Margua, finding comfort in the familiar musical qualities of their language.

"Did you sleep well?" Agnes asked hopefully from where she was feeding slivers of wood into the belly of the tiny countertop stove.

"Yes, I think so." Cassidy blinked, remembering suddenly what had woken her. She thought she'd heard her father calling for her. "I…must've had a dream."

The sound of Daphne yawning made them both look around. Fully dressed, but still half-asleep, Daphne slumped into one of the chairs, plopped the 'missing' notepad on the table in front of her, and yawned again.

"I had a dream, too. I dreamed I was being chased through the coral reef by a lightning eel with big, brown eyes." She shook her head ruefully. "That's the last time I have a snack right before going to bed."

Agnes turned away to hide her smile and Cassidy bit her lip. They'd been warning Daphne about her eating habits since their arrival, especially where surface food was concerned.

"Here." Agnes set a mug of the steep on the table in front of Cassidy.

"Are you still sore?" Daphne asked, her eyes now wide.

Cassidy shifted uncomfortably, tempted to push the steep aside and pretend she didn't want it.

"Yes, a little," she reluctantly confirmed. "I haven't been taking the time to exercise like I should."

Daphne nodded sympathetically. "I found a large room further into the maze," she offered.

"How big?" There was hope in Agnes' tone.

"At least enough space for the three of us to practice our taithís together. But, probably not enough for more than one suge taithí at a time."

Cassidy took a sip of the steep and worked her shoulders experimentally. "First thing tomorrow?" she suggested.

"Agreed."  Daphne and Agnes spoke at the same time, then they all laughed.  The sound of someone knocking at the outer door caught them by surprise.

"Ah, breakfast."  Daphne switched to the surface tongue, sprang to her feet, spun in midair, and hurried to answer the door.  They'd begun taking some meals in public since coloring their pink hair brown, but still chose to eat in their rooms sometimes.  Like today, when they were all too stressed and preoccupied to want to be responsible for not slipping into their native tongue with an audience of uninformed Wood Fairies.

"Morning," Gallica greeted as she wheeled in the breakfast cart.  She'd nipped down to the kitchen early so she could breakfast with them.  "Did everyone sleep alright?"

Cassidy assessed Gallica in a glance, deducing from Gallica's drawn face and less-than-perky tone that the young princess hadn't slept well at all.

"More or less."  Daphne chuckled at her own cleverness.  "Will you be joining us?" she half-invited as she transferred a telling fourth plate from the cart to the table.

"I was hoping to."  In an effort to keep her hands still, she slipped them into her pockets.

Cassidy felt more than saw Gallica's nervous glance in her direction and stifled a small, worried sigh.  Bad enough that she'd allowed her personal feelings to jeopardize intertribal relations; there was also a very real chance that her relationship with Isaac's entire family was damaged beyond repair after her plain words to Isaac. Taking a deep breath, she smiled at Gallica, as an additional invitation for her to join them.

"I'm a bundle of nerves." Gallica slid a fourth chair over from the desk and seated herself across from Cassidy. "I thought the waiting would get easier the closer it came to when we're expecting them to reply to your message, but I seem to tense up a notch with every passing hour." She found that extremely frustrating. As a Wrangler counting down inevitably meant she was drawing closer to a tangible danger, like chasing off a spider or hornet, but at least she could take comfort in knowing there would be a conclusive result.

"I know just what you mean!" Daphne declared, taking the warming lids from Cassidy and Agnes' plates and stacking them on the cart. "It took me so long to fall asleep last night that I didn't manage it until this morning!" They all chuckled with her.

Cassidy surreptitiously watched Gallica while taking a few bites of the fried potatoes and scrambled robin's egg. Swallowing was the hardest part of eating that morning. Her many cares and concerns seemed to have her by the throat, restricting it uncomfortably.

"Will it be alright if we join you?" Gallica blurted.

Cassidy nearly choked on her juice. Agnes and Daphne both rose to leave, intending to give them privacy for the discussion, but Cassidy lifted a hand to forestall them. Clearing her throat carefully, she motioned for them to retake their seats.

"You may as well hear this," she murmured in Margua. Then, in the surface tongue, she addressed Gallica. "When you say *we*, whom do you mean?"

Gallica carefully set her fork aside, feeling strangely as though she'd just committed an unknown tactical error.

"As you will recall, Isaac was present during the sending of the message. My parents and I had duties elsewhere that prevented us from attending." Gallica noted the subtle shift in Cassidy's posture, the slight lift of her chin. "We've all cleared our schedules in anticipation of the response to your message and, with your permission, would prefer to be present. In this way," she concluded in a rush, "the reply can be shared with us as quickly as possible."

Cassidy closed her eyes as thoughts began pounding against the inside of her skull, shouting for her attention. She'd rationalized allowing Isaac to remain, to see their equipment and witness it in use. She'd even agreed to leave some of it behind, trusting the Wood Fairy Royal Family not to breach their trust by inspecting the equipment while they were gone. The lightning reservoir, of course, was safely locked in Agnes' room, refilled and ready to go. But how could she pretend to be keeping her tribal secrets if she did not object to this? If she did not find some way to prevent anyone else from seeing—and possibly questioning—today's event? Yet this was surely a reasonable request from the Wood Fairy Royal Family.

Conflicted, Cassidy opened her eyes.

"I would discuss this with my nurses. Will you pardon our speaking in our own tongue?" At Gallica's surprised nod, Cassidy looked from Agnes to Daphne. Speaking in Margua, she began to share her thoughts. "Water Fairy law states that we must first protect the secret of our tribe's existence. Then the secret of our access portals. And finally, at all costs, the secrets of our lightning science. We came here to assist a prince, one of a handful of surface fairies who knew already that there was a fifth fairy tribe. Circumstances forced us to remain, but we have adapted by changing the color of our hair, wearing glasses to hide our hazel eyes, and trying to blend in." Pausing to make sure they were with her thus far, Cassidy took a deep breath before continuing. "The harsh weather has removed the greatest danger of our breaking the second law by leading them to a portal, yet here we find ourselves face to face with the question of how to keep the third law under the circumstances."

"I would rather die than break the third law," Daphne stated grimly.

"A noble sentiment." Agnes sighed. "Unfortunately, the choice here is not so clear cut as deciding between betrayal and death. Instead, we hover between betrayal and insulting those we hope to call allies."

Gallica frowned when Daphne did, though of course she couldn't begin to guess what they were actually saying.

"I suppose it must seem a trifling request to them," Cassidy agreed. "To deny them access could strain our relations with them, both for the remainder of our stay and for any future negotiations."

"May I ask Gallica a question?" Daphne interposed.

Cassidy considered the request momentarily before motioning for her to proceed. Ordinarily, she would have insisted on hearing it and relaying it herself. Today, however, she decided to take a chance on the intelligence and aptitude that were the very reasons she'd chosen Daphne as the third member of her team.

"Would you and your family be willing to remain in the outer room until the reply is received and recorded?" Daphne asked Gallica.

Gallica leaned back in her chair, struggling to keep her confusion hidden. She wouldn't have bothered to ask permission if her mother hadn't suggested it. And now they were being asked to wait outside, as if they were interlopers?  It took her a few breaths to separate her offended pride from what was actually important.  Number one: sending a message to the Water Fairy Tribe hadn't been her idea.  Number two:  even if it had been, she'd never have been able to accomplish it on her own.  Number three: she'd seen for herself the benefit of having even limited access to Water Fairy medicine.  Number four: after everything Cassidy, Agnes, and Daphne had done for the wounded Wranglers, Gallica owed them a debt she doubted she could ever pay.  The list went on, but Gallica had what she needed.

"I'll tell my parents," she acquiesced quietly.  Rising, she nodded to Cassidy.  "By your leave, m'Lady."

The lump in Cassidy's throat after Gallica left felt as large as the roll sitting uneaten on the serving plate.

"Well done," she complimented Daphne.  "An excellent compromise."  Since there was no way to make the council's reply come any sooner, she tried to think what she could possibly concentrate on for the next few hours.

"I think it's time to exercise."  Agnes rose, ignoring their previous agreement to begin tomorrow.  She hadn't seen Cassidy this agitated since the review board ordered her to demonstrate her first scientific discovery.  Thankfully, though, she remembered how Cassidy got through the waiting that time.

Daphne, her appetite gone as well, hastily recovered their dishes, then followed Agnes and Cassidy's example, hurrying to her room to change into something less restrictive. Agnes had a lightning-powered watch pinned to her blouse when she emerged from her room a few minutes later. Cassidy gestured for Daphne to lead them to the room she'd discovered, and they slipped quietly away from their quarters, shutting the door firmly behind them.

Cassidy sneezed as soon as they entered the room, which was empty except for untold decades of dust.

"Ugh. It is *so* dry here!" She wiped her nose on a kerchief and resettled her glasses. She was amused to realize how automatic the gesture was by now, as if she'd always worn them.

"It could be worse," Agnes pointed out pragmatically, beginning her stretches. "It might not be as humid as Noddfa, but at least we have the moisture from the tree."

Conceding the point, Cassidy joined Agnes and Daphne in their stretches. They took turns assisting each other with the two-fairy stretches, feeling more like themselves by the minute as they went through the familiar motions. Cassidy's back stopped twinging about halfway through, and she was happy to line up with the others for the taithí.

Like a forest of seaweed, they bent forward and backward, side to side, avoiding imaginary attacks. Protecting their wings, too, from their imaginary assailants, by keeping them tucked, they used their arms and legs as counterbalances as well as to strike back. The final move was to bend so far backwards that they transferred their body weight to their arms and lashed out with both legs. Flipping themselves over, twisting in the middle and landing lightly on their feet, they balanced themselves with their outstretched wings as they transitioned back into the defensive stance with which the form began. They began and ended at exactly the same time, their fluid motions barely stirring the dust.

One taithí led to another: the crab, or floor defense; the octopus offense; the evasive eel. If not for obligations elsewhere, they might've gone on until they dropped from fatigue.

"It's nearly time," Agnes announced unhappily after checking her watch. "If we hurry, we will have time to clean up and change."

Despite their best efforts, they were not the first to arrive.

Isaac greeted them in the hall outside the empty service room. "My parents will be here shortly," he advised them. "Along with Stuart and Gallica."

Agnes and Daphne discreetly slipped into the service chamber to reconnect the lightning reservoir, leaving Cassidy alone with Isaac.

"I need to apologize." He waited briefly for her to respond, but when she refused to look at him, he slipped a finger under her chin, applying just enough pressure to bring her head up. "I mean it." He reached for her glasses, the action finally prompting a reaction in the form of a black scowl. "Easy," he murmured, his eyes locked on hers as he carefully removed her glasses, allowing him to see directly into her stunning hazel eyes for the first time in weeks. "I got caught up in my feelings for you." Realizing he was practically whispering, he cleared his throat. "I deluded myself into thinking that a solution to our conundrum would present itself. In fact, I convinced myself you'd already decided to stay." He exhaled slowly. "I forgot about the treaty. I forgot about," he shrugged, embarrassed, "the rest of Fairydom." His hands still near her face, he ached to touch her cheek, but denied himself. "I'm appalled at my arrogant, selfish behavior. And I wanted to let you know that I will do everything I can to make the rest of your stay here as…unencumbered as possible. I give you my pledge."

Cassidy's eyes burned with repressed tears, yet she refused to blink. The escape of a single tear would burst the dam irreparably, and she would find herself leaning on Isaac for support while her aching heart wrung itself dry of tears.

"The fault," she forced the words to come, "is not entirely yours, Your Highness." Somehow, she could say no more. She accepted the glasses when he bowed and handed them to her, but could not bring herself to put them back on.

"Cassidy!"  Agnes' urgent call reached them through the partially-closed door.

Alarmed, Cassidy handed the glasses back to Isaac and hurried into the room, closing the door behind her.

"What is it?"  She chose Margua to offset the remote possibility that Isaac would find a way to listen in.

"The device began working the instant we connected it.  One command, over and over."  Agnes swallowed hard.  "We're to transmit a locating signal."

Cassidy caught hold of Agnes' arm as the room began spinning.  Hunger, fatigue, shock—they all hit her at once.

"Obey," she whispered.

Daphne hit the switch that activated the built-in signal, then hurried over to wrap her arms around Cassidy.  Agnes did the same, so that they were sandwiching Cassidy between them, warming her in the hopes of preventing a full collapse.  They all looked around in astonishment as the machine began emitting a high-pitched beep that rapidly accelerated until it was a single tone.  Then, it stopped.

"They're here."  Cassidy rested her head against Agnes' shoulder, resisting the temptation to laugh.  "It's impossible, but they're here."  She took a steadying breath.  "We'll need blankets and something hot for them to drink. Daphne, please see to it."  Tentatively, she straightened away from Agnes.  "I'm alright," she reassured her anxious friend.  "Disconnect the lightning reservoir and cover the machine while I inform King Walter that," she choked back a hysterical sob, "we have guests."

Isaac charged into the service room, dragging a protesting Cassidy along with him. "You're sure they're in the shaft already?" At her nod, he growled, "Then they need our help." He was reaching for a safety harness when his wingboard bumped him in the back of his head. The service shaft was barely large enough for rescue maneuvers without such an encumbrance. Scowling, he tossed the harness to Stuart, who caught it deftly. "I'll man the wheel," Isaac volunteered.

He pulled Cassidy over to the wheel, explaining as he went. "The water that comes through our pumps in the winter is frigid. The tree and ground insulate it enough to keep it from freezing, but just barely. Anybody in the water," he pointed at the service shaft, "needs to be gotten out of the water as quickly as possible." He flipped the lever that set the wheel mechanism to release the safety line.

"Yes, but…" Cassidy didn't disagree; she just knew that, once again, there were going to be too many outsiders witnessing Water Fairy science at work.

"Ready?" Isaac cut her off, turning back to look at Stuart.

Stuart had expertly fastened on the harness almost before they reached the wheel and now he tossed the safety line up onto a pulley rigged near the mouth of the service shaft.  Nodding sharply, he backed up to the shaft.

Cassidy screamed when Stuart jumped clear of the edge and fell.

"It's alright," Isaac calmed her, one eye on the rapidly unspooling safety line.  A faint splashing sound barely preceded the line's coming to a halt, and Isaac's hand shot towards the lever.  Reversing it, so that the gears meshed, he waited tensely for a double tug from below, the signal to pull them up.

Cassidy and Agnes exchanged looks of horror at the noises that came from the shaft instead.  Agnes leapt forward, shoved her head into the shaft, and began shouting in Margua.

"Wait!"  Cassidy's hand on his arm stopped Isaac from racing over to the shaft as well.  "She's doing all that can be done."  Shouting 'friend!' over and over was little enough to do, but it was all they had.

Isaac's gaze fastened on the safety line as it jerked twice.  "Grab the other handle," he ordered Cassidy, pointing at the far side of the wheel.  "And go!"  Together, they cranked the wheel around and around as rapidly as they could, their bodies bobbing up and down as the huge, whirring wheel drew the safety line up, up…

"Hold!" Stuart's voice caught them at odds, Isaac up and Cassidy down.  But they held exactly where they were.

"I've got him!" King Walter's strong voice cut through the ensuing silence and prompted Cassidy to lift her tired head. The instant she spotted the ensign on the diver's shoulder, she recognized the three diagonal blue stripes on the pink background. She should—it was her family insignia!

At her gasp, Isaac looked sharply towards her.

"Release the line!" Stuart ordered. "There are two more to fetch!"

Isaac dropped the locking bar and hit the release lever, plunging Stuart once more into the dark service shaft.

With a sob, Cassidy rushed over to where Agnes was standing by the rescued Water Fairy, a strange look on her face. Cassidy's hands trembled as she unzipped the top of the diving suit and gingerly peeled back the rubbersap hood, revealing his short-cropped pink hair and familiar hazel eyes.

"Breathe," she murmured in Margua. Deftly, she released the catch on his nose mask, removing it and letting the clean, fresh air in. One could endure recycled air only so long. She hated to think how long in this case. "Breathe." His hands reached for hers and she clasped them to her chest. "You're so cold."

"Here!" Daphne popped through the door to the service room, an insulated jug hanging from each arm and a bag in one hand. "Warm doctor's water."

"Does that taste as terrible as it sounds?" Cassidy asked, relieving Daphne of the bag, which contained large tin mugs. Doctor's water, as they called it, was bitter enough when chilled. As fantastically restorative as it was, she didn't envy the divers having to choke it down warm.

"Worse." Daphne grimaced and set the jugs on the nearest flat surface, shoving some tools aside in the process. "Still, it will help."

Cassidy filled a mug, took a deep breath, and turned back to where she'd left her diver. Catching Isaac watching her, she took another deep breath. She was grateful to see that Walter had joined him at the wheel. Agnes and Daphne were wrestling the second diver out of the shaft, and she could see that Stuart was pale and shaking with cold.

"Wait!" she called before Isaac and Walter could release the line again. Cassidy sternly forbade herself to look down into the shaft. "Drink this," she ordered Stuart, offering the mug with one hand and holding onto a safety bar with the other. "It tastes horrible," she'd gotten a good whiff of it by now, "but it's warm."

Stuart held his breath and drained it, then shuddered so violently that the line quivered with him. "Oh, that was gross!" Waving a hand at Isaac and Walter, he grabbed another quick breath before disappearing once more into the shaft.

"I hope you don't think I'm going to drink any of that," someone said in Margua.

Cassidy turned back to her diver. "You most certainly will," she informed him severely in the same tongue. Refilling the mug, she brought it to him. "Medicine is supposed to taste terrible, you know." Wrapping his hands around the mug to warm them, she guided it carefully to his lips. She laughed softly when he made a face after the first sip and gently smoothed his hair. "Drink it down," she commanded teasingly.

Isaac threw himself into turning the wheel for the third time, partly to take his mind off the ache in his side, but mostly in an effort to keep from watching Cassidy with her charge. Except he couldn't. When Gallica offered them a blanket, Cassidy wrapped it around them both. Even though it was a logical move, given how desperately cold the divers were, Isaac grumbled a bit on the inside. The man was at least twice her age! Which, he unhappily admitted, might not matter to Water Fairies.

Agnes did the same thing with her diver, a tall, willowy fellow with a strangely-shaped ensign on his shoulder—it looked like a midnight sky with a handful of stars sprinkled across it— though she also kissed his cheek once she found it, and whispered to him. Meanwhile, Daphne took charge of the third diver, distinguishable from the others only by the ensign on his shoulder (a scarlet background featuring what looked like a black quill) peeling off his hood and coaxing him to drink the horrid doctor's water. Isaac thought her manner was superbly professional by comparison to the others as she took his pulse and checked his pupils for responsiveness.

"Well." King Walter secured the wheel and looked about the room. Gallica was wrapping a shivering Stuart in a blanket, without even stopping to remove the harness. "Not quite the reply I was imagining." Fiona had already begun moving among them, refilling the mugs from the half-empty jug and seeing what else they needed.

"Nor I," agreed Isaac. Cassidy was finally going through doctor-like motions, and he was still jealous. Maybe it was the way she seemed snuggled into the stranger's arms that was making his temper rise?

Fiona appeared at Walter's elbow. "We need to get them into warm, dry clothes."

"I could be wrong," Walter hazarded, "but their…clothes look perfectly dry to me." It was quite interesting, really. Wrangler equipment naturally included waterproof gear, yet compared to whatever these three were wearing, it might as well have been made of barkcloth. The purpose behind the twin, raised straps on their backs eluded him completely, though they seemed to be connected to the tubes protruding from either side of the face masks they'd been wearing.

"Nevertheless." Cassidy wrapped the blanket more tightly about her charge, then came over to join them. "They will be significantly more comfortable in ordinary clothing." She knew that from personal experience. The rubbersap material was wonderfully protective while in the water; once out of the water it quickly came to feel restrictive.

"Of course," Walter agreed soothingly. "I'll send for some hooded cloaks and…"

"And have the entire city wondering what you want with them?" Fiona shook her head. "You better get them yourself. Isaac, you need to go to Stuart's quarters for a change of clothes for him, as well." She shooed them out the door. "Hurry!"

Cassidy started to return to her diver, hesitated and turned back. "Queen Fiona?" The formality seemed odd under the circumstances, but Cassidy needed her full attention.

"Yes, my dear?" Fiona lightly placed one hand on Cassidy's arm, grounding them both in that moment despite the multitude of other things that they both needed to be thinking about.

"I give you my word, we had no foreknowledge of these visitors."

"Thank you, Lady Cassidy." Fiona smiled and relaxed fractionally. The thought had crossed her mind. It was quite a relief to be able to set it aside.

Cassidy nodded, then hurried to rejoin her diver, who was already walking around the edge of the small room, leaning on the wall occasionally to rest. Slipping her arm around his waist, she held on as tightly as she comfortably could. Time enough later to sort out whether or not he was mad at her. They continued walking around the room, like Agnes, Daphne, and even Gallica, forcing the blood through the men's chilled bodies, until Isaac and Walter returned with their arms full.

Isaac arranged the damp blankets to create a makeshift privacy wall and helped Stuart change while Cassidy and the others wrapped the cloaks around the still rubber-clad divers.

"More comfortable clothes await you in the medical maze," King Walter promised.

"Thank you, Your Majesty." Cassidy looked him in the eyes. "Before we proceed any further, I should like to introduce you to your newest guests." Stepping aside so that the men were standing in a line, she began with the fellow to her left. "Sir Derrick, scholar of the Ten'rae region." Sir Derrick bowed his head, causing what was left of his thinning hair to raise and wave at the room in general. "Agnes' husband, tri-Baron Duncan Edgins, of the Seyth region." Baron Edgins, his arm firmly clasped by Agnes, clicked his heels together in the customary salute of his family, though the sound was completely lost due to the resinous compound that composed his swimming gear. "And Volt Clark, son by marriage of the Botere clan, Master of the sciences, and councilor of the Mugan region." She slipped her arm through his. "My father."

King Walter couldn't help noticing the slack-jawed expression on his son's face at this last announcement. Thankfully, Isaac was still with Stuart, and well behind the Water Fairies, who were all facing himself and Queen Fiona. *This complicates all sorts of things; unless or until it simplifies them.* He roused himself to return the introductions.

"I am King Walter, sovereign of the Wood Fairy Tribe. This," he slipped an arm about his wife's shoulders, "is my wife, Queen Fiona. Welcome to our home." The new arrivals surveyed him solemnly while Cassidy translated his greeting and he realized he was forgetting to breathe. At last, her father murmured something.

"We thank you for your hospitality," Cassidy related, "and apologize for any alarm our unexpected arrival might have caused."

Walter's smile broadened slightly, pleased by the acknowledgement of their part in the havoc they'd caused. They might cause even more turmoil over the next several weeks until spring, but at least things were getting off on the right foot.

"Over and done with," he returned lightly. "Come," he beckoned. "We can wait in the medical maze for their rooms to be prepared."

He frowned thoughtfully, his eyes darting to the unusual footgear the divers were wearing. It made him think of a frog's webbed foot, longer and wider than a fairy's. No doubt they were great assets in the water, but in Weetu, they would draw a great deal of unwanted attention. Dare he ask them to go barefoot?

Cassidy followed his gaze and smiled. "Let's take the flippers off," she suggested, dropping to her knees before her father. Her nurses followed suit, and in a matter of moments, the flipper attachments were discreetly bundled in the damp blankets with Stuart's soaking wet clothes. Rising, she made eye contact with Agnes, who smiled a little sheepishly. It was lucky the medical maze was so full of empty rooms, since Agnes and her husband naturally wanted to share a private room of their own. Beds and clothing, on the other hand, were probably going to be more difficult.

"Is this better?" Cassidy asked.

"Yes." Walter nodded approvingly. Now it looked like they were wearing black slippers, a relatively common choice in Wood Fairy footwear. "We can come back for your equipment later," he protested, spotting Baron Edgins leaning over the edge of the service shaft, hauling in the silver wire hand over hand.

"They feel it would be best to remove all evidence of our presence here," Cassidy returned.

Walter hesitated, then shrugged. Weetu's halls were always full of fairies going here or there, carrying this or that.  At least that would be one ordinary thing about the group.

"Remind them to keep their wings tucked under the cloaks, please," Fiona advised.  The pink edging on their wings wasn't quite as noticeable as their hair, however she saw no point in taking chances.

Cassidy quickly relayed the message, surprised to find she was so comfortable in her own disguise that she'd forgotten about that.  She hoped they didn't look too odd as they made their way through the halls.  King Walter and Fiona meandered along, not really holding their position at the head of the group, because that would make it a 'group;' which would in turn catch the attention of Weetu's citizens.  Gallica and Stuart did the same thing, fluttering slightly ahead of or dropping casually behind the group.  Both couples were a common sight in Weetu these days, and nobody took much notice of them.

Cassidy motioned for Daphne to join Agnes and her husband, in the hopes of breaking up the matching combinations of cloaked and non-cloaked fairies moving in the same direction.  That left Isaac and Sir Derrick coming along together in an awkward silence.  The entrance to the medical maze was just around the corner when someone called out.

"Hey, Doc!"

Cassidy released her father's arm and turned to answer Sugar's hail.  Her father kept walking quietly forward, and she was pleased to see Daphne slip forward to join him.

"Yes, Sugar?"

"Doc, I've been looking everywhere for you." He brightened when Isaac moved up beside Cassidy, lugging the roll of silver wire. "My dad needs the silver he loaned you for your experiment back. If you're done with it, I mean?"

Isaac grinned at him. "You have no idea," he gave an exaggerated groan of effort as he lifted the roll to offer it to Sugar, "exactly how done I am with hauling that thing around!"

Sugar laughed and tossed it over his shoulder as if it weighed no more than a standard-issue lasso. "Excellent! Bert's play opens soon, and the orders for fancy jewelry are coming in like snowflakes in a blizzard." He slapped Isaac's shoulder in a friendly fashion, taking care not to hurt him, saluted Cassidy, and flew off, whistling cheerfully.

"Hey." Catching Cassidy staring wistfully after the carefree Sugar, Isaac took her hand in his. "It's going to be alright."

"What is?" she asked, cocking her head to one side. She had a pretty good idea what he meant, she just needed to hear him say it.

"Everything." He gave her hand a friendly squeeze. "Come on, we'd better catch up." Without stopping to consider, he released her hand as they turned, and slipped his arm around her waist instead. It was no different from the way he might've walked along with Gallica if she needed a little encouragement, but he felt very self-conscious when he looked up and caught Cassidy's father watching them closely. "I've been thinking." His voice sounded so strange that he paused to clear his throat. "We'll obviously need to make some adjustments to your sleeping accommodations." They'd rounded the corner leading into the maze by now, so he gestured vaguely towards the rest of the group. "What would work best?"

Cassidy hesitated, vaguely aware that something was wrong with what she saw when she looked at the group. Her concern dissipated when Sir Derrick's cloaked figure moved away from the public water fountain and followed the others. He would've blended in just fine with the others stopping to drink from it.

Impressed that Isaac was anticipating their needs, Cassidy smiled up at him as she allowed him to lead her along. "You're too generous." A flash of emotion in his eyes, quickly suppressed, made her look away. It wasn't going to be easy for him to keep his promise. The least she could do was try not to make it any harder. "I know Agnes and her husband would prefer private rooms, if that is possible. Daphne and I will be perfectly comfortable in our current quarters, of course."

"Of course," Isaac agreed to have something to say.

"Supposing that the rooms aren't spread too

far apart," she continued tentatively, "I think my father and Sir Derrick would choose separate rooms for themselves."

"Hmmm." Isaac scratched his chin thoughtfully. "If they didn't have so much luggage, it would be easier." He winked good-naturedly at her when she looked up and was rewarded with a smile. "But I think we can arrange that."

She stopped as they were about to reach the others. "Thank you. For taking us all in. For behaving as though we're not taxing your resources."

Isaac took a half step away from her and clasped his hands behind his back. *Friends*, he reminded himself.

"You're more than unexpected guests." His voice betrayed a little of what he was trying not to feel, but he kept going anyway. "You, Agnes, and Daphne, you're already a part of Weetu. As for your father and the others…they're welcome, too, just as my father said." He could get lost in those eyes, he thought irrelevantly. "Our future is bright." Too late, he realized what he'd said and how it sounded. And that he'd mean it exactly that way, under other circumstances.

She swayed towards him fractionally before she could stop herself. That was a direct contradiction of what she'd told him and what she'd been telling herself, so she hastily retreated to arm's length. *Blast his husky voice!*

Cassidy and her nurses made their bedrooms available to the divers for changing purposes, even though that meant waiting in the crowded common areas with King Walter and the others. Isaac politely kept his distance, feigning a deep interest in the files on Cassidy's desk. Since she kept no patient files there—and knowing that the reports on the local medical resources were all written in Margua—Cassidy made no objections.

Besides, her mind was mostly occupied with the first impressions being made on her father and his committee. The beds (thankfully, she'd taken the time to make hers that morning!) and wooden chests of drawers in each room would tell them this was where she and her nurses slept. It was much smaller than their quarters at home, and lacked the awesome view of the sea—or anything at all. Truthfully, that was one of the main differences between the winter habitations of the surface tribes and the Water Fairy underwater domed cities. The vistas under the sea were enormous and ever-changing, constantly reminding their tribe that they were a tiny part of the whole. Now that they were seeing how the surface tribes spent their winters, Cassidy wondered what they would think.

The three bedroom doors opened almost simultaneously and the men stepped out. Volt spoke tersely.  In Margua.

"My father requests an audience with King Walter and Queen Fiona."  Cassidy translated stiffly.

Walter considered.  He'd found a page on their way over from the water system, and sent a message to his aide that he would be unavailable until further notice.  A meeting of this magnitude should take place in his offices, particularly given with whom he would be dealing.  His experiences with Cassidy made him suppose that Water Fairies were, on the whole, formal and dignified.  Ah well.  If his aide hadn't already taken the afternoon off, he was about to.

"I will grant it gladly.  Fiona and I will leave first and await you in my office."

Cassidy spoke to her father, who nodded gravely.  A few moments after the king and queen had left, she shooed Gallica, Stuart, and Isaac out as well.

"We'll be along shortly," she promised.

A quick assessment of the new arrivals showed her that their clothes fit well enough to pass the offhand inspection of anyone they would pass on their way to the king's office, but she knew the official messenger pouch her father carried would not.  Made of treated eel skin, it was waterproof when closed, and it's shiny, textured surface was wholly unlike anything that could be found in Weetu.

"Here."  She helped him back into his cloak.  "Keep it closed in front, so that your bag won't be visible."

"We should draw as little attention to ourselves as possible," agreed a subdued Agnes as she likewise helped her husband back into his cloak.  His private reaction to her brown hair still stung; nevertheless, she could not allow that to jeopardize what they'd all protected for so long.  She looked up in surprise when he caught her by the wrist and stepped closer.

He mouthed, "I am sorry," and reached up to smooth her wavy brown hair.  Leaning close, he murmured for her ears only, "Forgive me?"

Cassidy was relieved to see Agnes' face light up in a smile.  Hard as Agnes tried to hide it, Cassidy had known something was wrong.  Once they were all ready, they made their way to the king's office, using as many side tunnels as they could, but still having to pass through the large common area where Sugar had startled them earlier.  As always, Cassidy smiled at the sight and sounds of the large, round water fountain.  The water trickled out through a hole at the tiptop, meandered like a stream through a lovely carving of a forest, and eventually collected in the basin at the bottom.  She'd once asked Isaac how they kept it from overflowing, and he'd explained that the basin rested on a spring system.  As it filled and grew heavier, a mechanism partially closed the hole at the top; as it emptied and became lighter, the process was reversed.  Hardly an example of advanced engineering, it nevertheless impressed her as an example of Wood Fairy ingenuity and their love for beauty.

Volt strode into the office, discarding his cloak as soon as the door was securely closed behind them.  The king and his family were clustered near the only desk in the room, so Volt decided the chairs facing the desk were meant for Cassidy's party and his committee.  Taking the one furthest from the door, he moved it so that he would better be able to see both the desk and the witnesses.  Edgins and Derrick did the same.

King Walter watched curiously as the men rearranged the furniture without a word, then seated themselves.  It made him uneasy to see how easily they overlooked any possibility that their actions were at variance with Wood Fairy custom.  However, he wasn't convinced he would have been able to pinpoint the source of his discomfort if Cassidy and her nurses had not politely looked to him for permission before taking their seats.

*Polite.*  Such a simple word for such a complex concept.  Wood Fairies, Silver Fairies, Plant Fairies, Sky Fairies…they all had different customs.  With the crystal clarity of hindsight, Walter now wished he'd used some of his own time with Cassidy to learn Water Fairy customs.

Walter and Stuart seated Fiona and Gallica

before taking their own chairs. Flanked by his family, Walter felt a little better and yet woefully unprepared. This time, it was he who looked to Cassidy for guidance.

She glanced at her father before addressing the waiting Wood Fairies. "Councilor Clark and his committee have come at the behest of the Water Fairy ruling council to initiate diplomatic relations with you, King Walter, and your tribe, the Wood Fairies." She waited a beat, then continued, "In the spring, when travelling resumes on the surface, we intend to begin exchanging emissaries with the other tribes. Discreetly, of course."

She wondered what they were going to do with the *advena*, but there had been no time to ask. Releasing the thousands of detained fairies and their descendants would relieve the growing strain on Water Fairy resources, to be sure. On the other hand, for many of the younger *advena*, the 'surface' was something they'd only heard about in stories. With which tribe would those of mixed tribal heritage choose to align themselves? Which tribes would accept them? And…well, could the surface tribes handle the coming mayhem?

"I see." Walter was reeling. How could she speak so calmly about drop-kicking Fairydom into a veritable hornet's nest? Trade agreements with the Sky Fairies regarding weather and water, transport and shipping, tribal histories—*everything* was going to change.

"They have an official letter to that effect." Cassidy held her hand out to her father, who opened the eel skin messenger bag and produced a folded document. She caught a glimpse of a dozen or so additional documents inside the bag, but kept that to herself.

Rising, she brought the letter to King Walter, expecting him to break the seals at once. She found herself smiling on her way back to her chair because he instead began examining the two, unusual seals. The handful of seals she had seen while at Weetu were made using different colors of wax: brown for the Wood Fairies, periwinkle blue for the Sky Fairies, etc. By contrast, the crimson wax that was used for official Water Fairy business looked very flashy and bold. Almost…arrogant?

Isaac leaned forward to get a better look at the letter as his father accepted it. He half-expected to see a dozen separate seals adorning the document's flap, one for each of the ruling council members. Catching Cassidy squinting at him, he decided he could wait until later to satisfy his curiousity.

Walter did his best to keep his worry from showing as he accepted the packet of thick, greenish paper. It…smelled. Pushing that from his mind, he looked over at Volt.

"Why now?"

Volt's gaze dipped to the unopened letter in

Walter's hands even before Cassidy could translate the question. The two men remained motionless for several seconds, considering each other. Volt spoke to Cassidy in Margua without taking his eyes off of Walter.

"Lady Cassidy's contact happened now." Cassidy spoke in the third person to more fully confirm that she was just relaying her father's words. "We have been considering this for some time."

Walter promptly looked at Cassidy for confirmation. She looked tentatively at Volt. Volt would've ignored Walter's inquisitive frown if not for the hopeful tilt to Cassidy's head.

"It only became common knowledge recently," Volt told her in Margua. Earlier that day, to be precise. After his nephew, Kuntza gave his report of his time visiting the Sky Fairy Tribe, Volt's own mother had discovered over a hundred Sky Fairies hiding from winter in an abandoned mine. One of them had been treated for lightning poisoning, but they all were most cooperative, freely answering questions about conditions on the surface.

Added to that was the testimony of Prince Cambrian of the Sky Fairies, who Kuntza had the audacity to bring back with him. In the end, the councilors who still balked at the idea of resuming relations—despite clear evidence that the other tribes were no longer warring—were finally persuaded to agree upon being assured that lightning would still remain their closely guarded secret.

Walter deliberated briefly before returning his attention to the letter. That wasn't the information he'd been after, and he was reasonably certain Councilor Volt knew it. However, if they wanted to be cagey about the reasons behind the Water Fairy's world-shaking decision, that was fine with him. For the moment. Breaking open the seals, he was astonished to find that it was written in the common language. Short almost to the point of brusqueness, it outlined the mission of the committee and their mandate to act on behalf of their tribe.

Finished reading it, Walter handed the letter to Fiona. Leaning back in his chair, he asked himself to whom he would assign such sweeping authority; and in what dire straits he would have to find himself. This was not a simple, mundane assignment, like renewing the Plant Fairy contract for Wrangler units. Ultimately, it would reshape Fairydom. And the three fairies sitting opposite him were trusted by their tribe to help decide what shape it wound up in.

Cassidy, familiar enough with the Wood Fairy Royal Family to know that they would all read the letter, spent the time trying to puzzle out the answer to Walter's question. For several reasons, she was inclined to believe her father's declaration that this was a well-planned decision on the part of the council.  Except that it didn't add up. Even scouring her memories of the last few decades with her new understanding, she was unable to find the subtle hints she would've expected.

In the past, the council had eased the tribe into decisions, big or small.  Where were the specially prepared speechmakers, assigned to sway public opinion on the subject of the 'warlike' surface tribes?  The increased emphasis on teaching the surface tongue and customs?  The meticulously improved security measures, that no one would really understand until ambassadors from the surface began arriving?  She glanced over at her father and forgot everything she'd been thinking.

Isaac, surreptitiously watching Cassidy over the top of the letter, was alarmed to see her face change from pale to white.  Following her gaze, he looked at her father. Making the short mental leap to the idea that something was drastically wrong, and remembering how much they'd all just been through, he handed the letter back to his mother.

"With your permission, Father."  Isaac rose as he spoke.  "I should like to be excused so that I can check on the progress with our guests' rooms?"

Walter accepted the letter from Fiona and passed it to Gallica.  It was technically bad etiquette to let Isaac jump up and leave.  Trusting

Isaac to have weighed that already, Walter nodded for him to leave anyway.

"Councilor Volt." Walter turned his attention back to the matter at hand. "I realize it's unnecessary to point out that we will have to proceed with a great deal of caution. It's been generations since the idea that the Water Fairy Tribe might actually exist has been considered credible. I think the best way to begin would be to introduce you to my chief advisors at once." He felt Fiona's hand lightly squeeze his elbow at the same time that Cassidy gave a tiny shake of her head without missing a beat in her translating. "Immediately after breakfast tomorrow, that is," he amended. They'd completely missed lunch, now that he thought about it. A couple of hot meals and a good night's rest should do a world of good for the committee after their strenuous morning. Fiona must've thought so, too, for she gave his elbow a double squeeze of approval.

Cassidy responded privately to her father's request for access to the tribal histories she'd mentioned in the original message, then relayed their acceptance of King Walter's proposal. She and her ladies curtsied while the men bowed to each other. Catching her father before he reached the door, she lifted his hood back into position. Once they were all safely hidden again, she led them through the tunnels back to the maze.

"Perfect timing!" Isaac grinned at them as

they entered the tunnel where they'd been staying. "If you'll follow me?" A few rooms further into the tunnel, he paused to indicate the entrances newly-fitted with doors. The bulk of the rooms in the medical maze were originally used for preparing medicines, experiments, and so forth, so they hadn't required doors.

"Councilor Volt." Isaac pointed to the nearest door. "You'll be quartered here. Sir Derrick," he pointed at the next door. Made confident by Cassidy's prompt translation, he smiled directly at Agnes. "I'm afraid the next suitable rooms are a bit further along," he told her, pointing at another door. "If you and Baron Edgins find it to your liking, I'll see to transferring your things."

Agnes translated for her husband, Duncan's, sake. She was pleasantly surprised at Isaac's thoughtfulness. There were an abundance of abandoned rooms in the maze, to be sure. Having not one but *three* cleaned, furniture moved in, etc., all in such a short amount of time was very generous of their hosts.

"We thank you," she murmured in the surface tongue.

"Think nothing of it," Isaac smiled. "I'll arrange a light repast to tide you over until supper, which I suppose you'll be taking here?" He couldn't help looking at Cassidy as he asked. For the first little while after she and her nurses arrived at Weetu, they kept to themselves as much as possible.  Only after Rosie suggested coloring their hair and camouflaging their wings had they begun to venture out.  He hated to have them—especially Cassidy—restricted to the maze again.

Cassidy nodded.  "Yes, thank you."  Aware that her father was watching them curiously, she murmured something in Daphne's ear before responding to her father's unspoken command to join him in his rooms.  "If you'll excuse me?"

Isaac bowed courteously and suddenly found himself alone in the tunnel with Daphne.

"How'm I doing?" he asked, trying to smile at the affable young woman.

"Marvelously," she assured him.

"But?" he prompted, remembering that Cassidy had given her some instructions.

"Lady Cassidy thought I might assist you with selecting the menu?"

Isaac managed a real smile at that.  "I thought she liked our food."

"Oh, she does."  Daphne shrugged.  "We all do.  It's just that some of the dishes take a little getting used to."

Isaac laughed aloud and offered her his arm. "That makes sense," he agreed.  "I guess you eat a lot of fish?"

"That's true."  Accepting his arm, Daphne flew alongside him.  "But it's mostly the different spices your cooks use that make the beef and pork taste so different to us."

"Wait.  You have cows and pigs?"  Isaac had

to remind himself to keep his voice down as they exited the maze.

Daphne flushed, wondering if she should've mentioned it. Not that their island ranches could remain a secret for much longer, with the way things were going.

"Not very many," she answered at last.

"Fascinating." Seeing that he'd made her uncomfortable, Isaac smoothly changed the subject. "Frankly, I'm glad for your help. I was going to suggest roast robin and mashed thips with sweet corn, but now I'm not sure."

"It sounds delicious to me," Daphne smiled, relieved to be on a safe topic again. "However, I think the committee would prefer a hot soup. Perhaps robin soup, with noodles?"

Cassidy, who'd remained near the door until Isaac and Daphne's voices faded, now smiled at finding her father examining the glowing mushrooms on the ceiling.

"What do they call these?" he asked, looking down at her as he gave the mushroom's cap an assessing poke. Seemed in good health. They gave off a sufficient amount light, but they tinged everything green! Not the dark wood walls and furniture, but his hands and her face looked frightful. Not to mention her hair.

"Foxfire," she answered. "They grow these mushrooms all over Weetu. There is even a special team of Plant Fairy gardeners that does nothing but care for them."

Volt smiled at her affectionately. "I've missed you, Daughter."

She flew up for a hug without further invitation. "Oh, how I've missed you!"

Volt eased them down to the floor, where he pressed his cheek to hers and smoothed her hair. He could tell from the fierceness of her embrace that she was more than just glad to see him; she *needed* him. They'd never been apart for this long before. A few days here and there, a week at the most, on the rare occasions that their duties took them away from home.

"Forgive me," he murmured. "But your hair is truly atrocious."

She burst out laughing as she pulled back, glad that he was teasing her.

"It is a necessity," she informed him, still laughing. "If we are to come and go as we please, to visit our patients, and so on, we must appear to belong."

Volt took note of the word 'patients,' meaning plural, and thought back to the letter he'd found waiting on his bed the night she'd vanished. It still hurt to think about it. He'd had a long conversation with his nephew, Kuntza Botere, before finally reconciling himself to the fact that his daughter, chum, and confidant, chose to pack up and leave without consulting him. It made sense, in a way. As a tribal councilor, he'd have been obligated to order her to abide by the strictest interpretation of the treaty until the full council could be gathered and consulted. Which would've meant that Prince Isaac, the handsome young fairy who couldn't seem to keep his eyes off Cassidy, would've gone without treatment until spring, when it almost certainly would've been too late.

# Chapter 14

That evening, after supper, Volt called for the others to join him in the nurses' quarters.

"We realize," Volt began once they were all arranged, "that we took a great risk in coming directly to Weetu without first communicating our intent. However, the council determined that circumstances have reached the point where our continuing to remain separate and aloof is no longer the wisest course." Opening his bag, he lifted out one of the sealed documents. "This is our mission, as given to us before we left the underwater portal at Praia."

Cassidy accepted the document with slightly trembling fingers. It was only right that the council should have provided it, rather than leaving them with the second-hand instructions of the three-member committee, yet she felt the weight of her tribe's trust coming to rest with even greater force on her shoulders as she broke the seals.

"By command of the Water Fairy ruling council," she read aloud for Agnes and Daphne's benefit, "the medical party currently under the head of Lady Cassidy Clark shall be joined to the committee—Councilor Volt being the head thereof—sent by this council for the purposes of initiating formal contact with the Wood Fairy Tribe.

"All matters of negotiation with said surface tribe achieving a majority consensus of the joint parties, shall be considered accepted by this adjunct council, going into force at once and being entered into Water Fairy official diplomatic records at such time as they shall be received."

It was signed by the current members of the council. As always, the tribal motto emblazoned across the bottom of all official documents sent a rush of emotion straight to Cassidy's eyes and nose, making them burn when she repressed them. *Dignum fiducia nostrae*, which translated in the surface tongue as 'Worthy of our trust.' As much declaration of fact as promise of fidelity, the motto challenged every Water Fairy operating in an official capacity to serve to their utmost. Their own wishes were to be set aside in consideration of the tribe's welfare.

"Now then." Volt folded his hands and set them on the table. "We have established formal contact with the Wood Fairy Tribe's royal family. Tomorrow we shall meet the king's advisors. Under the circumstances, we will naturally not be able to reach the entire tribe for some time. That makes it all the more important for us to use our time to meet and solidify our relations with the citizens of this particular city. That way, they will give a favorable report of us in the spring when they travel to the other cities. I, for one, think that we should discuss our next step."

"What did you have in mind?" Cassidy asked apprehensively.

"We should have the king introduce us to the city at the next assembly."

Derrick snorted his disapproval of Volt's bold suggestion.

"I'm sure they will, when it is time." Cassidy tucked Derrick's behavior away to be thoroughly assessed later. "We must await the king and queen's discretion," she stated firmly. "To do otherwise would needlessly jeopardize our relations with the royal family. Not to mention that we can spend the time between now and then in familiarizing you with their ways and them with our ways. It has been so long since guests from the surface were welcome among us that our own tribe will have to relearn hospitality, and...."

"Cassidy." Volt leaned forward earnestly. "Our tribe is not ready for the level of intrusion you seem to be envisioning."

"Forgive me." She shook her head, troubled by his choice of words. "I distinctly remember telling King Walter for you that our tribe was aware of the council's decision." Granted, she'd then assumed a great deal. Incorrectly, it appeared.

"What we said," Volt corrected gently, "was that our tribe only recently became aware that the council was contemplating the resumption of intertribal relations." Shocked, Cassidy barely heard what he went on to add. "It will still be some time—possibly a very long time—before our tribe is fully prepared to accept what we're doing."

"Why your eagerness to be presented to this city, then?" Cassidy heard the bite in her tone and took a deep breath. "You have some reason for expecting the Wood Fairies to be more welcoming than our own tribe?"

"A very good reason." Volt was disturbed by her reaction to his explanation of how he'd evaded the king's prying. "First and foremost, our tribe has completely faded from the memories of the surface tribes. With them, there will be no lingering presumptions, no foregone conclusions dooming us to failure before we begin. Our introduction to them should go favorably." Still seeing skepticism in his daughter's eyes, Volt forced himself to look at the faces of the others. He'd almost forgotten they were there.

Sir Derrick was a perfect example of the attitude Volt had just described, with his arms folded across his chest and a disapproving scowl on his face. From previous debates, Volt knew that he didn't approve of *any* of this. If not for the council's direct orders, Derrick would still be in Cachora explaining why they should remain detached from the rest of Fairydom. It made him the perfect instrument for pointing out flaws in optimistic assumptions and further insured the tribe's best interests. Nevertheless, right now Volt was just grateful that he was letting them work through this instead of trying to usurp the conversation.

Daphne, on the other hand, had shifted slightly so that her knees were pointing towards Cassidy. He might've expected that the naïve young woman would feel defensive of her hosts; he would have to help her understand he had no ill intent. Baron Edgins and Agnes, in the best tradition of happily married couples, somehow each managed to wear the same uncertain expression in their own way.

Volt disciplined a sigh. Their body language told him as plain as words that none of them agreed with his proposal that they be introduced to the city as soon as possible. While he wasn't ready to concede the central point, but he would get farther faster with the full support of his committee, which now officially included Cassidy and her team.

"Trust the king and queen to know what is best for their tribe," Cassidy advised, breaking the short silence. "Let us teach you what we've learned about their ways during our time here. Study the histories." Gesturing at her father's messenger bag, which still contained several missives, she postulated, "Negotiate trade agreements with the advisors if you can. But let's not fry the fish before it's caught."

"Yes." Volt half-smiled at the old expression.

"It's late.  We should rest if we're going to meet the advisors in the morning."

While Cassidy noticed that he didn't yield the point, she didn't press it, either.  He would do what was best when the time came.  He always had.  Whether any of them would get any rest that night, on the other hand, was debatable.

Cassidy tossed and turned for an hour before going out to the antechamber.  On her way past Daphne's door, she thought she heard soft giggling.  No doubt there would be another library book to return tomorrow.  But for now, there were piles of reports on her desk to go through.  Reaching for her ink bottle and quill, she started on the pile labeled *Medicinal Plants*.  She was just closing the last file from that stack when she heard someone at the outer door.

"Good morning," Agnes greeted, poking her head into the antechamber.  Once the door was shut behind her and the food cart, she switched to Margua.  "I brought breakfast!" She'd gone to the kitchen early to be sure she got enough for all of them, and left word for whomever was assigned to the task that morning.  "You fell asleep on the desk again?" Taking in Cassidy's disheveled state, she repressed a smile.

Cassidy gave up trying to look cheerful. "How could you tell?" she asked, rubbing the back of her aching neck with one hand.

"Experience." Agnes handed her the mug of warm steep she'd brought along. "Sip that while you change for the day."

Cassidy groaned and got to her feet. Taking the mug with her, she continued rubbing her neck on her way into her room. The steep finally eased the kink in her neck by the time she'd finished stepping into a fresh set of slippers. She felt almost like herself when she came out to join the others for breakfast.

"Morning!" She smiled at her father, yesterday's discussion fresh in her mind. They'd disagreed many times in the past, but never about anything so important. At least they agreed on one important thing long, long ago—never to remain angry with each other. It felt good to face the new day together again.

"Will you be requiring a translator again today?" Agnes asked Volt, offering him the plate of acorn bread toast.

"Yes, I think so," he nodded, taking two slices off the top. He eyed the bowl of oatmeal a little warily before taking a bite. "We stand to learn much more by hearing all that is said instead of just what they want us to hear."

Cassidy chewed and swallowed before suggesting, "Then perhaps you would do best to assign a translator among yourselves. While the advisors will know one of your party speaks their tongue, they will likely be less careful."

Taken aback by Cassidy's suggestion, Volt

shoveled a few more spoonsful of the tasteless glop into his mouth before washing it down with some juice.

"Yes, alright. If you think that would be best."

"It would also allow us to make our usual morning rounds at the hospital," Agnes observed mildly. She agreed with Cassidy that there was no advantage in the committee's continuing to pretend not to speak the surface tongue.

Volt wiped his mouth on his napkin. He could hardly object to that, especially after listening to Cassidy talk on and on about her patients while they talked in his rooms before supper last night.

"Established routines should be maintained," he asserted before Derrick could do what he did best—take the opposing side.

A bit deflated by his taciturn response, Cassidy still managed a smile for Daphne. She would suggest that she and her father breakfast alone tomorrow, to give them a chance to discuss things privately.

Volt watched in surprise as all three of the women looked up at a rhythmic rap on the door. Delighted to surrender what was left of his dish, he observed with interest how swiftly they gathered things back onto the cart. Clearly this was routine.

"I didn't realize it was so late!" muttered Daphne, stacking the final plate before she towed the cart towards the outer door.

Cassidy mostly closed the door to the antechamber to keep her father and the others from being seen. The hallway should have been clear, but she'd rather not take the chance.

"Ah, excellent!" Stuart's voice came from the antechamber. "Return this food cart to the kitchen and see that the dishes are thoroughly cleaned."

"At once!" A much younger voice agreed.

Cassidy heard the cartwheels rolling across the wood floor, then the click of the outer door closing.

"Lady Cassidy." It was still Stuart's voice. "May I have a word, please?"

Cassidy waved Agnes over to her position, then slipped through the dividing door.

"Oh!" She exclaimed in surprise. *Sir* Stuart gleamed from the freshly polished toes of his black knee-high boots to his sword belt buckle and insignia. Cassidy was more than a little curious about the various medals adorning his double-breasted jacket.

"King Walter's compliments, Lady Cassidy." He saluted her, touching his brown-gloved fingers to the front of the wide brim of his hat. Returning his hand crisply to its position beside his sword, he continued, "Sir Stuart of Ouray privileged to report as official escort to the Water Fairy ambassadors."

Wide-eyed, Cassidy just stared at him. Her mind refused to process this contradiction to the warm, companionable Stuart she thought she'd come to know. His friendly wink jolted her out of her stupor and she drew herself to her full height.

"I will inform them of your arrival." Motioning for Daphne to join the others as well, Cassidy inclined her head apologetically to Sir Stuart.

Once back behind the dividing door, Cassidy mouthed the word 'uniform' to Agnes, who gave Daphne a soothing pat on the shoulder.

"I hope you have chosen your translator," Cassidy hissed in Margua. "Your escort is here."

"Escort?" Volt frowned as he shrugged into his cloak. "We can't afford to draw attention to ourselves."

Cassidy couldn't help rolling her eyes. How Stuart could do anything but attract the admiring gazes of everyone he passed by was beyond her!

"Well." Volt drew his eyebrows together until he felt he had the right degree of glower. "Let's see."

Reluctantly, Cassidy opened the door and stepped aside. It made a lot of sense that King Walter would choose to honor these particular guests with a formal escort. Nevertheless, as a strategy for introducing them to the unsuspecting city, Cassidy thought it a rather bad idea.

"Councilor Botere." Sir Stuart saluted sharply. "Sir Stuart of Ouray reporting as your escort during your stay at Weetu." If Volt's glower fazed him, he wasn't showing it.

As she translated his words into Margua, Cassidy shot Agnes a look, even more surprised by this development. Surely he had more important things to do, like finish getting ready for his wedding?

Volt slowly clasped his hands behind his back, then, without actually taking his eyes off of Stuart, said something in Margua to Derrick.

"We thank you, but we do not," Derrick hesitated, as if searching his vocabulary, "un-der-stand. Does the king wish to make us known to the city?"

"Not at the present time, no."

"Then, why this?" Derrick pointed in Stuart's general direction.

Stuart remained at ramrod attention instead of looking down at himself. "The Wranglers are on parade today. We will not be unduly noticed."

Derrick looked with raised eyebrows to Cassidy, who reminded herself that he was playing a role, and translated Stuart's speech for them. After a short murmured conference, which consisted mostly of Volt expressing disappointment that the Water Fairy Tribe was *not* going to be revealed to the city yet, Derrick turned back to Stuart.

"We are ready."

Cassidy exhaled slowly as the door shut behind them. She had an uneasy feeling about letting them go without her.

"Come." Agnes tugged on her arm. "We have rounds to make."

So she did. She dutifully reviewed each chart, chatted with each patient, and did all of the little things she would normally do. At first, she intentionally avoided the idea of checking on Isaac. But, when they were almost at the end of their rounds and the others hadn't seen him, either, she began to worry.

"You two go ahead," Cassidy told them. "I'll stay around a little while in case he just got delayed by the meeting." Rolling her shoulders forwards and backwards to loosen them up, she picked up a clipboard and absent-mindedly began reading the file on her way to the patient's room. Her steps slowed as she approached the doorway. Was that…?

Isaac looked up from where he sat, chuckling over a story with one of Cassidy's spinal patients, and was surprised to find Cassidy watching them from the doorway. Her words still troubled him—*Even if I could stay, you wouldn't want me to.* He wanted to believe that her father's arrival the day before would somehow change her mind. Unfortunately, there was now his own pledge to keep him from pursuing it with her.

"How are you feeling today?" she asked as she entered the room, smiling at her patients.

Isaac just smiled back and let her focus on West.

"I'm feeling pretty good, Doc."  West let her take his pulse.  "When do I get to start therapy?"

Cassidy laughed and made a note in his file. "If you keep making progress like you have been, you'll be walking by spring."

Isaac, noting the light fade from the lad's face, grinned at him.  "I suppose you thought you'd be taking tumbles by now?"

West grinned back, feeling better with the teasing.

"I used to hate sparring," he admitted.  "But if it means I can walk again, I'll go rounds with the weapons master herself!"

Isaac laughed a little louder than the reference warranted, mostly because he'd so recently been in the lad's position.

"I'm sure you would," Cassidy inserted, recognizing braggadocio.  "For now, focus on being patient.  And," she took a palm-sized ball from her pocket, "I need you to squeeze this one hundred times with each hand after each meal." Scientifically speaking, the exercise was basically worthless.  Emotionally, however, it would do him good to have a task to complete.

"Right."  West took the ball eagerly and began counting aloud to himself as he squeezed it.

Cassidy caught Isaac's eye.  "I need to dress your wings," she told him, beckoning for him to follow her.  She carried the key to a specific exam room in her pocket, and took it out as they approached.  "Have a seat, please."  She slipped on a pair of protective gloves.

"Have you ever tried to sleep with one of these things on?" Isaac asked, lowering himself onto the chair. "I used to think I could sleep anywhere, anytime." He grinned.

Cassidy opted for a simple eyebrow raise, acknowledging him without expressing interest. Stretching his wing out onto the table behind him, she lightly palpated the wing membrane around the drying starfish sheets.

"It's healing well," she nodded. "Are you drinking your doctor's water as prescribed?"

"Yes, and it's not easy." Isaac made a face, but she didn't look up from the clipboard where she was making notes. Disappointed, he searched for some way to get her attention. "How's it look?"

"It's healing at a fantastic rate." She traded the clipboard for a jar and what looked like a paintbrush. Removing the jar's lid, she dipped the brush inside.

Isaac's neck began to ache as he craned his head around to try to watch her dab the wet brush along the starfish sheets. It smelled as awful as it had the first time.

"There." She ruthlessly squeezed the remaining rehydrating solution off the brush and back into the jar. "That should hold you for another day or so."

Not knowing what else to do, Isaac moved to stand between her and the door.

Cassidy avoided meeting his eyes by focusing on meticulously removing her gloves without getting the goop on her fingers. It not only stank, it had a tendency to color her skin an unbecoming shade of green.

"How did the meeting go this morning?"

Isaac frowned. "I didn't go."

Cassidy gaped at him, the gloves forgotten. "How could you not?!"

"Well…" He scrambled for a better answer than that he'd expected her to be there, and instead found himself offering weakly, "You didn't go, either."

Cassidy suddenly became absorbed in lifting the lid on the dirty linen basket and dropping her gloves inside.

"Cass?"

She closed her eyes. She must have been more tired than she'd thought. Even the awful nickname didn't bother her.

"Are you alright?"

"Fine." She nodded and reached for the clipboard. "It's just a lot to process."

"Really?" Isaac lowered his eyebrows and pursed his lips for effect. "Because I can't think why." Leaning back against the closed door, he folded his arms across his chest with a shrug. "It's not like you had anything to do with all of this history-making stuff that happens to be, um, happening." Her answering smile made him feel better than he had in days. Reminding himself that he'd promised they could be just friends, Isaac scratched his chin thoughtfully. "Thinking about this wears me out. C'mon." He took her by the hand. "I know what'll cheer us up."

"Isaac." She held her place. "Thank you, but I can't. My father and the others will be waiting for me back in our quarters to discuss what happened this morning. I just stopped by here to," she dropped her eyes to the clipboard she was still holding, "keep up my routine."

"Sure." Isaac willed himself to release her hand. He couldn't. "I'll walk you back, then," he suggested.

"Alright."

The silence as they went was deafening. Until they reached the general admission area, that is.

# Chapter 15

"Easy," Rosie soothed her patient who was struggling to breathe. Wiping beads of sweat off the ambassador's forehead, she inadvertently caught his green hair between her fingers. Softly, she smoothed it back down. "We're getting a khella preparation for you." A nurse arrived, carrying a cushion to put between the patient and the hard wooden bench he was sitting on, but Rosie waved it away. She'd already sent for a wheeled chair; if it didn't arrive soon, she was going to have this patient carried into a private examination room.

"Rosie." Isaac paused, frowning.

Spotting him, Rosie motioned for one of her nurses to take over.

"Rosie, what's wrong?" Cassidy asked, taking note of the worry lines between Rosie's eyes as she approached.

"That man is the Plant Fairy in charge of our greenhouses and plantings." Rosie jerked her head in the general direction of the patient she'd just left. "And I don't know what's wrong with him."

"Is that unusual?" Cassidy asked, confused. She had only practiced medicine for a century, but in her experience it was common to struggle with diagnosing a general ailment. *Especially* for patients of a mixed tribal heritage! She looked again at the patient. By all appearances, he was not of mixed heritage; not in the last few generations, at least. And really…it was odd that he seemed in perfect health aside from his wheezing. She frowned without realizing it, as she tried to remember why that was so important.

"It is during the winter, when he's in the same environment day after day," Rosie answered, shoving her hands into her jacket pockets. "And in a man his age. By now any allergies should've presented, but his record shows a clean bill of health. What's more," lowering her voice, she took a step closer to the others, "he says he felt fine until last night."

"You mean this just," Isaac shook his head in disbelief, "appeared out of nowhere?"

"Exactly." Rosie shook her head. "I might attribute it to his time in the greenhouse, where mold could theoretically be building up since it's so damp, but this doesn't look like any reaction to mold that I've ever seen."

"The greenhouse?" Isaac shot a worried look at the patient. "That would mean any or all of his assistants are experiencing the same symptoms. They could be stranded in their rooms, unable to breathe…"

Rosie held up a warning hand and carefully looked around the admission area for anyone who might've overheard him. She had enough trouble without adding gossip and the inevitable hypochondriacs to the list of things to be done in connection with this case.

"I have already sent runners to check on them." She stuffed her hand back into her pocket. "As I said, I don't think that's what this is, but I don't dare take the chance of being wrong."

Cassidy looked at the man with new interest. Right now, a mystery ailment sounded much more appealing than her nerve-stretching tribal duties. Of course—she took a mental step back—the man was Rosie's patient.

"I'm sure you'll figure it out," Cassidy smiled reassuringly. "It's probably an inherited condition that he's somehow triggered." She silently began reviewing all of the Plant Fairy respiratory ailments with which she was familiar. Regrettably, the number of unmixed Plant Fairy *advena* was dwindling, and she couldn't remember treating or reading about any cases like this.

Rosie cocked her head to one side. "That could be," she agreed, sounding hopeful. "I'll review his family's files." The preparation arrived just then, and Rosie went back to her patient.

"Isaac?" Cassidy tucked her hand through his elbow without noticing. "What's khella?"

"Hmm, where to start." He resumed moving them in the direction of her quarters. "It's a member of the wild carrot family. The Plant Fairies harvest the seeds in the late summer, dry them, and export them for medicinal uses." He scrubbed his hand through his hair, trying to come up with something more interesting to say. "Properly prepared, it can soothe coughs and ease pain." He still sounded like a dictionary entry. "They're kind of pretty, actually. Uh, the plants, I mean," he clarified when she cocked an eyebrow at him. He gestured with one hand as if lifting aside a curtain to show her. "They look like enormous white lace handkerchiefs draped over these really tall stems, whole forests of them. And when the wind blows, they all bend with it, like they're dancing with some giant, invisible partner." A passing nurse gave him an odd look, and Isaac sheepishly dropped his hand to his side. "I guess that sounds pretty strange to you, though."

Cassidy chuckled, having also seen the nurse's reaction to what they'd overheard of Isaac's imaginary tableau.

"Not really." She shrugged as they turned off into her destination tunnel. "I've never seen wind, but I have seen entire seaweed beds swaying with the tide while a saldo of seahorses frolic around the coral reef."

"That sounds beautiful." Moved more by the light in her eyes and the warmth of her voice as she spoke fondly of her home than he was by the description he couldn't quite picture, Isaac cleared his throat before daring to speak again. "What color is the seaweed?"

"Oh." Cassidy was grateful for the neutral question. "That depends. Some beds are green, others pink or blue. There are even red and brown seaweed."

"I didn't realize that your world was so colorful," he marveled.

Cassidy looked up sharply when someone addressed her in Margua.

"How long has *this* been going on?" Sir Derrick sneered from where he stood by her door. His eyes flicked back and forth between them disapprovingly.

Cassidy grabbed her recalcitrant temper by the ear and ignored Sir Derrick as she dropped a half-curtsy to Isaac, her stiff slate gray skirt puffing up around her waist.

"Thank you for walking me back, Your Highness."

"Thank you for the enlightening conversation, Lady Cassidy." Isaac bowed in return, and sternly admonished himself not to let his irritation at the man's tone show. After all, he really knew nothing about the intratribal dynamics of the Water Fairies. "Sir Derrick." He acknowledged the man with a brief nod before fading back the way he'd come.

"We have lost valuable time to your flirtation," grumbled Sir Derrick as he yanked the door open. "See that it doesn't happen again."

Cassidy brushed past him, her head held high. This was not the time or place to remind him that he had no authority to give her orders. Besides, these were unusual circumstances. While she would certainly require him to address members of the royal Wood Fairy family and herself with respect going forward, as members of an *officially* appointed council committee, they should at least try to work together.

Volt didn't even look up from where he was seated at Cassidy's desk, reading through the Plant Fairy tribal history. It was truly fascinating to see how far the surface tribes had come since the last authorized contact with them. They lived peacefully now. So much so that this history was exceedingly dull. Well, it would've been, if not for the detailed accounts of the trade agreements between the Plant Fairy Tribe and the others. That helped him begin to fathom what surface goods and services were worth.

"We have too much to do to waste time finding fault where there is none," he lightly rebuked Sir Derrick, having only heard his last few words. Marking his place in the history, Volt closed it and rose. "However, now that we're all here, we have much to discuss." Offering Cassidy his arm, he led the way into the next room, where they made themselves reasonably comfortable around the table again. "In regards to our meeting this morning, I think that the kings' advisors took the news amazingly well."

"Even Minister Eldwell?" Duncan grinned. King Walter was waiting for them when they arrived, his advisors facing him warily, apparently concerned about the emergency meeting. Their complete and utter shock when King Walter revealed what had been a king's secret for so many generations was something Duncan would not soon forget.

"He was…the most incredulous," Volt acknowledged. The portly minister had stared, slack-jawed, for several seconds after he and the others removed their hoods. He might've been seriously considering inspecting their pink hair for himself when the king invited his advisors to read the Water Fairy letter of introduction.

"They couldn't even agree on when to let us begin negotiations," Derrick grumbled.

"That's logical." Daphne gulped a little when they all looked at her. "The surface tribes are interdependent, with long-standing trade agreements. If we offer them something they already have trading agreements in place for, they will have to choose between our terms and those of the tribe with whom they've dealt for generations."

Cassidy looked down at her hands to keep from laughing aloud at the way Derrick was gaping at Daphne. She'd chosen Daphne for many reasons, including the fact that her youth more often than not was mistaken for foolishness.

"Well said." Volt cleared his throat. "I am beginning to agree that we have a great deal to learn before we can properly serve our tribe." He smiled at Cassidy as he spoke.

"But how can we?" Duncan asked, gesturing at the walls about them. "We hardly dare venture out of our rooms."

"Indeed." Volt cocked his head to the side. "At least we can be sure that Sir Stuart won't be wearing his uniform going forward." The Wrangler's he'd seen strutting through the halls and corridors filled him with questions about the progress made by the Wood Fairy Tribe, yet Sir Stuart and the few he'd actually spoken with seemed quite reasonable.

"I suppose we could continue wearing our cloaks," Duncan proposed half-heartedly. "Though I confess, I do not like them."

"At least they are better than stooping to coloring," scoffed Derrick under his breath.

"Excellent suggestion!" Volt perked up immediately. "Why didn't I think of that?" He twitched the coarse brown sleeve of his cloak. "I too am weary of these things."

Cassidy's lips twitched in a spontaneous smile at the way Derrick's eyes widened in horror.

"We still have some coloring," offered Daphne impulsively.

"Truth be told," Cassidy inserted, "I've been noticing that we could all use a touch-up." She smoothed her curls. "T'would seem our roots are growing in pink."

Daphne sprang to her feet. "I'll go ask Rosie for some more."

"And we'll get things together here," volunteered Agnes. She looked at Duncan without moving her head. He hadn't actually agreed, but... "Be sure you bring enough," she admonished Daphne.

"Before we get started." Volt held up his hand. "One task we must all work towards is preparing this tribe to receive their *advena* when the time comes. Historically, Wood Fairies have had the most trouble adapting to their detainment, and it will be a relief to them as well as us to have them returned to the surface."

There it was, in plain Margua. Cassidy's chest constricted painfully. Her pulse rocked her body and she fought down the bile rising in her throat. The noise of the fabric of Daphne's dress rustling against itself as she left the room was deafening.

Agnes, noticing Cassidy's dilated eyes and erratic breathing, instantly diagnosed a panic attack. "Come along," Agnes smoothly drew Cassidy to her feet, turned her towards her room. "Let's get you changed out of your good dress." Closing the door on the sights and sounds of the others, Agnes gave Cassidy her full attention.

Cassidy lowered herself onto her bed, her death-grip on Agnes' arm pulling her along. Finding Agnes' other arm wrapped around her shoulders, Cassidy leaned on her friend for much-needed support. Coming face to face with the inevitable revelation that the *advena* existed was overwhelming her nervous system. All of her brain-lightning was fixated on the thoughts of the causal sequence of events that announcement would unleash, to the exclusion of other needed functions, like breathing.

*Even if I could stay, you wouldn't want me to.*

She closed her eyes and focused on what she knew: how her body should be functioning. Her lungs should be functioning at the rate of two hundred breaths each minute. Her heart, at a resting rate, should beat two hundred times per minute. She should be able to recite the known lightning metals from worst to best or best to worst.

"Silver," she whispered, beginning with the best. "Copper." She forced herself to breathe. "Gold. Aluminum." Her control gradually improved as she went down the list. "Lead," she finished.

Agnes leaned closer to listen when Cassidy began to speak. She couldn't help smiling in relief as she recognized the recitation. Nevertheless, she held very still, lest she should break her concentration. Several seconds after she'd completed the list, Cassidy sat up straight.

"Thank you," she whispered to Agnes. "For getting me out of there and," she took a deep, unsteady breath, "for staying here."

Agnes patted her back lightly. "Of course, my dear. Of course."

"I've read about these attacks, of course." Cassidy dug a clean handkerchief out of her dress pocket and wiped her nose and mouth on it. "Most unpleasant to actually experience one."

"You're handling it very well," Agnes reassured her. Panic attacks were pretty rare, but she, too, had read enough on the subject to know Cassidy wasn't quite clear of the cave. "Do you know what brought it on?"

Cassidy closed her eyes, inadvertently squeezing out one of the tears she'd been holding back. It would sound so selfish if she admitted being worried about Isaac's reaction to the truth.

"The *advena*. Releasing them after all of this time." She shook her head. "They've been mourned and buried by their relatives, replaced in their functions. Essentially, they've ceased to exist on the surface. How will they live? Where will they live? What will they do and for whom?"

Agnes squeezed the hand she still held, cutting Cassidy off before the panic returned.

"What can we do about that?" she asked, trying to find a response that would give Cassidy some control over the situation. "Can you think of anything?"

"They need help." Cassidy's eyes fluttered open. "Our help. Oh," she turned to Agnes quickly, "I don't mean just you and me. I mean, our whole tribe. We've detained them against their will, we caused all of this because of our fear of being revealed. *We* must make it right."

"That may not be possible." Agnes held her breath. Better that Cassidy should work through that now, while they were together, than to have it strike her while she lay in bed, unable to sleep.

"If I have at least made the effort, then my duty is discharged."  She wrapped a finger through a stray curl as she often did when deep in thought.  "I have to talk to my father.  He may know when and how the council plans to tell them they are free to leave."

"But first," Agnes caught her by the arms. "You have to change so we can recolor your roots."

"Oh."  Cassidy looked down at her plain barkcloth dress.  "Yes, I'd better.  This isn't much to look at," she began unbuttoning the cuffs, "and that's why I like it so well!"  Agnes laughed and went out, closing the door behind her. Cassidy changed quickly so she could rejoin the others and was in time to hear Derrick debating with her father.

"I am only stating facts," Derrick growled. "For the last several generations, the *advena* have been permitted to seek employment as servants and laborers."

"We made that decision to benefit them," Volt scowled, intentionally including himself in the ranks of the deciding body, even though it had happened before he was born.  He felt convinced that the original council members who decided to detain the *advena* to prevent them from exposing the Water Fairy Tribe's existence had never expected the *advena* population to grow to this number.  "To allow them to be more than peddlers or island farmers.  It doesn't make them a lower class of fairy."

"But it does present a problem in the form of how their leaving will impact our culture."  Derrick waved his hands expressively.  "Our own tribesfairies will have to fill the void, which means they will have to leave their higher pursuits of education and the sciences.  How do you think that will make them feel?"  He turned his faintly purple face towards the others, including them in the question.  "Do you think they will feel happy about being deprived of their birthright?"

"What of the birthright of the *advena* born on the surface?" Cassidy quickly challenged.  "We've deprived them of their freedom.  And not just them, but also their descendants.  We have hundreds, thousands of *advena* to whom the 'surface' is nothing more than a story their grandparents tell them."

"Exactly!"  Derrick smacked his fist against his palm.  "Exactly what I tried to make the council see before they sent us on this mission.  What loss will it be to those who've never even thought of the surface if they never see it?"

Aghast, Cassidy stared at him.  The firm planting of his feet, the earnest bent to his upper body, his raised eyebrows, it all spoke to his being absolutely serious.  To his believing every word he'd said and everything they implied.

"You want to make them drudges?" she whispered in horrified comprehension. She refused to succumb to the emotions swelling over her this time. This she could fight, here and now.

"They already are! And it will cripple our economy to remove them." Derrick's voice nearly cracked as he pleaded with her to see his point. "We must finally make their position in our culture official."

The outer door opened before anyone could respond.

"Here it is," Daphne sang out. "Are we ready?" The sight of Volt and Derrick glaring at each other was enough to dampen even her enthusiasm for the project. "It can wait," she assured them all, though she doubted any of them heard.

Chapter 16

"It's going to be strange to see you with brown hair," Cassidy remarked as she carefully tucked the waterproof cape around her father's shoulders and buttoned it.

"I can well believe that." He tried to smile. After declaring an uncomfortable adjournment to Derrick's tirade, they'd retreated to his quarters, leaving Agnes and Duncan in charge of the coloring process in the nurses' quarters. "Cassidy." He caught hold of her hands before she could turn away. "Please believe me. Derrick was not appointed to accompany us because we of the council agree with him."

"Then…why?"

Volt's heart twisted painfully at the hint of tears in her voice. "Because he sees only our tribal interests. Duncan and I will negotiate as fairly as we can, yet none of us has experience with this process, these circumstances. Derrick is here to remind us that we are not here to fit in, but to stand out." His eyes fell on the bag of coloring on the counter and he sighed. "So, naturally we agree to sacrifice our tribal colors in order to blend in."

Cassidy dropped her gaze. Tugging her hands free, she went over to the sink.

"You can still change your mind," she pointed out. "Your cloak awaits."

Volt forced himself to stop and ponder before responding.  He felt it would be wise to color his hair and tribal points because then he could travel Weetu freely, experiencing the culture for himself.  That appealed to the student inside him as well as the statesman.  Was it enough?   Or was he doing his mission a disservice?  What would the Wood Fairy King, his advisors, and the ambassadors from the other tribes think of his decision?  He must consider that as well.

Cassidy already knew what he'd decided before he opened his mouth to speak.  She could read it in the disappointment on his face.

"I cannot."  Shaking his head, he unbuttoned the cape and tossed it aside.  "I have been appointed to represent our tribe in a most delicate circumstance.  I must look the part."  Running his fingers through his hair in frustration he added, "I will hear daily reports from each of you."

"And Duncan?  Derrick?"  She unstopped the sink and reached for a towel on which to dry her hands while it drained.  "Should I go stop them as well?"

Volt shrugged.  "It is my voice that will be heard as the representative of our ruling tribal council, even if it is through a translator."

She grinned impishly.   "Then wait here. You've just given me an idea."  Partly for the sake of letting Duncan experience a coloring and partly out of a perverse desire to see Derrick's discomfort, Cassidy flew straightaway to the theater. She felt more than a little silly for not having thought of this solution sooner, like before she'd colored her own hair.

"Ah, Doc." Harry set aside the equipment he'd been mending. For the hundredth time. "What brings you to our little nook?" The stage was relatively quiet compared to the chaos that would reign tonight, when they gave the first official performance  of *Winter Delayed.*

"I have a favor to ask." Cassidy flashed him her most brilliant smile. On second thought, it might've been better to ask Bert to obtain these for her, but she was already here, so… "I noticed during the dress rehearsal that some of you were wearing..." She stopped, at a loss for what to call it. "Different hair?"

"Wigs?" She nodded and he grinned. "That's right." Harry smoothed his hand over his ultra-short haircut. "It adds to the realism." He held up a finger and cocked his head to the side. "It also takes less time to swap out a wig than to stop for a recolor in the middle of a performance!"

"So clever!" Cassidy laughed with him. "But wherever do you get your wigs?" she asked.

"We make our own. Sure," he nodded when her eyebrows went up. "We've got from every tribe here. So if a wig starts looking a little old or threadbare, we just set up a hair cutting day."

"How resourceful!" Cassidy's mind was racing. There were a handful of barbers in Weetu, but how did one *make* a wig? "Could you not purchase them?"

"That we could." Harry chuckled as politely as he could. "Except that we find it, um, suits our purposes better to make them as we need them." Viewing the tilt of her head and slight narrowing of her eyes in puzzlement, Harry tried to find a way to explain what he meant without actually saying it. "Wigmakers can be a bit fussy, you see. They want advance notice, or they only carry the fanciest, most expensive materials, the sorts of things that would wear well at an occasional ball or banquet, but wouldn't really hold up to nightly use in performances."

"Yes, I see." And she thought she did. He'd worked the subject of expense into the conversation quite neatly. She folded her arms across her chest. "I suppose, though, that the wigmakers also have to account for, well, a closer scrutiny." She nodded at the distance between the stage and the first row of seats, "You do have that advantage, so to speak."

"Tell me, Doc." Harry leaned forward, his interest piqued by her detailed, continuing curiousity. "What's your real interest here? Got a patient that needs a wig?"

Cassidy fought back the blush that was threatening and managed a faint smile.

"If I did?" She raised an eyebrow noncommittally, working hard to resist the urge to wipe her damp palms on her dress.

"Then you ought to know a doc can get most whatever they need or want during a winter at Weetu. But you don't, do you?" It was his turn to be puzzled. Why would a well-known doctor be coming to him for easily available information? Oh, sometimes the youth of the city came around, asking foolish questions about the supposedly glamorous life of a trouper. This, though; it was different. "Wait." He reached out to catch her by the wrist when it seemed like she was about to leave without answering. "Your pardon, Doc." He snatched his hand back, cursing himself for the breach of etiquette. "I meant no offense…"

"None taken." Cassidy blinked at him in honest surprise.

"Thanks." Harry eyed her warily before deciding to take a chance. "What do you need, Doc? A green wig? A blue one? Don't have to tell me what for." He held up both hands, palms forward, to emphasize that. Better if she didn't, to be honest. "You helped put Phil Girard and his thug, Dizzy, somewhere's they can't harm the troupe anymore. I owe you."

Cassidy studied his dark green eyes before taking a deep breath. "A brown wig. For a man."

Harry weighed the situation for a split second, then nodded. "Easy enough. What's his hat size?" A fitting would be best, but then he couldn't deny knowing for whom she wanted it. Besides, it was common practice amongst troupers to make wigs on a flexible mesh base that would give within a size or two so they didn't have to redo the lot when so-and-so got a role with a different color.

"Why, it's…" Cassidy almost laughed at that. "Probably the same as yours."

Harry shrugged. "If you say so, Doc. Just keep in mind that wigs wear best if they're not too loose or too tight."

"Understood."

Harry looked around the stage as casually as he could, then picked up the equipment he'd been working on. As far as he could tell they weren't being watched, which was good. This conversation was taking longer than maybe it should, if folks were to believe it wasn't about something important.

"Does your fella have any hair?"

Again she repressed a laugh.

"Yes, a full head of hair." Her gaze flicked to his short-cropped hair.

"Better cut it close," Harry recommended. "I'll make it extra loose in case. Come back tomorrow and I'll have it ready, along with some eyebrow and wing dusting powder."

"Thank you." Cassidy could've hugged him in her delight, but decided not to given the way he'd reacted to touching her wrist. "Very much." Feeling decidedly awkward, she pivoted and flew away. It wasn't like at home, where she was surrounded by servants of her house and could ask what she pleased because they had an understanding. Somehow, despite Harry's perception of an obligation to her, because of the enormity of her need for the wig, she considered herself a bit in his debt.

Back in her father's quarters, she explained what she'd done and produced a pair of medical scissors. They'd always had a servant do it before, so she had absolutely no experience, but under the circumstances…they both agreed to letting her try to cut his hair. Several nerve-wracking minutes later, she set the scissors aside and brushed him off before removing the cape.

"What do you think?" she asked hesitantly.

Volt stared at the mirror on the far wall for a few heartbeats before he was able to force himself to stand. He'd never thought himself a vain man, and yet, he was reluctant. He began practicing things to say in case it looked terrible, all short on one side or jagged on both…

Cassidy exhaled in relief when his reflection peered at itself, then smiled at her.

"Well done!" Volt cleared his throat, aware he'd been a wee bit too enthusiastic in his congratulations. "You have a positive talent for this, my dear." He kissed her forehead and hugged her close. As her arms slipped about his waist, it was almost like they were back home.

"That might be overstating things a bit," she chuckled from the warmth of his embrace. "I'm just glad you look presentable."

"You know, this situation intrigues me." He rested his cheek against her hair. "I'll be able to slip out and about Weetu while everyone thinks I'm sequestered here. What shall I see, I wonder."

She laughed with him and some of the pressure eased off her heart.

"You'd better wait for Agnes or myself the first time or two," she suggested. "The customs here are different enough that you'll still stand out."

"Alright," he agreed amicably. "How about joining me for breakfast tomorrow? I understand from Daphne that there are several public eateries here."

"Well, that's true," Cassidy agreed. "But we would have to find some work to do first."

"Work?" Volt stepped back so he could see if she was teasing him. "Don't these fairies know what money is?" he asked, seeing that she was quite serious.

Cassidy laughed. "Of course. They just see it differently than we do. Rather than exchange semi-precious metals or jewels all season long, they exchange service for service."

"Ah. And these 'semi-precious' metals you mentioned." He raised his eyebrows. "Do they account them the same way that we do?"

"Not at all," she shook her head vehemently. "Gold is worth more than silver here." Water Fairies judged the value of metal by its ability to carry lightning. Thus, gold was their third most prized metal, after silver and copper.

"Really?" Volt scratched his chin. "How strange."

"I know!" she concurred promptly. "They use gold for making jewelry and adornments. Copper, too, though they also use it for utensils and some weapons. And I'm not even sure I've seen aluminum."

"Well, well." Volt squinted at something, possibly the future. "I think perhaps we shall not have as much trouble negotiating trade agreements as I originally anticipated!"

She chuckled. "So long as we have something they want," she reminded him.

"Oh, of course we do. Our medicines! Our fine seafoods and volcanic glasses. That's just to name a few things!"

Cassidy hugged him. After so many weeks away from his voice, she could've spent hours listening to him, even if he just droned on about trade negotiations. Except that the water clock already showed that they were approaching the hour of the play.

"I have to go," she sighed. She felt his reluctance to part as well in the way that his arm tightened about her shoulders. "There's a play tonight, you see. I know the playwright, so I promised I would go, and…"

"Yes, yes."  Volt patted her shoulder.  "You must keep up your expected activities."

"I wish you could come, too."

Volt smiled at the thought.  "No, it's better that I spend the evening reviewing the histories with the others.  We have only begun scratching the surface."  He brightened at a thought.  "Of course, if you'd like to come by afterwards and tell me about it, why, I'll probably still be awake."

"Just like I used to," she smiled.  "After a lecture or presentation."

"Well, not exactly like that."  He winked at her.  "I don't know how interesting you'll find this play.  Fiction and all."  He led her over to the door.

"I've already seen the play's," her brows furrowed as she hunted for the right term and then translated it to Margua, "practice run.  It's actually about what Kuntza reported on, at least, what these fairies know of it.  Tonight I must go so that I am seen."

"Oh?  Well, um, I hope you have a good time anyway."  Bewildered, Volt opened the door for her.

"I'll see you soon," she smiled and went up on her toes to kiss his cheek.

Swiftly, she flew the short distance to the door to the quarters she now shared with Daphne.  There were splotches of brown drying on one wall, and a spoon lay half-under one of the chairs in the infirmary.  Frowning, she made her way further in, her eyebrows rising as she went.

"Daphne?" she asked, finally spotting the girl. "What happened?  It looks like a squid went off in here!"

Daphne bit her tongue savagely.  "No, Miss," she didn't bother getting up from where she was scrubbing the floor.  "Sir Derrick did."  Ducking her head, she resumed scrubbing.

Cassidy rubbed her forehead as she surveyed the scattering of brown dots from the coloring, a broken ceramic vessel, and various other bits and pieces.

"Daphne."   She began shaking her head before she even made eye contact with her. "Leave it, alright?  We'll let the coloring dry overnight, then sweep up…what's left in the morning."

"You're sure?" Daphne asked.  She'd been scrubbing as much to vent her temper as anything else, but now she wasn't sure if she wanted to finish what she'd started or forget the whole thing.

"I'm positive," Cassidy assured her.  "If we hurry, we can change for the play and go together."

Daphne looked down at her fingers, which were wrinkly, and red where they hadn't been colored brown.

"Well, I…sort of promised to go with one of the librarians."

"You did?" Cassidy ordered herself to keep a straight face. "You'd better hurry, then, look at the time!"

Daphne grinned, lunged to her feet and hugged Cassidy impetuously.

Cassidy laughed and hugged her back before she could pull away.

"Now hurry along," she mock-ordered, slipping the scrub brush free of Daphne's hand as she released her.

Despite Cassidy's best efforts, she heard the doors slam behind Daphne's exit well before she was ready.

"Oh dear," she sighed, giving her curls a final fluff. "Well, I suppose I shall just have to be late." And she was, for the corridors were filled with other fairies hurrying to the play. Judging from the way Isaac smiled when he first saw her, he certainly didn't seem upset.

"You're one woman I don't mind waiting for," he smiled down at her as he curled her hand around his elbow.

Blushing, she tried to distract herself by keeping her eyes open for Daphne as Isaac led her into the theater. Tonight, though, they were sitting in the boxes near the stage. The view of the stage was magnificent. The view of the audience, however, was at best half-restricted. Consoling herself that Daphne's friend would surely take good care of her, Cassidy nodded at the king and queen, and settled into her plush chair to watch the show.

The curtain rose on time, unlike at the dress rehearsal. Harry, wearing his blue wig and a reasonable facsimile of Prince Cambrian's crown, rushed onto the stage, waving papers in his hand.

"Father!" he addressed the much-older fairy staring out a window painted on the scenery. "I have terrible news!"

Much to her surprise, Cassidy found herself drawn into *Winter Delayed* this time. The story flowed effortlessly through the first 'act,' as she'd learned to call it, and she applauded with the others as the curtain descended on the ringing speech about how they had to restore the seasons, even if it did mean risking their lives. The royal woodwind orchestra switched from its rousing musical reinforcement to a softer, almost lulling tune, just loud enough to cover the scrapes and bumps coming from behind the curtain as the stage crew set up the scenery for the second act.

Isaac, delighted to find Cassidy sitting on the edge of her seat, wished Bert had accepted the invitation to join them in the royal box. It was a bit crowded already, but if he hadn't insisted that he was needed backstage, they would've found room.

"No, thank you." Cassidy waved away the tray of nectars that a servant had flown up for them.

Isaac accepted one, then set it aside after a sip.

"Enjoying yourself?" he asked Cassidy softly. Similar, hushed conversations were taking place all around the theater, a very good sign that the audience didn't want to be completely shaken free of the play's enchantment.

"Immensely," Cassidy nodded. "I had no idea that it would be so different tonight!"

"I know!" Isaac chuckled. "I've been to hundreds of opening nights and the excitement always catches me by surprise."

"Shhhh." Cassidy touched him reprovingly on the arm as two candle-bearers walked out from the stage wings, paused in the center to bow to the audience, then strolled along to their respective opposite sides. "The curtain's about to rise."

Isaac obediently leaned back, but found himself more interested in watching Cassidy than the play.

The second scene opened on the Sky Fairy docks. Enormous windships loomed over the stage in exquisite, painted detail. A single spar poked out through a strategically placed hole, enhancing the effect. Three fairies were grouped at center stage, Harry and two Cassidy didn't recognize. They appeared to be deep in discussion as a fourth fairy ran…no, lurched onto stage. Cassidy frowned. Was it the lighting or was that fairy's face turning purple?

Isaac came halfway to his feet as Cassidy lunged to hers. Turning to see what she was

staring so hard at, he looked just in time to see
the 'messenger' drop to her knees, then fall flat on
her face in full view of the entire audience.

# Chapter 17

Ignoring the scattered cries and laughter of the confused audience, Cassidy launched herself over the railing of the royal box and flew to the stage.

"Don't touch her!" she commanded, startling Harry and the others as she landed. They scattered before her and she dropped to her knees beside the prone trouper. Leaning over the body, she relaxed a little when she saw the young actress was still breathing. Barely. "Call for Daphne," she ordered Harry. "Don't gape at me," she barked, reaching with two fingers to check her patient's neck pulse. It was best to give him something he could do without training. "Just shout the name until she comes." Her pulse was dangerously fast and thready. Even in the relatively large neck vein, it was like trying to detect a twitching silk filament located just under the skin.

As Harry finally obeyed her, she reached inside her vest to pull out a slim case. There was no time to transport this patient anywhere, let alone wait for a khella preparation. She really had to take some time and figure out what one of those was. Biting her lip, Cassidy carefully selected a needle from the case.

"You two, don't stand there like dolls! Fetch a blanket or some way of carrying her, any way at all. We have to get her to the hospital." They bounded off, looking relieved at having something to do.

"Here I am!" Daphne landed beside her, either accidentally or by design, so that she was between what Cassidy was about to do and the audience.

"Roll her over," Cassidy ordered her. "Undo the top few buttons and monitor her respiration."

Daphne quickly did as she was told, grasping the trouper's far shoulder and using all of her strength to pull it towards her own body. Cassidy did the same with her hips, so that they were able to turn her without too much difficulty. Daphne busied herself with the younger girl's wings, which had sagged out of her costume and were at risk of being crimped between her body and the floor.

Concealing her actions as best as she could from the curious eyes of the other actors, Cassidy inserted the treated needle into the young woman's upper arm, counted to five, and withdrew it. Wrapping the needle in her clean handkerchief, she returned it to the case, where it no longer fit, and hoped fervently that whatever the girl had wasn't contagious. There'd been no time for safety precautions. No time to do more than grab the one needle that *might* help her breathe.

"Miss!" Daphne hissed her horror when she saw what Cassidy had done. "You should've used my gloves." She patted a bulging pocket.

"Never mind." Cassidy pushed her curls back off her forehead. Figured. The one night that week that she'd gotten her hair to look presentable. "Her breathing?"

"Better," Daphne admitted. Slipping her hand under the young actress' neck, she raised it slightly to clear her airway. The hat she'd been wearing as part of her costume came off, letting her naturally blue hair spill out. "I think she'll be alright."

"For now." Cassidy scowled at the actress, then leaned in and carefully opened one of her eyes. "Her pupils are dilated." *Her silver eyes…*

"Gutsy little thing," Harry observed, rubbing his palms together worriedly. "Never breathed a word to me about not feeling well."

*Breathed…* Cassidy's mind latched onto the word. First, the Plant Fairy gardener; now this much younger woman? What was going on? The symptoms weren't identical, granted… If her diagnosis was correct, the entire city was in danger. So much for the hope that it wasn't contagious.

Daphne helped Cassidy out of the way when the others returned to scoop up the actress, and whisk her off.

"Ladies and Gentlefairies!" Harry shot a glance at the wings, where his second gave him a nod. They were ready to start the second act over. Addi was being taken care of, so he had to take care of business. Clearing the stage was the logical place to start. "Cheers for Doctor Cassidy!" He didn't quite wait for the enthusiastic ovation to die down before he continued, "And now, with our dear comrade getting the best care, we shall continue the show!" Harry grinned wryly to himself as he recognized a few members of the stage crew scattered around the edges of the crowd, loudly applauding the idea. Right then. On with the show!

Cassidy remained for an instant, thinking hard, then hurried after the actress, Daphne at her wingtips. They skimmed over the tops of a group of fairies, forcing several who had lifted off slightly to try to get a better view of what was happening to duck back down or get knocked over.

Isaac, forced to remain where he was for the time being, fought to keep a scowl off his face. As soon as the music resumed, he leaned forward to hold a whispered conversation with his father.

Cassidy, meanwhile, arrived at the hospital mere moments after the straining actors.

"Not there," she snapped when they tried to lower her onto one of the wooden benches in the general admissions area. "Follow me." Careful not to touch anyone, Cassidy hurried to an open exam room. "Put her there," she indicated the bed. "And wash your hands!" She glowered over their shoulders until their hands were washed to her satisfaction, then she scrubbed her own hands vigorously.

Daphne was ready with a clean towel when she turned around, and stole the medicine case before Cassidy could protest.

"I'll examine this while you take care of her," she promised, then dashed out the door. Weaving nimbly through the startled fairies in the area, she vanished down their hallway.

Cassidy wished she could stick her head under some cold water, but it wouldn't really help. With Daphne rushing to study the tiny sample of the actress' blood from the needle, Cassidy tossed the damp towel aside and reached for a pair of examination gloves.

"What's going on here?" asked a nurse, poking her head in. She was in charge while Rosie searched for some case from before either of them could remember and she didn't take kindly to hospital rules being flouted. "Who is that girl?"

"Get out," Cassidy ordered crisply. "Send for Rosie if you must," she turned to glare the indignant nurse down, "but warn her that any who enter risk their lives." She watched with satisfaction as the nurse paled almost to white and retreated hastily.

"Cassidy." Agnes landed outside the door, Duncan immediately behind her. "I heard what you said. Are you certain?"

Cassidy looked at her patient. The purple tinge had faded from her face, but she was still struggling to breathe.

"We need hot water and towels," Cassidy told Agnes.

"Then you get them." Agnes stepped into the room.

"I've been vaccinated," Cassidy reminded her once she'd gotten over her astonishment.

"And I've actually had it," Agnes pointed out, tugging the gloves off Cassidy's fingers. The weaker version of the disease with to which Cassidy was exposed as a child had an excellent history of protecting the recipient, but it wasn't a chance she thought they needed to take. Yet. "She's a mix?"

"Yes." Reluctantly, Cassidy allowed herself to be pushed out of the room. "Silver Fairy mother, Sky Fairy father."

"How…do you know that?" Rosie's startled voice asked. "And *what* have you had?"

"It's a long story." Cassidy swallowed hard. "But…" She looked pleadingly at Duncan. There was so much to be done!

"Go," he urged, slipping off his jacket and rolling up his sleeves to his elbows. "I also have had it." Slipping past Agnes to the sink, he meticulously scrubbed his hands and forearms before reaching for exam gloves.

"Order your nurses to give him whatever he asks for," Cassidy told Rosie firmly.

Rosie looked past Duncan to where Agnes was carefully examining the patient. Then, she nodded to her head nurse.

"Bring us masks," Duncan instructed. "And start boiling water."

"Come on." Cassidy began pulling Rosie along after her. "Show me your other patient." *That's specific.* Wearily, she scrunched up her eyes. "The Plant Fairy you gave a khella to?"

Rosie did so, terribly worried when Cassidy's face turned the color of ash as they entered the room.

"Keep everyone out of here from now on," Cassidy ordered. Wishing she'd waited for a mask herself, she slipped on an exam glove before she gingerly lifted his eyelid. Like the actress, his pupils were dilated. Checking his pulse, she found it to be weak and rapid. Pushing aside the sheets, she bared his arm. Large, yellow spots dotted his bicep.

"What are *those?*" Rosie asked, her shock penetrating her professional veneer. "Those weren't there before." She thought she'd read of symptoms like that an age or two ago, but the memory refused to surface. Respiratory diseases weren't all that uncommon on the surface, and that was part of the problem. She'd spent the better part of the day hunting unsuccessfully through old case histories. By the time she sorted through them all, it might be too late. Unless…she looked hopefully at Cassidy.

"Uraren Sukarra." Cassidy dropped the glove on the floor and grimly reached for the soap. "That glove, these sheets, anything that's been used in the treatment of this patient needs to be either boiled or burned.  Preferably burned." Eschewing the towels on the counter, she left the room and plucked one off a stack of freshly laundered ones.

"Is it that contagious?" Rosie asked, her voice barely loud enough to be heard even by Cassidy.

"We need to alert the king."  Cassidy threw the towel she was using into the room she'd just left. "Quickly."  Remembering how she'd scolded the nurse, she winced.  Adding panic to plague was a stupid thing to do.

And so it was that *Winter Delayed* was interrupted twice on its opening night, for as discreetly as the page approached the royal family, and as quietly as they left their box, it did not go unnoticed.  Murmurs rippled through the crowd, swelling around the edges where there was standing room only.  One strange fellow, hearing the questions and theories and speculation, discerned the fear underneath.  Smiling, he faded back until he was able to slip away down the hall.

In the king's office, the small group that hastily gathered was much too large for Cassidy's taste.  She remained back by the door and refused to be drawn closer.

"Stay away," she warned Isaac tightly when he started towards her, concern etched on his face. Judging by how her stomach was sinking towards her toes, things between them were about to go from 'complicated' to the 'impossible' she'd been predicting.  "I've just been with a patient," she paused, corrected herself, "two, actually, suffering from an extremely contagious disease."

King Walter slowly seated himself.  His shoes pinched his toes as his weight shifted, and he knew he wasn't imagining this.  He looked at Rosie to confirm or deny Cassidy's statement.

"I'm not sure, Your Majesty."  Rosie shoved her fists into her jacket pockets.  She didn't do helpless well.  "I know these symptoms are on record somewhere, but," she shook her head.  "I haven't been able to find them as yet."

"Trust me, Your Majesty."  Cassidy's voice was firm.  Her gaze never wavered from his.  "Weetu is in grave danger unless we can find the source."

"Source?"  Walter seized on the idea.  "We can do something to stop it, then?"

"There is a very good chance of it, yes," Cassidy nodded, unwilling to deal in absolutes until she had proof in her hands.  "And maybe, even save these patients."  She stressed the uncertainty of that second half.

"How?"  Fiona's wings twitched with an eagerness to be about it.  She would've ripped off her own fabulously embroidered jacket and torn it into bandages right then and there if Cassidy asked it of her.

"First we have to question those who know our patients.  Find out what the last thing they ate or drank was, and when and where they did it."

She held up a hand to forestall Stuart and Isaac as they started towards the other door. "But we must be extremely careful. The symptoms present themselves differently in each tribe. Exposure to the disease is a very real danger, as is causing a panic."

"The play." Gallica stiffened. "The actors will receive congratulations at the end." Catching sight of Cassidy's upraised brows, she explained, "The audience will go up to compliment them, to shake their hands, so forth."

"Potentially allowing the disease to be spread throughout the audience," Rosie finished for her. "With your permission, Your Majesty?" She nodded toward Cassidy. "She knows more of the disease than I do, but I can at least prevent this from happening." At King Walter's nod, she left, careful not to touch Cassidy as she passed her.

"Do you have it?" Isaac's question reverberated through the suddenly still room. "Have you caught it?"

Cassidy met Isaac's gaze directly.

"That is highly unlikely. We have a treatment for Uraren Sukarra," she gestured impatiently at the blank looks on their faces, "which is our name for this disease. I received a vaccination against it when I was born."

The door behind her suddenly burst open and Volt charged in. He nearly collided with Cassidy, whom he quickly wrapped tight in a hug.

Watching them, Isaac wondered if contracting this strange disease might not be worth it if he could just hold Cassidy for a moment. She looked so tired.

"King Walter." Volt tossed aside his hood and his carefully laid plans for undiscovered observation and addressed him in the common tongue. "I just learned what is happening from Daphne. I wish to help."

Walter frowned, disturbed to learn that Volt had been deceiving them, however slightly.

"As I was saying." Cassidy stepped forward, putting herself between her father and the king. Somehow she found a moment to be grateful to her grandmother, Damaris, who insisted that they practice speaking the common tongue. If either she or her father had her cousin's stilted speech, they would stand out like hammerhead sharks in a school of clown loaches at a time when they didn't need additional distractions. "We absolutely have to find the source. Also, we need to locate any additional patients so that we can isolate them as quickly as possible. The symptoms will vary not just between tribes, but between combinations of tribes." When Walter continued to stare at them with troubled eyes, she added, "My father and I know all of the symptoms."

"What do you need?" The question was a significant indication of Walter's trust in her, for he was clearly no longer certain how far he could trust Volt.

"Rosie has already gone to separate the actors from the audience. The Plant Fairy's friends and colleagues may be more difficult to locate."

"Some of them will be at the play," ventured Gallica.

"And others will be in the greenhouse," Isaac agreed.

"Any of them who aren't in either of those places are most likely sleeping or eating at the Plant Fairy restaurant Landare," Stuart finished.

"Let's divide the tasks," Cassidy suggested. "Father, go with Gallica to the play. You can work with Rosie to examine the troupers as well as any Plant Fairies in attendance. Stuart, round up everyone you can find and send them all to the Landare. While you're waiting for us to join you, try to find out who was the last fairy to see our Plant Fairy patient before he became ill. But don't touch anyone! Especially not if they're having trouble breathing."

"And you?" Isaac asked, hardly daring to hope.

"I'll go to the greenhouse with you. We might get extremely lucky and find that the water there is the source."

"The water?" Walter asked sharply.

"Yes." Cassidy squared her shoulders. "Uraren Sukarra translates to the common tongue as 'water fever.'" She had to work hard not to squirm under the intensity of their gazes. "And someday I'll explain why."

"How do you know so much about how it affects the surface tribes?" Walter persisted.

"We know that," Volt stepped up, taking Cassidy's hand in his, "because we have a significant population of surface fairies living among us." Ignoring the gasps and gapes of shock, he continued, "The *advena*, as we call them, arrived on our islands and in our waters over the eons, claiming to be the victims of windship crashes and other calamities. To preserve our secret, we detained them and their descendants."

Cassidy was curiously aware of Isaac's cold, unblinking stare. At least, she told herself, one more secret is out.

Walter held his breath to keep from saying something he would regret. When he thought he was in control once more, he waved them all away.

"Go. Do as she says." Walter watched as they split up, each of them going to the place they suggested. He noticed that Volt went with Stuart. "What do you think?" he asked Fiona quietly as the doors swung closed.

"I cannot think." Fiona pressed her fists to her eyes. "Ten minutes ago we were enjoying a new play. Now, we are facing…a plague?"

"Yes." Walter leaned back in his chair, turning his face towards her. "I think it is safe to call it a plague. But why now? We haven't had anything remotely like this in generations." Suddenly agitated, he shoved his chair back and got to his feet. "Rosie couldn't even recognize the symptoms!"

"Unless they brought it with them." Fiona could hardly bring herself to voice the thought. To arrive offering peace while plotting to destroy them? She shuddered.

"Ah, yes. That is a terrible possibility." Walter began striding up and down in front of the fireplace, chafing under the spatial restraints of his office. "Yet again we must ask: why?"

Fiona didn't answer, for she had none.

"Perhaps they are punishing us for taking Cassidy in. We know she left without permission."

"That's completely illogical." Fiona frowned. "It also suggests this is intentional."

"How do we know it is not?" Walter countered. Gesturing broadly he asked, "And can we expect logic from a society determined to wipe us out?"

"We don't know that they are." Fiona suddenly shook her head. "Nor will I believe that they are until we have more proof." She held up her hand when Walter opened his mouth to raise another point. "I mean it. I know Cassidy, and so do you. She's intent on helping us. Her father is as well."

Walter pinched the bridge of his nose to relieve some of the tension in his forehead.

"I hope you're right, my love. I do hope you are right."

# Chapter 18

Still in the nurses' quarters, Daphne fiddled with the microscope, trying for a third time to force it to show her something less definitive. Less condemning. Less…so obviously what it was. She'd briefly teased herself with the idea that there wasn't enough blood on the needle to test. But if that was the case, the results would've been inconclusive, not blatantly obvious.

Straightening away at last, Daphne rubbed the back of her neck. There was nothing for it. She was going to have to find Cassidy and Councilor Volt. And probably the king and queen. And tell them what she'd found. Her feet seemed made of lead as she left their rooms. She was about to close the door behind her when she heard a faint sound. A *click*. Looking around in confusion, she found that the hallway was empty except for herself. She shivered inadvertently, suddenly struck by how far the emptiness stretched before and behind.

Shrugging it off, she closed the door. Then she had a thought: Agnes! They'd all been at the play tonight, for Duncan and Agnes had decided to attend at the last minute. Cassidy was—who knew where by now?—but Agnes was most likely at the hospital. She'd recognize the symptoms easily since she'd once had it. Smiling, Daphne spread her wings and took off.

At that exact same moment, Cassidy was dutifully following Isaac towards the greenhouse. He hadn't said a word since they left the king's office and she didn't try to change his mind. She'd had a few nasty shocks of her own in her life, not even counting this outbreak. Allowing him to process the news of the *advena* in silence would likely save them both a lot of grief in the long run. Not all of it, but a lot of it.

Isaac paused in front of a heavy wooden door and shoved it open. Standing well back so they wouldn't touch as Cassidy walked past him, he also kept his eyes fixed on what was inside the room. He was still stuck inside the tree, away from the sun and wind, it was true. However, this was the closest he could come to pretending otherwise. He closed his eyes for a moment, inhaling the rich scents of damp soil, fresh growing plants (it was like he could smell the color green!), and the subtle hint of maple that lurked behind it all. They soothed him as nothing else could've at that moment. And he needed soothing. His lungs burned like he'd inhaled ice water. He couldn't breathe, let alone think.

Cassidy gasped, overwhelmed by what she saw as she entered. Reaching out with her fingers, she touched the blanket of rich, green moss that ran up and around most of the sphere-shaped room's walls and floor. At the far side of the room, barely visible around and between rows of growing plants, she saw something else, something unlike anything she'd ever seen before.

"What is that?" she asked, pointing at the large, ragged ledges. They weren't white, exactly. Some of them even had a tinge of very pale blue.

"That's rock tripe," Isaac answered tightly.

"Rock tripe?" she repeated, bemused. "What an odd sounding name."

"Yes, I guess it is. I hadn't thought of it before." He found himself filling the awkward silence with additional information. "We hauled a few pebbles up a century or so ago so we could grow it in here. The domestic variety doesn't grow nearly as large as it does in the wild, but it retains all the medicinal properties. Not only that, it can be used to stretch our food supply in the winter." As they walked further in, her breathless wonder persisted at each new-to-her item that they encountered. Isaac almost forgot his anger in the answering, until they came around a row and found themselves face to face with a Wrangler apprentice.

"Where's your master?" he growled at the unsuspecting lad.

"Thank you." Cassidy smiled sweetly when the lad pointed up at a distant white blob.

Forgetting himself, and angry with her for being kind where he hadn't but should've, Isaac took her by the elbow and pulled her along with him.

"Isaac!" she protested, alarmed. "Isaac, let go!"

He stopped abruptly. Looking down at where he was touching her bare skin, he hesitated, caught between not wanting to be anywhere near her and the intensely irrational desire to defy her. How could he have been so wrong about her? Just because she was beautiful and smart, he'd assumed she was...better. She'd always been cagey, though. What else didn't he know about her?

Carefully, Cassidy straightened her arm, her elbow coming loose from his fingers in the process. Without saying another word, she picked up her skirts and left. She couldn't comfort him even if he was willing to let her try. All that was left was to put some distance between them.

Frustrated, Isaac wished there was time to visit the woodshed and work off some of his energy. He was never more aware of his wingboard than now, when he was forced to walk while she flew away from him. He aimed a hard kick at a nearby bucket—and connected. Using energy he couldn't spare, he clamped down on himself hard, holding in the howl of pain. *Stupid. Stupid, stupid, stupid,* he congratulated himself as he limped after Cassidy.

Cassidy, her heart hammering with half a dozen different emotions, flew up and over the rows of vegetables that lined the greenhouse. It was really just a round hole in the tree the size of a middle-aged hermit crab.  She could see that now.  She could also see the huge, white object ahead of her more clearly now.  She shivered. Was the temperature dropping?  Or was she still feeling the aftereffects of Isaac's glare?

"Hello!"  She called to the fairies hovering near the white object.  Squinting at it, she wondered dazedly if it was what they called a *moon*.  She'd never been to the surface before coming here.  Not even to visit the small farming islands.  But she'd heard of the sun and the moon, how they lit up the sky.  Funny.  She'd thought they were round, not flat.

"Hello, there!"  A broad-faced Plant Fairy grinned at her. "Hey now, a bit cold, ain'tcha?" He started to offer her his jacket, glanced at the ice window behind him, and thought better of it.  "Wait down there!" he called, pointing to a small equipment shack about halfway up the slope to the window.  "Won't be a minute!" Turning back to his apprentices, he tapped the nearest pad of paper.  "I guess you two ought to know how to measure the window by now. Ah!"  He quelled their excitement with a lifted finger.  "Work separate and check your figures against each other before bringing them to me when you're done.  And remember.  This," he gestured at the greenhouse around them, "is the most important place in Weetu right now.  So get it right."  Nodding emphatically, he turned and whisked himself off to check on his surprise visitor. Probably the mother of some apprentice hopeful who positively couldn't wait until next spring but hadn't been old enough last spring.

Cassidy performed a quick visual examination as the fairy approached her, lighting softly on the wooden boards that lined the area. He looked alright. Unless he was a mix, perhaps a Plant-Wood? Then his incubation period would be much longer.

"Well now. Ross is the name. And what is it you've come to see me about, ma'am?" Ross hung his hat from a peg in the shack.

"It's about, um," Cassidy stumbled over her words, trying desperately to recall the name of the Plant Fairy patient. She'd seen it on the door to his room. Hadn't she??

"Loji." Isaac leaned against the end of the row where he'd stopped at a safe distance. "Loji, your colleague. He's taken ill."

"How's that?" Ross scratched his chin with one dirty paw, eyeing the prince thoughtfully. Something was up. "He was fine last time I saw him."

"Which was when?" Cassidy leapt back into the conversation.

"We ate lunch together at the Landare. Why?" Ross folded his arms across his chest. "Don't try to tell me the food there made him sick, I'll never believe that." He took a deep breath.

"Oh, no." Isaac interrupted before he could get any further in his declaration of loyalty. The Plant Fairies were fiercely devoted to the one restaurant in Weetu dedicated to their cuisine. "That isn't it at all."

"No, of course not." Cassidy took her cue from Isaac while silently hoping that Stuart and her father didn't find the restaurant's entire clientele in dire straits. She wasn't sure which would be worse—locating the source at a restaurant that served a fraction of the city's occupants or at the greenhouse that supplied every cook fire. At least the disease might be cooked off a bit in either case. Which felt wrong, somehow. Like she was missing something. "And he hasn't been back here since?"

"Not likely," Ross huffed. "Just started his three days off."

"I see." Cassidy nodded briskly. As if in afterthought she asked, "Did anyone else eat there with you?"

"Nob'dy. We were busy exchanging updates before I come on."

"Thank you so much for your time." Smiling brightly, Cassidy turned to face Isaac. Searching his face and not liking the pinched lines around his eyes and faint sweat marks near his hairline, she made a decision. He might be walking again, but he wasn't yet at full capacity. Drawing him a few steps away from Ross, she instructed quietly,

"I need you to report to your father, please. Tell him that it isn't the greenhouse after all." Glancing around, she mused aloud, "I was pretty sure it wasn't as soon as I saw all the moss."

"Right, it cleans the water." Isaac bridled at her surprised look. "Basic Wrangler training involves clean water. How and where to find it, so on."

Cassidy allowed herself to smile up at him for an instant, impressed once again with the Wranglers she'd so underestimated. True, his condescending tone made her cringe, but she hid that as best as she could.

"Wash your hands as soon as you can," she advised. "I have to get to the Landare."

"Wait! I..." Isaac started to run his fingers through his hair, but caught himself in time. "How will you find it?"

"I'll ask a page for directions. Or read one of the signs! Please hurry." Clasping her hands together to keep herself from unnecessarily touching anything, Cassidy exited the greenhouse promptly. Lifting off, she flew up to the next level as quickly as she could, aiming for the collection of restaurants she knew about. "Pardon me." She stopped almost in front of a few Plant Fairies coming from that direction. "Am I going the right way to find Landare?"

"Yes," the tall one answered sourly, "but it's been closed."

"Sir Stuart said something about the water pipes needing maintenance," offered the woman beside him.

Cassidy's vision blurred for an instant. A restaurant, serving for hours after the first patient was discovered. Except…these fairies were alright? She summoned the strength to listen again and was glad she did.

"Right in the middle of our meal?" the tall one complained.

"It's winter," the woman pointed out philosophically. "It would've been in the middle of *some*body's meal no matter when they did it."

"Thank you." Cassidy flew around them, resuming her course. They were already eating when Sir Stuart arrived. They both had green eyes and hair, with none of the skin tone discrepancies that hinted at a tribal mix recent enough in their family history to alter the incubation period. It didn't make sense. She had to get to the restaurant.

"Hey!" The tall one called after her. "It's closed!"

"Oh, let her go," shrugged the woman impatiently. "Maybe she was meeting someone there or wants to get a menu or something."

Oblivious to their confusion, Cassidy zipped along the hallway, tilting her wings to slow only when she spotted the Landare's elegant sign. The tables were empty, the light-green leaf-like tablecloths still covered with half-eaten meals and mugs.  The hair on the back of her neck began to rise as she walked towards it.

"Move along there."  A bored Wrangler stepped between her and the restaurant. "Landare's closed for now."

"I'm Doctor Cassidy," she tried to explain.

"Sorry, Doc."  He tipped his hat, more than a little awed to discover with whom he was speaking.  "Please to meet you and thanks for what you've done and all."  He hooked his thumbs through his belt loops.  "Landare's still closed."

"Stuart!"  She called around the Wrangler's shoulder.  He had to be inside.  "Stuart!"

Stuart popped out from behind a partition deep in the restaurant.

"Let her in, Staud!" he ordered, beckoning to Cassidy.

"Thank goodness."  Cassidy darted around the Wrangler and joined Stuart at once.  As she'd expected, her father was already at work.  She hadn't expected to find a handful of white-clad cooks watching him, though, their arms across their chests in defiance.

"They refuse to leave," Stuart muttered when Cassidy looked from the cooks to him.  "Believe me, I tried."

"Doesn't matter."  Volt waved Cassidy over to him.  "Look."

Cassidy leaned over the edge of the cavernous sink to see three separate tin cups, all filled halfway with water. They were all a milky white color and reeked of vinegar.

"From this tap?" she asked. Though she couldn't imagine why he would run three tests of the same tap. Her heart sank as he confirmed her suspicion.

"That one is from this tap," he pointed at the furthest to the left. "They draw all of their cooking water from here. The middle is from where they wash the dishes. And the last is from the little sink over there," he nodded to the far wall, "where they wash their hands. A very clean kitchen." He flashed a smile at the cooks, who exchanged looks before tentatively smiling back.

As she mulled over his response, she had to admit that she was stumped. It was unlikely that the disease could've survived being boiled or baked into the dishes served here, so she'd been mentally preparing to treat only half of those who'd eaten there. Finding nothing, though? There was still the actress, of course. Maybe Gallica and Rosie had learned something, another piece of the puzzle?

"Sorry, my dear." Volt patted her arm gently. "Our apologies for the inconvenience." Volt bowed to the cooks, taking care to keep his hood firmly in place.

"Just a moment." Stuart took them each by an arm and walked them to where they could talk privately. Judging by the indignant sniffs from the cooks, he'd have to do something pretty huge to rate a meal there in the future, but that was the least of his concerns. "We can't let them reopen yet," he hissed.

"Why not?" Volt was puzzled.

"Why not?" Stuart took a deep breath to keep from exploding. "All you did was draw some water, add milk, salt, and vinegar! And stir."

"That was all that was necessary," Volt stated simply.

"He's right." Cassidy held out both of her hands, palms up. "We can run the test again, but it would just waste time we don't have." Her mind took a short trip back to the hospital, where she trusted Agnes was getting all of the support she needed.

Stuart took another deep breath. "This disease. It couldn't have come in on the vegetables or other ingredients?" Water was everywhere in the food preparation processes and he figured they couldn't afford to overlook that possibility.

"Under other circumstances, perhaps. In the case of Loji, impossible." Cassidy realized she hadn't told them what she learned. "Isaac and I spoke with his colleague at the greenhouse. Apparently the last place Loji ate was here, but that was mere hours before he was brought to the hospital barely able to breathe." She looked back and forth between the two men. "There wasn't time for him to have done much else."

"Yes, too fast," Volt agreed.  "If the disease was in the food, it would be cooked, weakening it significantly.  It would take much longer to reveal itself in the patient."

"Which makes Loji quite fortunate," Cassidy concluded aloud.  The words sounded strange to her own ears, but not because they were false.

"What are you talking about?" Stuart asked, shocked.

Volt waved him away, recognizing her pensive squint.  "What is it?" Volt asked her gently.

"Had he contracted it through the food, a big, healthy fairy like him," she slowly turned away from them, her mind sorting through the facts at a dizzying speed.  Scanning the area before her, she searched for the answer.  "He would never have understood his danger.  The symptoms, which are so severe now, remaining much smaller, why, he could've ignored them.  He might've even overcome them.  This onset, so sudden.  He must've come in contact with a highly potent form of it."  The source had to be close by.  It *had...*  Her thoughts jerked sharply to a halt.

Volt followed her gaze and inhaled harshly. How had they missed that?  Granted, it wasn't sticking out of the wall next to the entrance to the Landare. Still!  It was huge.  The entire ring of restaurants was formed around it.  The fairies in the area flocked to it.  He swallowed hard.  There were several around it right now.

"What?"  Stuart looked as well, only without seeing anything unusual.  Sheepishly, he released his grip on his sword hilt and began scanning more carefully.  Staud was still guarding the entrance, and the traffic near the Landare had dwindled down to nothing, so it wasn't that.  The other restaurants were doing good business, which was normal.

"The fountain," Cassidy whispered.

Stuart suddenly could see nothing else.  It was a child's winghop to the fountain from the Landare.  From…every restaurant he could see. Too much salt in your dish?  Smile politely at the waiter, then quench your thirst at the fountain. Meeting friends to eat together?  Rendezvous at the fountain and take your pick of restaurants.

"No."  Cassidy's hand clamped down on Stuart's jacket, preventing him from charging into the circle and spreading panic.  "Have Staud and a few other Wranglers gather those who are drinking, ask them to come to the hospital.  Tell the Wranglers to be polite, but insistent.  And send a page to have them shut the pipes to the fountain down."  Nonchalantly, she slipped her arm through her father's.  "It looks as though we will need the Landare's kitchen a little bit longer."

# Chapter 19

"Where should we start?" Cassidy asked her father quietly once the crowd had been cleared away. Another crowd had gathered around the edges, leaving their meals to satisfy their curiousity. Cassidy would be glad when winter was over and they had other things to occupy their time. Her head nearly snapped off her neck when she heard Daphne calling for her.

"Lady Cassidy!" Cassidy waved her over and the Wrangler blocking her entrance was smart enough to move out of the way.

"What is it?" Cassidy asked, alarmed at the heightened color in Daphne's face. Had she accidentally been exposed to the disease?

Daphne held up her hand and took a couple of deep breaths, demonstrating her uninhibited lung capacity.

"I have new information." She was about to whisper in Cassidy's ear when she caught Volt's eye. Her face pinked again until Cassidy caught her by the elbow and pulled her over between herself and Volt.

"Say on," Volt encouraged. He'd never spent much time in Cassidy's lab, which probably explained why this charming girl seemed so intimidated by him.

"The tests that I ran on the virus." Daphne's voice was so soft that they had to strain to hear her.  "This type isn't naturally occurring.  I checked several times."

Cassidy looked at her father, who was staring at Daphne.

"Could you repeat that?" Volt asked, forgetting himself enough to put his hand lightly on Daphne's arm.  "I swear I heard you say that it was," he paused, glanced around and switched to Margua, "*not* naturally occurring."

Daphne just nodded.

"Derrick."  Cassidy's mind made the leap in less time than it took for a whisker of lightning to cross a standard operating gap.  "It has to be," she insisted in reply to her father's startled expression.  The details might be lost in the shadows of his hood, but she could feel the shock roiling off him.  "Who else?"  She took a half step closer when he didn't answer.  "*Who else* even has the knowledge to be able to do this?"

Volt's shoulders sagged in defeat.  He knew he hadn't done it, and was grateful to Cassidy for not suggesting that he had.  Duncan?  The man hadn't a mean bone in his body.

"Where is he?"  Daphne took a step back as they both lifted eyebrows in her direction.  "Wait, I haven't seen him since I colored his hair."  She, too, had switched to Margua.

"His hair."  Cassidy felt a twitch coming on.  "With his hair colored the same brown as everyone else's, he will blend in, vanish!"

"But not escape."  Volt gestured at the area

where they were standing. "This whole city is sealed off, shut down for the entire winter." He shrugged. "Derrick is just prolonging the inevitable."

Over the hubbub of whispers and questions shouted at the Wranglers, Cassidy thought she heard someone wheezing. Was she imagining things?

"Sugar! Oi, somebody! Sugar can't breathe!"

"Stuart!" Cassidy summoned him without hesitation. "You have to…" She coughed, cleared her throat, and resumed in the common tongue, "You have to search Weetu for Sir Derrick." She watched Stuart's warm brown eyes grow cold as the implication sank in. "Take my father with you. He knows Derrick by sight." She registered Stuart's nod and lifted off. "Daphne, with me!" Wings pumping powerfully, she cleared the crowd of onlookers and swept toward the Eagle. Her worst fears were confirmed when she saw Skite bending over Sugar's slumped form.

"Sugar!" Swooping close, she landed mere finger-widths away. "Daphne, quickly. Fetch me some hot, wet towels." Sensing Skite hovering nearby as she gave Sugar a cursory examination, she resisted the inclination to tell him to get lost. "Give me a hand," she ordered instead. Together, with a great deal of straining and a few grunts, they were able to roll Sugar over onto his back. "Is that his hat?"

Skite scooped it up and offered it to her, then followed her pointing finger and rolled it up under Sugar's neck.

"Easy, mate," he murmured, wiping sweat off Sugar's forehead. He gripped Sugar's hand and looked him in the eyes when they flickered open. "Doc Cassidy's here. You'll be alright."

Cassidy swallowed the painful lump in her throat at Skite's words. Reaching for Sugar's shirt buttons, she gestured at his belt, which was fashionably cinched around his narrow waist, emphasizing the breadth of his shoulders.

"We have to ease his breathing," she explained to Skite, who nodded but was already loosening the belt. "Alright, now. Daphne and I, we're going to try to warm him with these towels," she took the towel that Daphne handed her. "It won't be enough. We have to get him to the hospital. How can…" She broke off when Skite abruptly rose and whistled sharply.

"Wranglers, at the ready!" Skite seized the nearest table. Together with some of the others, he had it flipped over in a twinkling. The legs, which were designed for easy removal, were kicked off and set aside. "Ready, Doc?"

Wide-eyed, Cassidy and Daphne got out of the way while the Wranglers formed up around their fallen comrade.

"And, heave!" Sugar was tenderly transferred to the makeshift stretcher without disturbing a single of the hastily-laid hot towels. "Grip it good, lads," warned Skite, the self-appointed leader of the group. "Ready? Up!"

Cassidy bit her lip, regretting her many unkind thoughts towards Skite. He might be a roughneck and a jokester, but clearly there was much more to the man than she'd given him credit for.

"Come along," she murmured to Daphne. As burdened as the Wranglers were, the women had to move swiftly to keep up. Cassidy was impressed more than once as a fresh Wrangler slipped in to spell another, all while keeping the table perfectly level.

"Rosie!" Cassidy was surprised to find Rosie back at the hospital, and more than a little relieved. "Rosie, we know exactly what is happening."

"Does that mean you know how to treat it?" Rosie watched in mild amusement as the Wranglers formed up around the admissions desk and eased the table onto it.

"We do." Cassidy caught a glimpse of Agnes. "Excuse me. Daphne, keep Sugar under those hot towels." Dashing across the room to where Agnes stood, Cassidy was astonished to see a bandage wrapped tightly around the woman's arm. "You already know?" she squeaked.

"Daphne came here first," Agnes explained, continuing her steady cranking of the homemade centrifuge Duncan had slapped together. "I drew blood from Duncan and myself to be sure we had enough."     Assuming, of course, that the gearwheels they'd pulled off the laundry machine didn't come loose from the braces they were attached to and that the center disk continued spinning.   Once the components of the blood were separated, she should be able to extract what she needed for the vaccination.

"You are the best!"   Cassidy gripped her friend by her uninjured arm, came up on her toes, and kissed the older woman's cheek.

"Tosh, now," Agnes laughed.   "We're doing what has to be done."   They'd gotten some strange looks from the nurses at first, to be sure. Those had stopped, however, when Rosie got back with Gallica and several troupers in tow. "Two of the troupers were showing early signs, so I quarantined the lot of them.   They're not very happy about it."

"No, I shouldn't think so."   Cassidy sobered.

"Isaac popped in a while ago, too, so I sent him and Gallica off to check door-to-door, in case anyone needs help and can't get to it." Satisfied with the appearance of the glass tubes of blood, Agnes stopped cranking.   Gingerly, she slowed the center disk, stopped it.   "Have you found the source?  Was it the Landare?"

"We did.  It was Derrick."   Folding her arms across her chest, Cassidy cocked her head to one side.   Changing to Margua, she continued, thinking aloud, "I am still in shock.  He made his position towards the *advena* plain enough, but to do this, to doom dozens, or perhaps hundreds of innocents to die?"

"They're not innocent to Derrick." Duncan had appeared at Agnes' elbow, carrying a tray of freshly sterilized needles and syringes. "Thinking back over what he said at the council meeting, I shudder to think we agreed to bring him."

"Why, what did he say?"

"He denounced us all as traitors for not enforcing the treaty. Fought with every word he knew to convince us that coming here, reopening diplomatic relations was the wrong thing to do."

*The treaty...* A cold chill prickled along Cassidy's spine. She promised herself that they would find Derrick—and was not at all reassured.

"Why?" Cassidy found Agnes and Duncan both looking at her and realized she'd voiced her thought. "Why would he come here, pretend to agree, and then trap himself in a city with no exit?"

"That's a good question," Agnes agreed, setting aside one of the prepared syringes. "There's no way in or out of here until spring."

Cassidy choked on her own gasp.

"The water pipe." Duncan spoke through clenched teeth. "We came up through the water pipe that feeds the whole city, did we not?"

Over the thundering of her pulse in her own ears, Cassidy heard someone call her name. She didn't stop. The thundering grew louder and louder until the *crack* of Derrick's door slamming open surpassed it.  He wasn't there.  The rubber suits, which he'd offered to store while they were there, were spilled across the floor in one corner. One was missing.

Numbly, Cassidy flew to her own bedroom and opened the chest at the foot of her bed.  The hilt of her suge was cool in her hand as she left, heading for the maintenance pipes.  Her wingtips brushed against more than one blissfully ignorant fairy as she wended her way through the halls, her suge carefully hidden in the folds of her skirt. The traffic finally eased off when she turned away from the commercial areas and soon all was silent but the sounds of her own wings beating.

"Sir Derrick!  Show yourself!"  She flung her challenge ahead of her as soon as she saw the open door to the maintenance room.   Her slipper-shod feet made no sound as she slipped closer. "Scholar of the Ten'rae region!"  She spat the words.

He appeared suddenly in the doorway.  He leaned out, reaching for the door, to pull it shut. Releasing the coiled blade of her suge, she took two running steps forward, brought her arm forward and flicked the weighted end towards him.  He yanked his hand back, leaving the weight to dig a furrow in the flat panel of the utility door.  Flapping furiously, Cassidy charged the door, but she was too late.  His suge in one hand and a glass vial in the other, Derrick faced her.

"Let it go, girl," he snarled. "Turn around and run away before I have to hurt you."

"I think one of us running away is enough," she ground out. The liquid she could see sloshing inside the vial had to be the virus! How could she get it away from him? Unfortunately, he did have a slight advantage in that he had discarded his cloak, leaving him wearing just the thick rubber diving suit, which would provide more protection than her party dress. Of course…neither of them were wearing the traditional suits of armor.

His hand twitched and she jerked her head to her right, narrowly escaping the length of his razor-sharp blade that whipped past her face. Responding automatically, she sent her own suge snaking in towards his undefended belly. He could never have brought his blade into position in time, but metal shrieked against metal as he managed to deflect the weighted end with the elongated handle on his weapon.

"Enough!" he bellowed, his tone tinged with fear. "I refuse to waste my time sparring with you."

She hadn't stopped moving. Spinning out of his suge's return path on her left, she raised her suge arm up over her head. Tucking her wings, she allowed the blade to circle above her head, then released a rapid-fire volley of cuts in his direction that sent him scrambling out of the way. He escaped, more or less. His decision to protect the glass vial cost him the messenger bag he was wearing over one shoulder. The same strike pierced the rubber suit and left him with a deep cut on his upper arm.

"Very well." He kicked the bag aside and attacked, his thinning hair floating above his head like a traveling bed of stringy brown seaweed.

While the room's ceiling was too low for either of them to try an aerial assault, there was more than enough room for the rolling combinations he launched at her. Cassidy blocked slice after slice, sidestepped a flick, and walked into a backhand-reverse that sent blood streaming from her shoulder. It was almost identical to his wound. Gritting her teeth, she did the only thing she could think of. Flipping her grip into the air, she caught her suge by the ricasso, the slightly thicker and duller section of the blade immediately below the handguard.

She used the hilt of her suge as she might've used a dagger if she'd had one, deflecting the next flurry of strikes as she closed the gap between them. At the last second, she noticed him shift his feet, unintentionally signaling a cutback. She didn't have to see behind herself to know that his blade was curling around itself, travelling towards her undefended back.

At the same time, he raised the vial, threw it at the open shaft that led to Weetu's water supply.

"Coward!" she screamed. Switching the hilt to her left hand, she made a desperate decision.

Gathering her full concentration to the single move, she forced fear and anger aside. Stepping forward with her left foot, bringing her body in to alignment with the slowly spinning vial, she flicked her suge forward, the metal and leather from the damaged handle digging into her palm. It moved about as rapidly as a lazy sea horse, laboriously raising itself off the floor and meandering in the general direction of the vial.

In the back of her mind, Cassidy thought she heard someone shouting, but dismissed it as unimportant. Stretching, stretching like a starfish basking in a warm current, her suge reached for the vial. Pain began to register in her right side, but she shoved it away, holding her position while the suge's weighted end made contact with the disease-filled vial. It barely grazed the vial, shifting its course only fractionally. But it was enough. Instead of disappearing down the water shaft, it careened off to one side, striking the room's far wall and shattering there. Its contents stained the wood a sick yellow-green as it ran down the wall.

"No! You fool!" Cassidy heard the voice clearly now. It was Derrick, cursing her. "How dare you interfere with the justice of the Water Fairy Tribe?!" He went on, but it was all meaningless. Even the pain in her side was meaningless.

From the corner of her eye, she saw him draw his arm back, his suge glistening in the dim light as it followed suit. She didn't hesitate. Her suge shot towards his chest in a simple backhand flick. He could easily have parried it—if he hadn't left himself wide open. The weighted end sank home. His arm, heavy now, fell to his side. He fought to hold onto the handle of his suge, but it slipped through numbing fingers and clattered to the wood floor.

Staggering over to the small equipment table, the blade of his suge whispering along behind her, she dropped to her knees and leaned back against it. Because she couldn't bear to watch him lie there without breathing, she closed her eyes.

"Cassidy!"

Her eyes flew open at the sound of Isaac's voice.

"Stay back!" she ordered. "Stay," she drug a breath into her one intact lung, "out of," another breath, "this room." The disease in the vial was meant for water dispersal. Nevertheless, even such a small quantity, exposed to the air, could easily be dangerous to the vulnerable surface fairies.

"Cassidy." Her father's voice reached her an instant before his hands. He scooped her into his arms, held her close. Wiping the bloody froth off her lips, he almost began to cry.

"Uraren..." Her breath failed her. Exerting herself, she raised her hand to point at where several small pieces of the glass vial had embedded themselves in the wall.

"Well done, my darling girl." Raising his head, he took stock of the situation. The weighted tip of Derrick's suge was still in her side, causing the blade to rattle softly against the wooden floor as she inhaled and exhaled. "Easy," he murmured soothingly. He hadn't come this far to watch her die. "Isaac! Cover your mouth and nose and come to me at once."

Isaac ripped the sleeve from his shirt and bound it around his head, leaping to obey like a first-year Wrangler apprentice.

"Carefully, follow the blade to its handle. Touch **nothing** but the handle. You must carry it while I carry her."

Again, Isaac obeyed, his heart pounding painfully in his chest as he automatically noted the numerous contact scars on the walls and scrapes on the equipment now scattered liberally across the floor.

"I have it!" he announced. He would gladly have traded places with Volt, given the chance.

"Stay by my side." Gathering her close, Volt rose and strode towards the door. "Stand aside!" His commanding tone swept the Wranglers from the path ahead of them. Spying Duncan, he jerked his head towards the room he had just left. "The disease is splattered over the far wall. It must be sterilized at once." As an afterthought, "Dispose of the body while you're at it." He hated giving such dirty jobs to his friend. There simply was no one else.

Isaac, who'd given low-voiced orders for the Wranglers to evacuate the area, now moved a step or two ahead of Volt, clearing the way as they entered more heavily trafficked areas. The curious onlookers didn't help, and it was all he could do not to vent his fear in their direction. When he looked over his shoulder and saw that Cassidy's skin was taking on a blue tinge, the medical area seemed further away than at the beginning of their journey.

"Rosie!" Isaac's voice projected his fear.

"What is it?" Rosie came out from where Agnes was showing her how to inject the vaccination. "What's happened…" She broke off abruptly as Volt came into view. "Prepare the first surgery," Rosie ordered the nearest nurse, "for a traumatic pneumothorax."

"Sugar should make a full…" Agnes, exiting the room to see what was going on, stopped mid-sentence on seeing them.

"You know this injury?" Volt asked, following the nurse. He stopped just long enough for Agnes to sever the suge blade with a set of heavy shears, as close to Cassidy's side as possible.

"Know it?" Rosie permitted herself a modest smirk even as she eyed the malicious-looking weapon that Agnes was gingerly gathering up. "I could perform this operation in my sleep."

"Then if you would assist me, please?" Volt asked. Rosie beckoned and he followed her towards the nearest operating room.

Daphne intercepted Isaac as he tried to follow them into the room.

"You can't go in there." She put both hands on his chest, tilted her chin up until she could see his face, and made sure she got his attention. "Isaac! You-cannot-go-in-there." She used tiny pauses between the words for emphasis. "Councilor Volt is one of the finest surgeons I've ever known, but they have enough to worry about right now."

"No no no!" Isaac raked his fingers through his hair. Torn by conflicting emotions, he watched the door shut, closing him out. It didn't help that he knew this was a relatively routine procedure for Rosie, a common injury among Wranglers. He still would've thrown something if everything in his immediate vicinity wasn't either alive or nailed down. Nothing was certain until after the surgery.

"Isaac." Daphne didn't dare soften her tone. "Settle down." The phrase worked well enough on the children who came to visit the library every week, but she hardly dared breathe as she waited to see how he would react.

"She can't die," he whispered. "I'm not..." He looked down at Daphne without seeing her. "I'm not ready. We... I..." Words swarmed in his brain—words of anger for what he'd just learned about the *advena*; words of fear at the thought of losing her; all the words of love that would mean so much more now that he knew at least one of her tribe's dark secrets.

Chapter 20

"Isaac?" Daphne touched his shoulder gently and nodded at the door to the operating room. "They're done."

Isaac leapt to his feet, searching for Rosie.

"Isaac." Rosie caught his arm and drew him gently aside while a pair of male nurses stepped into the operating room to relocate the sleeping Cassidy. "Isaac," she repeated, giving him a gentle shake to draw his attention from the inside of the operating room. "The surgery was a success. She'll be fine," she assured him soothingly.

"When can I see her?"

Rosie smiled patiently. "She's still unconscious. It will be some time before the anesthesia cloud lifts."

"Yes, naturally." Isaac watched as the nurses carried Cassidy past where he stood. It was unnerving how still she lay. He had some experience with anesthesia himself and knew Rosie was right. There were things that needed doing in the meantime. "If she wakes before I return, will you please tell her for me that I'll be back as soon as I can?"

"Of course." Rosie watched as Isaac walked away.

"What did he want?" Volt asked, careful not to drip on her skirt as he dried his hands after washing up from the surgery.

"Offhand, I'd say he wants to trade places with Cassidy," Rosie responded quietly.

Volt turned to look after Isaac, but he'd already rounded a corner and disappeared from view.

Isaac reached his father's office just in time to hear Stuart finishing his report about the fountain.

"I've shut the fountain down as Councilor Volt instructed me to and have four Wranglers watching to make sure nobody else drinks from it until after it has been sterilized," Stuart concluded.

"Very good." Walter flicked a glance in his son's direction. Something in Isaac's posture as he hesitated in the doorway told Walter he was looking for a private conversation. "Keep me posted on the recovery of the victims," he instructed Stuart with a nod.

"With pleasure!" Stuart accepted his dismissal and hurried off to catch up on the news about Sugar. The last thing he'd heard was that Sugar had been admitted to the hospital.

Isaac acknowledged Stuart's passing nod, then closed the door behind him.

"You look terrible," Walter informed him, leaning back in his chair.

"Probably no worse than I feel," Isaac shrugged. "But I have an idea I wanted to discuss with you."

Walter watched as Isaac perched on the edge

of the nearest chair, elbows on his knees and hands folded.

"Sounds serious."

"I am," Isaac concurred. "Extremely serious. I've come to the conclusion that we have both an opportunity and an obligation to act on the information Councilor Volt gave us earlier about the Wood Fairies and other surface fairies who have been detained below the sea."

"How so?" Walter found himself leaning forward as well, drawn in by the intensity radiating from his son.

"It goes without saying that we are obligated to obtain their freedom as promptly as possible," Isaac began, "but we must look beyond that. What will they do? Where will they live? How can we help them reestablish their lives, especially those with family members who have mourned them as victims of windship crashes and buried them in their hearts?" Isaac paused to take a deep breath.

"Those are the same questions I have been asking myself," Walter confessed. "I'm grateful at least that we have spring before us instead of winter."

Isaac nodded in grave understanding. A massive influx of fairies to feed, clothe, and care for during the winter season would've been perilous to them all. Spring, summer, and fall, conversely, were times when there were never enough hands to get all of the work done and more than enough food to fill extra mouths.

"Therein lies the opportunity." Isaac couldn't keep himself from smiling. "My opportunity." He registered the subtle tensing of his father's posture, the faint lift of his eyebrows. "Grant me the privilege of overseeing their settling."

Walter studied his son through narrowed eyes. Isaac was intelligent, strong, and brave. A good prince. This, however, sounded like he was beginning to think like a king.

"I appreciate your enthusiasm, Isaac. Everything you've just said about what's coming is true and well-thought out. However, this is not a task for a single fairy. I will gladly appoint you to the reintegration committee, if that is what you want." Walter managed a smile. "Truthfully, I was already planning to do so. There should be a member of the royal family on such an important committee." The silence that followed his statement was so complete that he could hear the drops of water landing in the lower portion of the small water clock on the shelf behind him.

"You're right," Isaac agreed slowly. "It is too much for any one fairy. But I don't want to be on the committee. I want to lead it. Also," he continued before Walter could respond, "it won't be called the 'reintegration' committee. It will be the grafting committee." Swiftly he explained, "We will take our brothers and sisters and graft them back into the tribe, as precious offshoots that we want to nourish and help to grow."

Amazed, Walter turned the idea over in his mind.

"You would need a Water Fairy liaison." Walter frowned at him. "I don't suppose you had anyone special in mind for that?"

Isaac flushed. "This isn't about my feelings for Cassidy," he protested.

"And what are your feelings?" Walter pressed. "I saw your face when Councilor Volt announced the existence of the *advena*. Why, I rather thought you would be done with her after that."

"So did I!" Isaac exploded. "Until I saw her lying wounded in the pump maintenance room, her own tribesfairy dead not far from her, with his weapon protruding from her side." Isaac tore at his collar, popping off a button as he struggled to loosen it. "I love her, Dad. I hate what her tribe has done in taking prisoners eons after the war was ended, the treaty signed. Despite that, despite every up and down I've experienced while failing miserably to court her, I know now that I cannot bear to lose her." He inhaled shakily, the memory of her white face still fresh in his mind.

"All of that aside," Isaac squared his shoulders, "the future is coming. A future that holds Water Fairies, *advena*, negotiations, ambassadors, and probably every imaginable complication. I believe that heading this committee will not only help me win the woman I love, but that it will also help me forgive the Water Fairies for what they've done. And I need to do that if I am to someday reign over our tribe in peace with them."

Walter stared, wide-eyed, at his son. He'd made a calculated decision to call Isaac out in regards to Cassidy. Even so, he'd never expected the passionate declaration of love…nor the calm, cool assessment of Isaac's capacity to rule the tribe.

"Prepare a list of potential committee members," Walter ordered, deciding to see where this led. "I will compare it with my own and together we will select the final members." He hesitated, expecting an excited outburst, only to have Isaac wait—albeit with white-knuckled hands—for him to finish. "Continue as you are now, and I can almost guarantee you will head the committee.

"I understand," Isaac nodded. Wranglers learned to do things in steps, gaining more authority and responsibility as they proved themselves. His current duties as prince still allowed him plenty of downtime to relax with his friends and pursue other interests. The task he proposed to undertake would demand all of his time.

"I can tell you right now that the Minister of the Interior will be on the committee," Walter informed him firmly.

"Yes, I was thinking the same thing," Isaac agreed quickly. "His knowledge of our current settlements and areas designated for further development will be invaluable. However, I think the Minister of Trade will have her hands full with renegotiating our contracts with the other tribes, for food and other supplies. Therefore I propose we appoint her Chief of Staff to the committee in her place. Her insight into what business ventures will be most sustainable over the long-term will be critical as we help settle our brothers and sisters."

Walter tapped his fingers on his desk then reached for quill and ink.

"I have some time before my next appointment," he hitched his chair closer to the desk. "Whom else did you have in mind for the committee?"

Delighted, Isaac plunged forward.

"I propose we allocate an entire company of Wranglers to the task of protecting the groups as they come up, and to acquaint or reacquaint them with the dangers of living in the forest."

Walter looked up from writing Chief Allyn's name on the list. How had that not occurred to him? There were neither wasps nor antlions beneath the sea, to be sure!

"Do you think a company will be enough?" he questioned solemnly.

"If they rejoin us all at once, then no. But if we work with the Water Fairies to determine how many Wood Fairies there are, I believe we can arrange to have them all returned to us, in small groups, by mid-summer at the latest. The company can split the small groups into even smaller groups in order to teach and evaluate them more effectively." Isaac nodded as if agreeing with himself as he voiced some of the thoughts he hadn't fully worked his way through yet. "Ideally, those who aren't yet ready for life abroad in the forest will find homes in the more settled areas, where the locals can take care of them and teach them further."

Walter tapped the feathered end of the quill against the paper. "We still have to find a way to inform our tribe that the Water Fairies—and the *advena*—even exist."

"Yes." Isaac sat back in his chair. "Yes, we do."

# Chapter 21

Isaac dried his palms on his slacks before knocking on the open door. Volt looked up from where he was quietly studying and frowned at him over his corrective lenses.

"Yes?" There was no welcome in Volt's tone for all that he'd been expecting him.

"I'd like to speak to you for a minute, Sir. If you can spare one, I mean." Isaac wouldn't blame the man if he told him to go jump in the water shaft. It was three days since Cassidy's surgery and the first minute he'd been able to tear himself away from making preparations to welcome his tribesfairies back to the surface.

"Come in." Volt closed the file he was reviewing and leaned back in his chair. He knew next to nothing about this young man. Cassidy's feelings for him might be well-deserved, he realized that. Or, it might be a case of her naiveté betraying her. Most troubling to him was that he'd taken some time to examine his relationship with his daughter and found that he'd never really prepared her for this scenario.

"Thank you." Isaac shut the office door behind him, but didn't take the seat Volt indicated. What he had to say was best done standing. "I've given it a lot of thought, Sir, and I wanted you to be the first to know that I plan on marrying your daughter."

Volt's eyebrows twitched as he struggled to keep them from rising. He wasn't quite sure whether to be angry at Isaac's presumption or to laugh aloud at the culture disparity.

"Is it customary in your culture for the man to make this decision alone?" he asked, his amusement coloring his tone.

"No, I…" Isaac shook his head vehemently. "That's not what I meant."

"That's fortunate for you," Volt observed sardonically. "As I cannot imagine Cassidy taking kindly to such a dictatorial approach to her future."

"Neither can I." Isaac smiled slightly. "She's stubborn, to say the least." Taking a deep breath, he reminded himself he was dealing with a Water Fairy and tried a different angle. "It is customary, however, for a man to ask permission before he begins courting in earnest."

"And what you've done so far. All of this kissing she's told me about?" Volt folded his arms across his chest. "That was *not* in earnest?" He wasn't as angry as he was trying to appear. He clearly remembered his own courting days, and he'd stolen a kiss or two, though only from the woman he'd gone on to marry.

Embarrassed, Isaac reddened.

"She told you about that?"

"Naturally." She'd been coming out from under the effects of the anesthesia at the time, but Volt wanted to impress Isaac with the fact that

Cassidy wasn't alone and unprotected. He'd make that impression however he had to, even if it meant using a blunt object, but he hoped it wouldn't come to that.

"I…see." Isaac took another deep breath. "I probably shouldn't have kissed her, to be honest. Then, when she kissed me back, I knew I didn't stand a chance. I've already asked her to stay here, Sir. More than once. At the time, you weren't available, or I, um…" His voice trailed off. He wanted to say he'd have come right to Volt and declared himself. Except that now, looking back over his actions, he wasn't sure. "I didn't know I was in love with her. I mean, I thought I was, but," he shook his head slowly. "I should've known that love couldn't be that easy."

Volt scratched his jaw thoughtfully. It was the most intelligent thing he'd heard Isaac say as yet. He motioned again for him to sit and this time he did, being careful of his wingboard.

"I couldn't spend five minutes with your daughter without figuring out that she's one of the smartest fairies I've ever met. The sweetest, the dearest woman I've ever had the pleasure of knowing. Also the most attractive." Isaac forced himself to look Volt in the eyes. "And that's really all I knew about her. She never talked about herself or where she came from. I realized she was trying to guard her secrets, her tribe's secrets." He exhaled slowly. "Then, I got used to it.  I took it…her for granted.  I stopped trying to learn more and…"

"You mentioned something about it being too easy?" Volt interjected.

"Yes."  Isaac nodded slowly.  "She told me not too long ago that I wouldn't want her to stay and I thought she was crazy.  Then," he dried his palms on his slacks, "I learned of the *advena*."

"At which point you promptly proved Cassidy right," Volt interjected quietly.  He was relieved to see Isaac wince.  Admitting a mistake was usually the first step to learning from it.

"I really don't know how I could feel so protective towards her and behave so stupidly all at the same time."  Isaac ran his fingers through his hair.  "As I said when I came in, I've given this a lot of thought.  Before I came here, I had a long talk with my father.  He's agreed to allow me to oversee the settling of our tribesfairies when they return to the surface."

Volt was still pondering the statement and its implications when Isaac spoke again.

"I'd like your permission to see Cassidy now."

"I think that would be fine."  Volt glanced at the water clock, which he was still getting used to.  Such a clumsy device compared with the lightning-powered time pieces at home.  "She should be waking up soon from her nap."

"Thank you, Sir."  Rising, Isaac offered his hand to Volt.  He realized exactly how much the handshake would mean to him when Volt cocked his head and eyed his hand instead of taking it.

Volt had seen a lot of handshakes since his arrival at Weetu. If his observations were correct, it was an extremely versatile Wood Fairy custom, used in greetings as well as leave-takings. The increasing intensity of Isaac's gaze, though, told him that this would not be an ordinary clasping of hands. He rose as well.

Isaac gripped his hand firmly. He could tell he had a lot of ground to make up in the older man's eyes, but this was a good beginning.

Volt reseated himself as Isaac strode out of his office, shoulders squared and head held high.

"Chéile," he murmured to the memory of his darling wife, "I do wish you were here to see this."

Isaac made it all the way from Volt's office in the hospital to the door of Cassidy's quarters before his stride faltered. He tried to swallow, but his mouth was so dry that his throat stuck together. He needed something to drink. The nearest water was in Cassidy's quarters. On the other hand, the nearest stress-free water was in the public fountain. With Duncan's help, they'd identified how Derrick introduced the disease, sterilized the whole thing for good measure, and pronounced it fit to use again. Honestly, seeing the crown prince drinking there would probably do a lot to restore faith in it.

Determined not to surrender to his doubts

again, Isaac took the last few steps forward and knocked.

"Ah." Agnes stood in the doorway, demurely blocking his entrance. "I thought I recognized that knock." They'd used a special knock as code for a while when they first arrived, though they were mostly out of the habit by now.

"I'm here to see Cassidy." Isaac managed a small grin. "Councilor Volt said it would be alright."

"I'll ask if she'll see you."

Isaac abruptly found himself staring at a closed door again. It could've been funny if it wasn't happening to him. Gritting his teeth at the delay, he raked his fingers through his hair, this time to straighten it.

"She's feeling up to visitors," Agnes announced as she opened the door. "Please don't stay too long."

Isaac nodded dumbly and hurried in before she could shut the blamed door on him. He hoped Cassidy wasn't as mad at him as Agnes appeared to be! And yet…why wouldn't she be? He hesitated when he saw that all three of the bedroom doors were standing open.

"The first door on the right," Agnes quietly instructed from behind him. "We put her in my old room. It's a little bigger."

Isaac nodded gratefully and tried another smile. He was rewarded with a non-frown that didn't reach her eyes. Resolutely, he turned towards the room. His first glimpse of Cassidy startled him. The lower half of her face was encased in a black mask that he'd seen somewhere before. Tubes two fingers thick protruded from the boxy protrusion where her nose should be and ran down her body to something that looked like an empty quiver. He studied it for a moment as it inflated and deflated in rhythm with her chest.

"From one of the swimming suits?" He watched her nod slightly. "Does it help?" He smiled this time when she nodded. "I'm glad. I've got something I need to tell you and it's not going to be easy." He watched her eyes for some reaction, but she just blinked noncommittally. Reaching for the chair beside her bed, he made himself as comfortable as he could under the circumstances.

"I'd like to start by saying how sorry I am for the way I reacted to the news about the *advena*. You were exactly right about how I'd take it," he laughed bitterly. "Right at first, I was stupid enough to think I didn't want to see you again. Actually, I was angry with all of you, every Water Fairy that ever was or would be." Isaac laced his fingers together to keep himself from reaching for her hand where it lay on the clean white covers. This was hardly the moment. Not yet. "It wasn't until you and your father told us about the disease, including where it came from, and made yourselves so deucedly indispensable that…"  He tried to swallow again and choked. Spying the water pitcher on her nightstand, he got up and poured himself a glass.  He drained two before he thought he could go on.

"I needed that," he told her apologetically as he reseated himself.  "Thanks to you and your father, Duncan, Agnes, Daphne," he inhaled deeply, "all of you Water Fairies, there's clean water in Weetu again.  Even I couldn't stay angry after that.  So I began actually thinking for a change.  I'm never going to be happy about what happened, but I see now that only heartless fairies like Derrick ever could be.  And you are not heartless."  Leaning forward, he tentatively set his hand by hers.  "You're one of the bravest, most wonderful fairies in all of Fairydom.  I am honored to know you."  Her hand didn't move. He tried to tell himself that she hadn't pulled it away, but it wasn't at all comforting.  "Given time," he began to straighten away from her, "I hope you and I can become friends once more."

He froze in place as her fingertips grazed his. He was afraid to move until she took him gently by the hand and brought it up to her face, resting it against her mask.

"Cassidy."  He shifted forward in his chair until he was on its edge.  "I love you and I've been an idiot and I can prove it…well, not that I've been an idiot," he laughed a little.  "I think we have ample evidence of that already.  But I do love you and I need your help grafting the *advena* back into our tribe. Please?" He shook his head. "I can't do it without you." The words rushed out, leaving him breathless while he waited for her to respond.

Cassidy closed her eyes. Lifting his hand from her mask, she brought it back. Lifted it, brought it back. Isaac's eyes widened in shock as he realized that she was signaling him. He'd just lowered his shield and all she was after was…

"You want me to take your mask off?" His chagrin at mistaking her intention rose another notch or four when she opened her eyes and nodded. *Ample evidence indeed*, he groaned inwardly as he explored the edges of the mask with both hands. He remembered seeing her unhook her father's face mask, it just took him a minute to figure out where the latches were. "There." He started to lift it away, then paused to untangle the strap from her alluring curls. "Is that better?" He let her take it from him. In an effort at nonchalance, he observed, "Those latches are pretty stiff. Must make it pretty hard for a swimmer to take them off by their lonesome."

She smiled. "You should never," she coughed a little, her throat dry from the oxygen she'd been breathing through the mask's filtration unit, "go diving alone."

Discerning her problem, Isaac caught up the remaining clean glass and filled it halfway with water.

"Easy now."  Slipping a hand under her shoulders, he helped raise her off the pillows so she could get a drink without straining her side. "Let me do the work."  He sensed rather than saw Agnes in the doorway, but kept his focus on Cassidy.  It was terrible having her curls close enough to kiss and knowing he didn't have the right to.

"Thank you."  Cassidy let him ease her back onto the pillows and watched him set the glass aside before resuming the chair.  "I needed that." One corner of her mouth quirked up in a smile and she didn't try to stop it.  "What is grafting?"

"What?"  Isaac looked up from the hangnail he'd been examining. "Oh."  He ducked his head sheepishly.  "Grafting, it's something we do with trees.  And some shrubs."  He almost smacked himself in the face in frustration.  "It's a special cultivation technique for growing trees," he tried again, stopped.  That wasn't much better.  He decided to start at the beginning.  "We learned a long time ago that the best way to grow a new tree is to cut a piece from the old tree and plant it in another tree."  He chuckled at the surprised lift to her eyebrows. While there was more to it than that, he thought she had the general idea. "I guess it does sound kind of strange.  But," he hand-shrugged, "it works.  The cutting will not only start bearing fruit and nuts sooner than a plant grown from a seed, what it produces will be exactly like the tree it came from.  With a seedling, you can never be sure of that."

"I had no idea," Cassidy admitted. She frowned. "How will this help the *advena*?"

"I've asked to be put in charge of helping them return to the surface." He leaned forward, resting his elbows on his knees. "If I can find the right places to plant them, then I believe they will have a good chance of flourishing."

"I see." She nodded. It made sense. Of course, it wouldn't be as simple as it sounded. "You mentioned needing my help?" She watched him glance at her hands, then lift his eyes to hers. She wanted to hold his hand, too. She wanted the reassurance that they were going to be together, and not just as friends. Isaac now knew about the *advena*, the one secret she'd feared his learning. He'd even apologized for what she considered a perfectly understandable reaction.

It had just all happened so quickly. Too quickly? It was enough to make her head spin. How could she be sure of the feelings they both seemed to share? Let alone the impetus behind his sudden leap in understanding. She worried that her injury had played too large a role in that and wondered if his conviction would falter once she was recovered.

"I did." He couldn't hold back a full smile this time, embarrassed or not. "You know more about Weetu and Wood Fairies than any other Water Fairy. And you know all about Water Fairies, which none of us know much of anything about, including me."   He narrowly avoided sneaking in another apology for all of the time he hadn't spent learning about her tribe and their customs and, bluntly speaking, her.  "You're my first choice for partner in this."

Cassidy smiled back cautiously.   He was making very good sense.

"Of course," he slid his chair closer to the bed, "we'd have to spend a lot of time together." Tenderly, he took her hand once more.   "I'll probably be a complete nuisance to work with, pestering you with all sorts of questions about your home, your family, your childhood."   His voice softened as he continued more seriously, "Because I'll take any excuse I can get to do it right this time.  To show you that I want to be part of your life, not just for a winter, but for every day of the next several thousand years."  He lifted her hand, pressed her palm against his cheek.   "Hear the words of my heart," he implored huskily.

Cassidy stared at him, enthralled.  Of their own volition, her fingers moved to better cup his cheek.

Agnes cleared her throat from the doorway, breaking the spell.

"It's time for me to change her dressing," she announced, but she didn't enter.

Isaac smiled wryly.  It was going to be an uphill battle to win them all back over.  No surprise there.  Rising, he kissed Cassidy's hand

and carefully returned it to where it had been resting on the covers.

"I'll come by later with some ideas about where we might begin settling my tribesfairies. If you're up to company, I'd appreciate your input."

"Of course," she agreed. "I want to help with this however I can." She felt herself blushing as he continued steadily looking at her, his hand still on hers. It wasn't until she squeezed his fingers that he smiled and rose. Even as he walked away, she felt his presence in the room.

"He's a very determined young man," Agnes remarked as she closed the door.

"Yes," Cassidy agreed. "He has some good ideas about how to help the…" She hesitated, realizing she'd been about to say *advena*. That no longer seemed appropriate. "His tribesfairies settle into life on the surface," she finished.

"Wonderful." Agnes smiled, genuinely pleased to hear it. "Is that all he has ideas about?" She shook her head as Cassidy's blush heightened. "That's what I thought."

www.ingramcontent.com/pod-product-compliance
Lightning Source LLC
Chambersburg PA
CBHW061014120726

47910CB00006B/1936